❧ *Praise for* The Other Island: Ben's Story ❧

Ben's Story is a moving and beautifully written novel of Maine coastal fishing communities: a document of a way of life as it disappears beyond a far, watery horizon.

—PAUL DOIRON, author, *The Bone Orchard*, *The Precipice*, and *Knife Creek*

Growing up on the Maine coast, I've met the characters of *Ben's Story*, or at least their real life counterparts, the hardworking islanders with a deep love and pride for their homes, the fishermen who struggle with the ever-changing fisheries, and the summer people enraptured by the beauty of this state but rarely touched by the harsh realities of earning a living here. In *Ben's Story*, Barbara Lawrence tosses readers into this world, teaching them about the history and realities of fishing in the Gulf of Maine while wrapping them up in a bewitching story about love that endures the ravages of time and the changing tides.

—AISLINN SARNACKI, *Bangor Daily News*

I especially enjoyed *Ben's Story* for its detailed exploration of fisheries issues in the Gulf of Maine as the backdrop for an incredibly compelling story. Ben is a fishermen who is not afraid to ask the hard questions about why so many fish species have experienced dramatic decline. He works with scientists to help answer these questions, all the while fishing and attempting to make sense of the loss of a childhood love. Lawrence weaves the two parallel stories in a way that provides insight into relationships between people and place, between fishing and fish populations, between islanders and summer people. As a reader, you can't help but feel a connection between the grief of a lost love and grief over the loss of fish that sustained Ben's people for generations.

—NATALIE SPRINGUEL, Marine Extension Associate, Maine Sea Grant and liaison to Coastal Community Development Program of the National Sea Grant Network

Lawrence has captured a number of the subtleties of the intersection of different coastal cultures and woven it into a lovely love story, backed up by the fishing history of the time.

—ROBIN ALDEN, Executive Director, Penobscot East Resource Center, and co-founder of the Maine Fishermen's Forum

Islands of Time: I really like it. The story about a girl from away falling in love with a year-round kid from Maine, then coming back as an adult to reclaim her self, resonates with me. It's also a love song to the people and landscape of Maine.

—LINDA GREENLAW, *New York Times* best-selling author and swordfishing captain. Her most recent book: *Seaworthy.*

Penned by Barbara Kent Lawrence, a Maine resident who treasures the state and its people, *Islands of Time* is a multilayered love story, rich in emotion and introspection…Lawrence moves effortlessly between the 1950s and the present day as Becky's memories surface…people of all ages can relate to Becky's journey—her struggle to understand how past events, tragic and wonderful, have shaped her life, and how to move forward in the best way possible.

—AISLINN SARNACKI in the *The Bangor Daily News*

Islands of Time provides an amazing insight into the longstanding cultural divisions of the Maine coast and the possibility of transcending them through human compassion and understanding.

—WILLIAM CARPENTER, author of *A Keeper of Sheep,* and *The Wooden Nickel*

Islands of Time is a deeply sensitive and revealing work…I couldn't put it down! It is masterful the way Lawrence has woven the narrative so that it moves throughout time with such fluidity, while still pulling us forward into a better place.

—CAITLIN FITZGERALD, Actress: *It's Complicated, Like the Water, Masters of Sex*

For those who love Maine island life and enjoy a story that draws from the love of Maine, populated by real Maine characters, *Islands of Time* is a perfect read.

—Goodarticles

Barbara Kent Lawrence has written a page turner of a novel about first love, its loss and the near hopeless pursuit of recapturing that for which one was unprepared…Prepare for a day or night of non-stop reading.

—BARBARA LAZEAR ASCHER, author most recently of *Dancing in the Dark; Romance, Yearning,* and *A Search for the Sublime*

A good book is food for the soul, and for those who love Maine island life and wish for a novel that draws from the love of Maine coupled with a story rich in love, romance and passion, *Islands of Time* can be the perfect summer read…It's clear that Ms. Lawrence has used real life experiences of her Maine island life to give the book such depth, and the years she has spent understanding the cultural divisions of this island have been put to great use through the intricate characters she has built and brought to life.

—SCOOPASIA

THE OTHER ISLAND

BEN'S STORY

The sequel to ISLANDS *of* TIME

A Novel

Barbara Kent Lawrence

The Other Island: Ben's Story
©2017 Barbara Kent Lawrence

ISBN 13: 978-1-63381-096-9

This is a work of fiction. Names, characters, businesses, places, events and incidents are either the products of the author's imagination or used in a fictitious manner. Any resemblance to actual persons, living or dead, or actual events is purely coincidental.

Cover art: © 2016 *Looking Out* by William Bracken

Illustrations: All drawings of fish and gear, except as noted, are from www.NEFSC/NOAA.gov/lineart, which is a non-copyrighted source offering access to *Fishes of the Gulf of Maine*, (H.B. Bigelow and W.C. Schroeder, 1953) originally the fishery *Bulletin of the Fish and Wildlife Service*, Vol. 53

Designed and produced by
Maine Authors Publishing
12 High Street, Thomaston, Maine 04861
www.maineauthorspublishing.com

Printed in the United States of America

To BOB,
a gifted reader of people,
a loving and kind man,
and my best friend.

Other Books by Barbara Kent Lawrence:

Working Memory: The Influence of Culture on Aspirations, (Case Study of Mount Desert Island, Maine). Dissertation, Boston University: UMI, Ann Arbor, MI, 1998.

Bitter Ice: a memoir of love, food, and obsession, Rob Weisbach: Wm. Morrow Inc., NY, 1999.

The Hermit Crab Solution: Creative Alternatives for Improving Rural School Facilities & Keeping Them Close to Home, AEL, Charleston, WV, 2004.

Dollars & Sense: The Cost-Effectiveness of Small Schools, Lawrence, Barbara Kent *et al.*, KnowledgeWorks, Concordia, Inc. and The Rural School and Community Trust, Cincinnati, OH and Washington DC, 2002.

Dollars & Sense II: Lessons from Good, Cost Effective Small Schools, Lawrence, Barbara Kent *et al.*, KnowledgeWorks Foundation, Cincinnati, 2005.

The Hungry i: a workbook for partners of men with eating disorders, Greene Bark Press, Allentown, PA, 2010.

Islands of Time: a novel, Maine Authors Publishing, Thomaston, Maine, 2016.

ACKNOWLEDGMENTS

"Howard Wells has been much more than an *editor*." I wrote those words in 2012 just before my first novel, *Islands of Time*, was published, and they are even more true today. Howard is my beacon and prod, my guide and my goad. Together we've worked on four books, and I hope there will be more. He's a good man and editor, and I'm proud to call him my good friend.

My thanks to the gifted and hardworking people at Maine Authors Publishing, including David, Kristine, Nikki, Dan and Kelly, for helping me make the manuscript into a book I'm proud to have written.

With great appreciation to, and of, the fine people in Maine's many good local book stores, particularly Deb, Gordon, and Danica at Sherman's Books. Thank you for your kindness and support.

Many people have helped me learn about the fisheries and better understand the culture, tensions, and dualities of Downeast Maine. I am grateful for their generosity in sharing their time, knowledge, and experience. I could not have written this book without them, and any errors in it are mine, not theirs.

Robin Alden, Penobscot East Resource Center, www.penobscoteast.org

James Acheson, Professor, University of Maine, Orono

Gordon Bok, musician, for music of Maine to sing and write by

Douglas Cornman, Director of Island Outreach, Maine Sea Coast Mission

Barbara Fernald, resident of Little Cranberry Island

Des FitzGerald, aquaculturalist, author, consultant, and consummate fisherman

Linda Greenlaw, best-selling author and fisherman

Jonathan Labaree, Gulf of Maine Research Institute

Cynthie Luehman, reader

Sally Merchant, resident of Mount Desert Island

Kenneth C. McKinley, President and Chief Meteorologist of Locus Weather

Kathy Mills, Gulf of Maine Research Institute

Paul C. Scotti, author of *Coast Guard Action in Vietnam*

Natalie Springuel, Coastal Community Development Extension Associate, Maine Sea Grant at College of the Atlantic

Cindy Thomas, Librarian, Islesford Library

Joanne Thormann, resident of Little Cranberry Island

Michael Train, reader

Many new friends at the Maine Fishermen's Forum and the Penobscot Watershed Conference

To my wonderful family, and my dear friends Sheila MacDonald and Charlie Chatfield-Taylor, thank you for believing I could write this book.

THE BACK STORY

I love shrimp. The first winter after I moved to Maine in 1979, I was thrilled to find small, sweet Maine shrimp being sold from trucks on the side of a road near our house. I bought fifty pounds. For 79 cents a pound, I could afford to be greedy. What I hadn't realized is that they came with shells, heads, antennae, tails and, sometimes, eggs. It took me most of a three-day weekend to clean them. I loved them then, and still do, but now I have to call them Canadian shrimp because there are so few left in Maine waters that since 2013 Maine fishermen haven't been allowed to catch them. Warming water and intense fishing have removed Maine shrimp from the allowable catch and from my plate.

Now I also wonder where the fish have gone. As a child, I caught flounder off our float on Somes Sound, but there were none there when my children were growing up. Now I also ask why there are island-sized garbage patches circulating in the oceans, why trillions of plastic micro-beads from facial cleansers and micro-fibers from fleece enter the waters each day, why the corals are disintegrating, why the lobster are following the shrimp north, and where the cod, shad, halibut, mackerel, and menhaden have gone.

When I wrote *Islands of Time*, I didn't think about writing a sequel, but I gave my hero fisherman Ben Bunker a degree in marine biology because I'm a former professor and I care about education. After a long cab ride in 2013 with a former ground-fisherman who had recently lost his boat, his home, and his livelihood, I started thinking about what changes in the fisheries might have meant to Ben and his family. I started to ask more seriously what was happening to the shrimp, cod, and flounder about which I knew little. I started to think about writing Ben's story, and through him learning as much as I could about the fisheries in the Gulf of Maine and on the Georges Bank.

In the 1960s, environmentalists had to overcome the entrenched public perception that the rivers were immune to degradation caused by the dumping of toxic waste, over-use, and dams. I remember in the spring of 1966 driving back to college in Bennington, Vermont, and passing a river that was white with waste I later found out was effluent from a tapioca plant. The evidence was all around us, but we could not see it for what it was. The good news now is that such dumping is no longer allowed.

We have made progress, but we still must overcome the pervasive misconception that our behavior does not affect the oceans. What I have learned in researching *Ben's Story* is that we must change our behavior to save the oceans, and ourselves, and we must do it soon. It took only a few hundred years to decimate the extraordinary abundance of the western Atlantic that Basque fishermen discovered centuries ago. Fishermen in the late 16th and 17th centuries were already noting the disappearance of large cod and sturgeon; they argued with local magistrates to restrict new gear, like weirs and longlines, that made it easy to harvest enormous numbers of fish. Sometimes they won. In the late 18th and the 19th centuries, however, companies harvesting pogy and mackerel for oil to sustain the industrial revolution protested such restraints, and politicians helped them win. Unfortunately, scientists inadvertently subverted efforts to restrain overfishing because they insisted human beings were incapable of affecting the oceans. It was a convenient misperception that gill nets, purse seines, beam and otter trawls, and boats powered by steam were just more efficient and safer means of taking an endlessly sustainable harvest. Now scientists believe the oceans are depleted, but it is hard for the rest of us to admit our behavior is the cause.

We may never see the extraordinary plenty of the unspoiled western Atlantic, with schools of fish that extended for miles in all directions. We may never see creatures like seven-foot armor-plated sturgeon, 600-pound halibut, or six-foot lobsters, but we must not forget that they were normal in our waters four hundred years ago. We must force ourselves to see the ways in which we have diminished our world and its creatures and created an unacceptable new normal. Perhaps then we will be able to find ways to restore them to more than a shadow of what they once were.

This is a part of his story that Ben wants us to hear.

—Barbara Kent Lawrence
Camden, Maine
February 2017

Currents of the Gulf of Maine, courtesy of Gulf of Maine Census of Marine Life

BEN'S STORY

There be three things which are too wonderful for me, yes four which I know not; the way of an eagle in the air; the way of a serpent upon a rock; the way of a ship in the midst of the seas and the way of a man with a maid.
—*Proverbs* 30:18.

The history of cod fishing in the Gulf of Maine, particularly around Mount Desert Island and the Down East coast, begins with a tremendous diversity and volume of fish and ends in a marine ecological tragedy.
—NATALIE SPRINGUEL, BILL LEAVENWORTH, and KAREN ALEXANDER

There's more than one side to every story. There's a different story in everyone's living of the same story, and this is mine.
—BEN BUNKER, Islesford, Maine, 1998

INTRODUCTION

She's told you her story. Now I'll tell you mine. They are wound up in each other like the way I was in her from the moment I saw her. She stood high on the shore above our boat looking down at me. The wind played with her hair, and I wanted to be that wind. I tried to be cool, to stay cool, turned my head, just to show her I didn't care. But I was conscious of every step I took toward her as I rowed to the tide pools to help Grampie set up their float, drawn like a fish to the light. Well, to be precise, like little fish to plankton that are drawn to the light, and big fish that know the hunting is good when the little fish swarm.

I'm an islander, a fisherman, and a scientist. I've loved a lot of women, two of them good women. Becky was a light in my life, and part of my story. We came from two islands really—hers a world I did not know, and didn't want. The world of people who use *summer* as a verb.

Hard to know what Becky and I saw in each other, but she netted me that first moment. I loved everything about her. She only had to breathe, and I loved watching her. If she touched me, currents coursed through my body, and I wanted to hold her, just hold her. When she spoke, I felt as if she was playing me like a guitar, the chords reverberating into my soul. I longed for that voice, played it over and over in my head after. After? After what? Well, I guess that's the story, so I should just tell it.

CHAPTER ONE

"The bitch is back," Jason yelled out as he passed me on his way up the ramp to the dock. I tried to pretend I had no idea what he meant, but I knew. I knew he meant Becky. He was taunting me again. Like he did when we were young, taking the end of the lobster gauge he kept in his back jean pocket and digging it into my ribs. I always pretended it didn't hurt, didn't want him to think he could best me. I should have picked him up and nailed him to the shed door, but I've never been able to. Part of me was just like him, a part I feared, but that drew me too, so I looked at him and asked, "Now exactly which bitch would that be, one of yours, or one of mine?"

"That summer bitch—Becky. I always thought of her as the bitch who got you in trouble and then ditched you. Never heard from again. Just like a summer girl. So hoity-toity—nose in the air. I like 'em better with their tails in the air."

Thank God he turned and walked away, thinking he'd left me wondering and I would follow him. I watched his curious hitched gait as he walked down the road to his house. Leg twitched up in a trap hoist that left him dangling just long enough. Lucky it didn't rip him apart, but it sank the meanness deeper into him and put him on permanent disability. I watched him limping back to his house, empty because Katie had finally left, sick to death of him and what he did to her when he was drinking. He said she left with her kids and widowed mother to live on the mainland in Northeast Harbor while her children go to Mount Desert Island High School. Jason could find cold comfort in that lie, but maybe it was what he needed to salve his pride.

Let him have it, I thought, and stared at the mountains of Mount Desert. The mainland we call it, but it's not. It's an island, separated by a geological whim from the real mainland, a drowned valley stitched by a causeway. I thought of Katie cowering there with her mother, defiant, but scared. Scared Jason would show up one night and get inside the house she'd rented. I hope she's got a good lock, and a new dog.

I was pushing other thoughts in front of me to avoid thinking about Becky, but finally I let myself ask, Where are you, Becky Granger? Back in Northeast, that's my guess, but why now? Why so long? I remember my last sight of you like someone branded it in my head. Like the notch we take out of the lobster's tail to show we've taken its measure. That only lasts a few seasons before it grows out, I corrected myself. The notch you made has marked my measure for too many years.

The last time I saw her, in 1959, when we were foolish kids from different worlds, I watched her walk down the path to the house her parents had rented for the summer, the light in the entrance falling over the circling moths drawn to it, some of them seared then spiraling down. Some could rise again; others could not. Which one was I? I wondered. Before she turned, I backed into the bushes off the path to watch her. Drank her into me because I thought I would never see her again, my heart draining until I was cold and numb.

Then other memories took me over, and I could feel her in my arms, feel her body arching against mine. Feel her pull me into her and then cry out from pain. I wanted to hold her, tell her how much I loved her, but I couldn't. I didn't think she loved me, and I didn't know what love was then, anyhow. She made me feel as if I was something special and that I understood her in some way no one else did, but I didn't know why. I can still feel the roundness of her body in my hands. Literally feel it quivering against me. Something too precious to recapture or forget, though God knows I've tried.

I stared out over the Eastern Way wondering where she was now, and watching the boats, working boats crusted with crud and nets and rust. Some cleaner than others. Depends on who owns 'em, though the sailboats are neat rigs. Again, depends who owns 'em. The Phillips boat is always perfect—the sun shining on the deep-blue hull and the mahogany deck stoned clean and shellacked perfectly. The money makes a difference. Hiring two people to do the work of one makes a difference.

When the women cleaned one of the summer houses before the season, they used to do it with toothbrushes. They'd hand wash and iron every piece of linen—dish towels, curtains, everything. I guess that was necessary, but it cost. Problem is now that children who inherited a house can't afford to keep it the way their parents did. Some of them can't afford the big old hulk—cottage, they call it—anyhow or any way unless they rent it, and many of them share the cottage with their sisters and brothers. They expect the women to do the same work they did for their mothers, but in half the time and for a quarter of the money. All those labor-saving devices like washers and dryers don't really make that much difference when people have so much more stuff to clean than they used to. That's what the women say.

I sound like a nattering, scolding old man, but it beats thinking about Becky. I thought about her a lot when I was a kid, but I troweled so many layers over it that for long stretches she wouldn't even be in my dreams. Later I missed those dreams, missed the early mornings when I woke up and thought she was in my arms and we had made love—or whatever the hell it was then. I could skip the slow realization that I was in my own bed, listening to my wife, Abby, breathing, and sometimes I longed to go back to sleep. Four-thirty in the morning does come early, no matter what time of year, but it's some harsh when you're going out into the pitch dark and the cold of morning to work traps. Everything fights you—the cold metal on your bare hands and ropes frozen in coils on the deck. It seems the boat doesn't want to leave the harbor, either. The engine will cough or seize up. Chum doesn't smell so bad, though.

The night it happened, I walked back down to the dock in a trance, so many images racing through my mind, so many thoughts crashing and piling together like debris in a storm. When I got to the boat, Uncle Clem patted my back as I hopped over the gunwale and asked, "Hey, how was the picnic with your summer girlfriend? You're certainly looking rosy."

"Great, Uncle Clem," I told him. "Just great." I thought he could read through me, and I wondered if I looked funny. Rosy? Yes, I did. I panicked when I remembered Jason had told me that people got a rosy glow when they had sex and they smelled different, so I tried to stay downwind from Uncle Clem.

Uncle Clem may have heard the tired pain in my voice because he looked at me sideways and said, "Well, can't win 'em all. Best get back to work."

I worked hard on the ferry after she left, and then in the fall went back again to live with my Aunt Cissy and her husband, Uncle Albert, in Northeast Harbor so I could go to eleventh grade at the high school. That's where the high school was then, just for students in the town of Mount Desert and the nearby islands, including my island, Little Cranberry, and nearby Great Cranberry. Just after I graduated, they finally voted to consolidate the island high schools and build a new one outside Bar Harbor.

Because the new school was farther away from the ferry, it was much harder for the island kids to get home, so they had to stay with relatives or families that boarded them. I've heard now some of them don't find good safe homes, and there have been problems. But don't get me started on the school consolidation. It was a terrible idea, if you ask me, because kids need adults who know them and can inspire them to learn, not a big school where no one knows you. Seems that's more about perks for the adults than the students.

Aunt Cissy was a nurse in the health clinic and kept an eye on me. I'd lived with her and Uncle Albert since I started in ninth grade. I was a total cut-up. We pulled some really stupid pranks, Jason and I, Durlin, and even Ralph and a couple of the other island boys. The *Backside Boys*, they called us, because we came from the outer islands. It was tough not having use of a car or truck like a lot of the other kids did, but at least in Northeast we had enough friends from the islands to hang out with after school. Didn't do anything more for school than we absolutely had to. Said there was no point, we were going to make our fortunes fishing and didn't need book learning or even books.

We'd scrum around, getting into a little trouble, but nothing major. Halloween was a good time—throwing cereal and toilet paper and sometimes eggs on people's front doors, yowling and howling like wolves—scaring people, but I think they were just pretending, to make us happy. Worst thing we ever did was dump a box of old bait in a closet in the school. It smelled something awful, but no one ever accused us. I know they thought we'd done it, but they didn't have any proof.

Then Parents' Night when I was in eleventh grade, Mumma and Dad came over from the island. While they were busy talking with the teachers, Jason and I got talking about girls, and we both had to take a leak at the same time. We stood next to each other at the urinals in the boys' bathroom. We didn't see any other people there, and it was just a kids' bathroom, so we didn't bother checking the stalls. Jason said, "You ain't come clean with me, Chummy. You won the bet; she came over to the island, but there's more I want to know."

I'm not a good liar. What I'm thinking pastes itself on my face, and people who know me read it there before I even know. I remember thinking, Damn it, I should have taken that acting class in school. Other kids took it because people said it was really easy, but it could have come in useful.

"I want to know if you got her to second base when you saw her again last summer," Jason continued.

So stupid—he got hold of my ego and tugged. "Yeah," I replied. "Got more than that," and I turned to look at Jason to make the point, smiling my own taunt and looking like a cat that had caught a juicy mouse.

Jason was speechless for a moment. "All the way?" he asked incredulously.

"Yeah," I said again, so full of my own juices and the roiling secret I'd tried to keep hidden that it burst out of me.

"Well, I ain't paying you more for that. It was just the bet about getting a summer girl over to the island." He was nervous and exhilarated at the same time. A hideous grin washed his face as his eyes narrowed to slits. I wanted to hit him.

"Didn't expect you to," I said, zipping up my pants, instantly sorry I had said anything. "Got to find the folks," I added as I walked out of the bathroom. Just before I heard the thud of the door closing, I thought I heard a flush, but no, I told myself, there was no one else there. Telling Jason was bad, and I blushed so hard I sweated.

Friday I went back to the island for the weekend. I knew immediately when I saw my father that he was angry about something, but my mother didn't know about it. That told me it must be something really bad because Dad didn't want her to get upset. She gave me a big hug like usual, adding that supper would be on the table soon and she'd cooked some of the sweet little Maine shrimp I love that she'd frozen in the last season and put in our walk-in freezer. That freezer got us through some long winters.

After supper, my father said, "Benjamin," another tip-off because he called me that when he was mad. "I want to show you something I just got for the boat. Newfangled rig they want me to try out." Then he turned toward my mother as added, "We'll just be gone about half an hour, deah."

I wanted to tell him I had to do my homework, but I knew I had to follow him out the door. At first he was quiet, and then he said, "You stupid young buck. How could you be so stupid? She's a nice girl, Becky. We liked her fine when she came to your birthday picnic. She fit right in, and we liked her fine." He was quiet for a little while more, and so was I.

"We liked her fine. You liked her and you do what! Her parents are part of the crowd that charters your grandfather's boat. So you do what? You screw their daughter! Maybe get her pregnant. Have you thought about that, you stupid, stupid kid? Have you thought about what summer people would do to an island kid who got their precious daughter pregnant? Her family has money and power. You go up against that and you're a bug on the backside of a whale. What do you have to say for yourself?"

All I could think to say was, "How did you find out?"

That was really dumb. Dad exploded in anger. I thought he would hit me, and I know he wanted to, but instead he snarled, "You're grounded, young man. No more football for you. Or basketball neither. You can sit in your bedroom in Cissy and Albert's house the whole goddamned winter thinking about how stupid you are. When you're here, I don't want you out of your room except to work at the dock or help your mother, and you're not to tell her. She would worry so her heart would break—and I don't want her sick again. That's it. It's final." He wheeled around and walked toward the house, yelling over his shoulder, "You stupid little shit. You talked to that weasel, Jason, talk about a piece of shit, and you did it in the men's room while Joey Nelson was trying to take a crap. I've known him for decades. Hate to give him anything over me—but I'm some grateful this time."

There was nothing I could do or say. I thought about the long winter ahead. Missing football. Basketball. The world shutting down in my face. Mumma didn't know, and I couldn't tell her, though how I was going to stop her from sensing something was wrong I didn't know. Probably Dad would make up some other stupid shit thing I'd done that wouldn't frighten her so much. Becky—I couldn't write Becky—what would I say? I'd ruined everything between us. I knew she couldn't really love me, and when she came to her senses she'd be furious. She'd be hurt, too, and then I thought about her being pregnant. My God, that was a terrifying thought that sank deep into my gut and festered. I felt completely alone.

Sunday afternoon my father walked me to the ferry that would take me back to Northeast. We were silent until we could see the harbor. "Chummy, you've done something so stupid I can't fathom it. Can't even see how deep this could go. If she's pregnant, her family could get nasty. If they find out what happened. We'd better hope they never find out. But she's going to be angry and sad, and they're going to know that. If she tells. How old is she, Ben?" he asked suddenly.

"She just turned fifteen, or maybe sixteen," I said hopefully. I watched despair wash over his face, and I knew I really had been stupid, and said, "Dad, I'm so sorry. I didn't think. I don't know how it happened."

"It happened because your hormones took over your head," he said. "Shit happens. Ben, if the police get involved, it could be real trouble. Keep quiet and tell Jason you were just boasting and there's no truth in it. It's a lie, but we need to keep this quiet."

So that's what I did—I "admitted" to Jason that I had lied and boasted about something that didn't happen. Dad told Aunt Cissy and Uncle Albert, and they made me go to my room after I got home from school. We got into a routine. It wasn't totally bad. We'd have supper and they'd talk about their day just like normal. They would ask about my day, and I'd tell them it was fine and nothing special happened. Then I'd play with their kids for about twenty minutes and tell everyone I had to do homework. I'd sit looking out the window. I'd think about Becky and how she didn't know what hell I was going through. I'd get pissed off at the guys on the football team who'd made a fuss over me at first, but then got caught up in the season and forgot about me. I didn't really have anything to talk about or anyone to talk with. I didn't want to see Jason—guess that's obvious—but I couldn't tell Durlin or Ralph.

Two things happened. I took a course with Dr. A., who was a chunky old lady, but funny and smart. She taught a class about being an entrepreneur. We had to think of something everyone needed but didn't know they needed, then create a product to fit the need, build it, and design a marketing program. I had no idea what I was doing, but she said to go to the library to get ideas, so I did. The library in Northeast was six times bigger than the one in Islesford, and I'd never been there before. I wandered around trying to find something that seemed interesting, and after a while a man came up to me and asked if I'd like some help. I guess

I looked pretty foolish.

"Tell me what you're looking for," he suggested.

"Don't know," I responded brusquely, shyness shutting me down.

"That does make it more of a challenge," he replied, smiling. "So let's just go on a tour around the library and maybe you'll see something."

He walked me around to all the rooms where they had different collections, showed me the card catalogue and the magazines. "Explain the assignment to me," he suggested. After I did, he handed me a copy of *Popular Mechanics*, and I read it until closing time.

He told me his name was Mr. Pyle, and I should make a list of the things that I'd found interesting so he could help me come up with a topic. He figured out pretty fast that I was the boy Becky Granger went to see on Islesford, and that helped him see something in me. Later he told me that he'd been a teacher before he moved from Connecticut, and that I had smart eyes. No one ever told me that before, and by the time he said it, I had come to trust him, so I believed him. He added, however, that being smart wasn't enough. I had to use my brains to make the world better.

That seemed a heavy trip, but I enjoyed the flattery and his kindness, and slowly I began to enjoy reading. He'd suggest books—*Catcher in the Rye* and other books he called classics—that get assigned in school, but that I'd never bothered to read. When he suggested them, though, I thought maybe I'll like them because he knows me, and usually he was right. Holden Caulfield—now there's a kid I could identify with, even though our lives seemed so far apart. Holden wasn't sure of himself; he thought he was stupid, but he also thought a lot of what went on in the world was stupid. Sometimes the world seemed that way to me too. But Mr. Pyle didn't think I was stupid, and that helped me see maybe I wasn't.

I'd go to Grampie's library on the weekends to find new books, and I began not to miss hanging out with my friends so much and started to feel the pull of using my mind. Teachers began to notice I was spending more time on homework than before and getting better grades. When I met with Mr. Walters, the guidance counselor, to talk about life after high school, he said, "Ben, seems something fired you up a little while ago. You've done really well. What are you thinking about doing after you graduate?"

I told him I guessed I'd go fishing. Get a job as a sternman, then have my own boat, get married and have some kids and live on Little Cranberry. He looked at me through his metal-framed glasses and said, "Doesn't seem you're too excited about that."

I was quiet for a bit, and then admitted that I didn't know what else to do. Everything and everyone was pushing me to live on Little Cranberry and just do what we'd all done before—a bit of this and a bit of that, depending on the season—running the ferry, going after cod, haddock, and shrimp, a little clamming, and lobstering. The college-bound kids in my high school had always stayed to themselves, and no one in my family had ever gone to college. Grampie thought it might be a good idea, but he had different ideas from Dad and Mumma, particularly her, about my going away from home. I didn't know anything about college and certainly didn't know someone would pay for me to go. My family was lucky to have the ferry business. Made a good enough living. It was my island, my home, and I loved it. I loved my family—we're a big family—and I loved working on the water.

"Ben, you ever thought about college?" Mr. Walters asked.

"No. I don't know how I'd get in, or pay for it if I did."

"If you keep studying so hard, you might get some help."

So, the short of that one is he helped me apply for a scholarship and Grampie persuaded Mumma and Dad it was a good idea. Grampie promised that if I worked hard, he'd help by paying the expenses not covered by the scholarship. That is, if I could get a scholarship. Mr. Walters made out the applications so my parents could sign them, and I guess my personal statement, about having made a mistake but learning from it, impressed the admissions people. And I made sure to back it all up with those specific references Mr. Walters loved so much. I got into a few colleges, but Maine Orono gave me the most money, and it was lucky they did. I'd have been too scared to go to a college like Haverford, though Mr. Walters thought it would be a great place for me. It was just too far away—too much money, too much travel. Too far from home. Orono seemed familiar enough that I could bear it. In fact, I got to love it, and I could still get home on weekends like when I was in high school.

I remember Peedie, who was a year ahead of me, coming back from going to the University in Machias. That's a small place, but he never even got out of the car. Drove up with his parents from the mainland with all the stuff they'd gotten for his room. His grandfather had lived in Connecticut and thought college was important. They were some proud Peedie'd gotten in, but was he ready? Well someone thought he was ready for freshman year, but he didn't think he was, and he wouldn't get out of the car. Scared shitless. That could have been me, but I had another image growing in my mind. Becky planted it there, and Mr. Pyle and Mr. Walters helped it grow. I wasn't sure what I wanted to be, but I knew by then I didn't want to be like Jason. Lucky I knew him; the little twerp showed me who I didn't want to be.

The morning Jason told me she was back, I walked down the dirt road from the dock to my house, past Grampie's house. It was a tough place to walk past, always had been because I took Becky there, and it reminded me. Worse in some ways when Grampie and Grammie were alive, 'cause I'd go in and at some point we'd go to the library. I always loved the library, and I could see Becky standing in the doorway looking out at the beach when she came to the island for my birthday picnic. I watched her standing in the doorway like the figurehead on the prow of a ship. I remember wishing she had worn a dress so the light would flow through it and reveal a bit more of her.

She was wearing tan pants, but my boy mind undressed her anyhow, and I enjoyed the twinges of sex and pride that she was there and everyone was looking at her. She was blushing, trying hard to fit in. She did too—up to a point. I knew she was surprised by some things—Mumma so deferential, curtseying to her. Damn, that was funny. Funny to love two women from such different worlds. I can still feel Becky's shoulder where I put my arm around her, feel her hand in mine. I worried mine was so rough from handling the lines on the ferry. I wanted to kiss her. Could almost taste that, but I didn't. Too soon, I thought. Play her in like a crab on the end of a string. Bad image. Like a butterfly to honey.

It took courage to ask her to Islesford. I wasn't going to take Jason's dare right off. When I first saw her, she was staring at me from the bank overlooking the tide pools at her family's place. We'd just brought the float up the Sound to their dock, and I was supposed to be helping Grampie. I could feel her watching me. I remember spitting into a tide pool, an adolescent gesture of dismissal that, but it gave me some pleasure. I pretended I didn't see her. She was walking funny, sort of pigeon-toed and looking at her feet.

I planted myself in front of her for the hell of it—just to see what would happen. I remember looking at her hair blowing in the wind and that stupid orange life jacket concealing anything interesting that might lie under it. I wondered why she had to wear a life jacket on land, but then her father said, "When you learn to swim." She frowned, so I thought she was upset, but that seemed foolish to me. Lots of fishermen never learn to swim. Say they'd rather drown fast than slow. She had on a fancy blue sweater and those tan pants, and she looked ridiculously clean and boyish. I thought girls were supposed to wear bobby socks and white shoes and skirts. I was mesmerized by her long hair ruffled by the breeze off the Sound, and the sway of her hips when she walked. I don't think she did it consciously, but I loved watching her.

So I'm standing in front of her, expecting her to stop, and she bumps right into me. What luck! I got flustered immediately, though, and I couldn't think of anything to say. I looked at her standing in front of me and I wanted to put my arms around her and hold her against me. That would have shocked her, as well as Grampie and her father. We wouldn't have had much work out of the summer people after that. Well—I just got myself away as fast as I could. I can still feel the muscles of her back against my hand, and smell the sweetness of her where I touched her shoulder.

I don't know if I would have tried to see her again if I'd known how it was going to be between us, but whenever Grampie said that we had another picnic job, I volunteered just on the chance that it would be for her parents. It wasn't, of course, and I was so disappointed I went into a deep funk, and Mumma, who thought I was sweet on the Closson girl, figured she'd turned me down for a date. It was a good cover.

Then toward the end of that first summer, Grampie said there was another picnic job, and again I volunteered. When we docked, I scanned the crowd, the usual sort of crowd with their hampers and bags and bright shirts with collars and little embroidered lambs on the chest and wild Madras Bermuda shorts, or shorts with embroidered red lobsters. That's an odd uniform, but they all wear it. It's dumb looking, and the shorts don't even cover their knobby knees. When I did see her, I dropped the rope I was coiling, but I don't think anyone except her noticed. I blushed like a rose and learned what "hot under the collar" meant. I got her back, though, when she looked at me with those damn binoculars and I made a goofy face at her. She dropped the binoculars fast and they hit her on the knee, and it was lucky she had the cord around her neck. That told me she liked me. I wanted to ask her out right then, but I took my time.

Atlantic cod

CHAPTER TWO

I love Islesford, and I love the life I've made, but I did love Becky, and she's haunted me for years. There was a terrible vulnerability in her that I wanted to protect, to heal somehow. I knew it was dangerous for me, that she had the power to hurt me. Hell, I was sixteen—well, almost—and lust was a powerful motivator too.

I'd fooled around with some of the girls from high school. Smart enough, or lucky, not to fool around with girls from my island. That would have been kind of like incest—we'd been like brothers and sisters for so long in the same little school, and besides, word would have gotten around in a minute. Sometimes I think the wind takes words out of our mouths and broadcasts them, because rumors travel so fast. But no, I was always careful to keep my exploits to making out with mainland girls. I guess I wasn't bad looking, and the fact that my family had a good business, a long-time business, made me a catch, so I always had girls flirting with me. Got so I'd sort of experiment in playing them along.

Sure pissed off Jason because he looks like a wiry rat. I didn't see him that way when we were kids, and I liked the tricks he played on the teachers and other people on the island. I didn't like that he stole from the store, or shot BBs at summer cottages; he broke a lot of windows. Putting a snake in the teacher's lunch box or an eel in our school aquarium—now that was a laugh. Worst was when he got older and camped out in the summer cottages—his shack-'em-up shacks, he called them, and I guess he used them for courting. Well—not courting exactly, because he wasn't planning to get married. He got Katie pregnant, and her parents were so disgusted with him and her they might not have insisted that she marry him, but she wanted to, and that was her mistake.

Jason had a mean streak, but when I was young I thought he was powerful and smart. Now I see he was neither. He'd push around the little kids in school so they would do what he asked them to—get him his lunch pail, give him their cookies, little things; but when he was older at the high school he'd bully people into being scared of him—into giving him cigarettes, letting him spy on the girls in the bathrooms. He's pissed off just about everyone, but he's still from here. He's still ours, so we deal with him. When we were kids, Ralph and Durlin tried to keep me on a straight path, or at least pretty straight, and now we all try to help Jason in other ways, and 'specially Katie and the kids.

When I was a kid, Dad would come home from fishing, and Mumma would have been cooking and cleaning, mending and tending. She was tired; he was tired. Those were the best times. There's always something that needs fixing—nets, traps, buoys, the house. They'd sit and talk. We'd help with what we could. I got good at whittling pegs to hold the lobster claws, and my sister helped weave bags to hold the chum. Sometimes we'd go over to Grampie and Grammie's, and Grampie would tell us stories about when he was a kid sailing with his father and mother around the world. Maine captains took their families with them, and I don't think captains from other places did that. Children would study on the ship—learning about the places they went. Grampie's life as a kid seemed a lot more exciting than what I was doing in school.

Grampie said that his grandfather told him about when the fish were so abundant no one worried about them disappearing like we do now. He explained that fish around the islands were hardly touched, except by the few native people, until after the French and Indian war. When the first settlers came to Mount Desert from Massachusetts in 1761, they were astounded. Fishermen had already wiped out a lot of fish on their side of the Atlantic, and here they found fish stocks they hadn't imagined because they had never seen them in the Eastern Atlantic. Here they found everything they needed—tall trees for masts and houses, salt hay rich in minerals to feed livestock, and, most important, cod to salt for themselves and to trade. The stuff kept for months and it was a valuable resource before refrigeration. You've got to develop a taste for it, of course, easier if they start you as a baby chewing on it to soothe your gums. But soak it for twenty-four hours until the salt leaches out and you've got cheap, tasty protein.

The fishing wasn't so good to the west of Cranberry and Mount Desert because it had been intense even in the 1700s, and some places were already fished out of cod and sturgeon. The people who settled on Mount Desert couldn't believe the resources, but what we forget is that Europe had been that way too. Whites weren't the only ones to take more than they put back, more than could be sustained, but we were the most rapacious, and the seas became a place of slaughter. We forget that, and that's half the problem. We get used to what is left, instead of seeing what was; we've set a new baseline, a new normal that is far less diverse and rich than what was normal a generation or two before us. The memories disappear when the children die who heard the stories the old fishermen told. Grampie's stories made me want to understand what was happening to the fish and to us.

Where the rivers dump out into the bays should be the richest fishing. The river water mixes nutrients into the bays—there's lots of plankton there to feed the little fish like alewives and pogies. To the south of here, they call the pogy menhaden and even bunker, which is our family name. Comes from the French *bon coeur*, meaning good heart. I'm proud of that, but pogy is the Maine name for them. Those fish, and the smelt, cunners, and tomcod that we don't see now, used to feed the big fish like the cod. The cod eat the lobsters, clams, mussels, and scallops on the bottom, too, but they need to eat the oily fish, including the pogies and alewives, to get ready for spawning. That's why the fishermen harvest them for bait—it's what cod crave, and what draws them close to shore.

Grampie remembers his grampie telling him people fished differently back then, too. Families or neighbors would build a boat together, and the chandleries in Boston took shares, not cash, for the sails, cordage, and iron to outfit a boat. The fishermen used hand lines—two baited hooks on a hand reel—way into the 1850s. That's when the dory fishing and tub trawls started using long lines that had 500 to 1000 baited hooks. The boats weren't so big or specialized that you had to go after one type of fish, and families or neighbors paid shares. They didn't fish on Sundays. People all had other jobs—farmer, sailor, carpenter—and they fished for different species at different times of the year. They'd stop to take in the hay, or build a barn, and a lot of the boat hands were just kids in school.

And his grandfather told Grampie that until the Civil War, fishing didn't change much. There were still so many cod, pogy, mackerel, and flounder that only a few people could imagine them disappearing. I learned later that from 1793 to 1866, American cod fishermen got a bounty from the government for just fishing for cod because cod were such an important food. Captains had to keep logs to earn the bounty, so we know millions and millions of pounds of cod were fished out even in those days, just with the hand lines. Back then no one was adding it all up. If they had a bad year, they just thought the fish had migrated somewhere else and would be back soon. Most of the fish were caught close to shore, within twenty-five miles of home. Now the fish are so far offshore, fishermen in small boats can't catch them. Good thing we've got lobster.

A lot of things changed. Some fishermen noticed, but it was a long time before other people recognized the damage to the fisheries, or thought their actions might have anything to do with it. The settlers took down a lot of trees, and that let mud and other junk foul the estuaries. As the whale fishery killed off the whales, the industrial revolution was increasing the need for oil to lubricate machinery. Someone figured out you could also use pogy oil, so fishermen started catching them in huge numbers.

The fishermen knew that was going to cause problems, but other people didn't pay attention. In 1848 Maine fishing captains petitioned the legislature to close the pogy fishery to oil-factory seiners, but they didn't win. The captains of industry did. By 1879 there weren't any pogy to catch around here, just a few alewives and herring to draw the cod in to coastal waters, and not enough of them either. In the '50s though, when I was growing up, the fishing came back a bit, maybe because there weren't as many men to fish during World War II, and the fish rebounded. That gave us all hope for a while.

I was used to looking out from the harbor, seeing the mainland as the big wide world. Going to Willey's in Ellsworth to buy clothes for school was a big deal. Course I didn't need much—just a couple of pairs of jeans and a plaid shirt and good boots—but it was a trip off-island. That was so exciting they'd write us up in the *Bar Harbor Times*. "On the morning ferry—the Bunker family going off-island to buy school clothes. Guess school's going to open soon. My how those kids have grown."

I learned a lot my first year of high school, but not much of it out of books, and I got to know some girls from the mainland and other islands. Some of them flirted with me, some of them I went after. I didn't want to lead anyone on too far, though I did mess around with some of them. Sarah Brucker, now she led me on to places I'd only dreamed about, or heard about from older guys. She was older by three years, that made a difference, and she was walking sex. I met her when I was a freshman.

I think she specialized in freshmen. She was from Bar Harbor, and she had boobs held up by major steel construction, at least when she wore a bra, so they pointed right at you, saying, "Come here, you're mine."

I thought about burying my head in those boobs a long time before I did. She's the one who got me thinking about doing that. I admit the thought surprised me, but then I'd call it up whenever I wanted to and get an immediate hard on. That was an experiment in itself. Course, sometimes that happened when I didn't want it to. Chemistry class. Nothing sexy about that, except when you see two domes on the lab counter for some experiment. All the boys were whispering about how if you looked from a certain angle the domes looked just like we all imagined Sarah's boobs would look, though some guys weren't just imagining.

One day in the hall after class, Sarah stopped me to say she needed help with her brother's car. I saw some older guys snickering and one gave a thumbs-up sign, so I knew something special was going on. She said he'd loaned the car to her for the day so she could pick up some medicine for her mother on the way home. I would have followed her into Hell, my tongue literally wagging, thinking about sliding into her. She'd parked the car at the end of the lot where the football players parked, but they had taken the bus to their game in Ellsworth, so it was sitting in the lot with nothing and no one around it. "That's why I need you," she said in her husky voice. She smoked, and I thought that was pretty sexy too—it had lowered her voice so she sounded "mature." She said the problem with the car was that she couldn't get the back seat up and she needed to so she could pick up her kid brother and his friends after sports. Didn't even notice the different story about why she had the car.

We walked to the car, a 1956 Chevy 210. Cream and royal blue, sweeping fins, and a huge back seat. She walked close to me, edging nearer so our bodies were touching when we stood by the car door. "Sit there, I'll show you things you ain't ever seen, I betcha." She was right.

I opened the door for her like a gentleman, and she crawled in, almost sticking her ass in my face. Then she turned and when I put my left leg in the car, she grabbed my crotch and pulled the rest of me in under her. I let out a yowl of surprise and delight, and she hoisted up her skirt to show me she wasn't wearing underpants and unzipped her jacket. She wasn't wearing any underwear at all. It was a dream come true! Her enormous tits fell out in front of my face and, well, you can guess the rest.

It was quite an introduction to sex, and I let her introduce me quite a few times before she zeroed in on Jimmy Crank. Jimmy'd started the year late at the high school because his father was in the Coast Guard and had just been posted to Southwest from Hawaii. I was jealous at first, but then realized I'd "come of age" and would find other girls. I learned later that she parked that car there every day after classes, and the guys who worked for the school helped her with the back seat, and so did the football team. Screwing Sarah was an initiation rite. "Brucker's Fuckers," we called ourselves. And after she left school, she'd still come back from time to time and spend the day in the parking lot. I can't figure out why the principal never knew, but maybe he did. That was ninth grade.

But eleventh grade was totally different. I was in love with Becky Granger, and I was grounded. I shriveled up inside like a clam and didn't talk or flirt with any of the girls, and I started studying. "You're such a snob, Ben Bunker," Aileen said to me one day at school. "You've grown as uppity as the summer people. Think they'll think you're worth talking to if you study those books? I doubt it."

I looked at her, and I knew she was trying to flirt with me. She had her head down and her eyes fluttering up the way girls do, and her whole body was moving like grass in a breeze. I watched her boobs and hips doing this little dance in front of me, and I thought about doing a slow dance with her, but she interrupted this not unpleasant thought, saying, "I bet you wouldn't even go out with one of us local girls now. Just waiting for summer so you can impress the summer girls because you've read some books."

"Aileen, don't be daft. I just screwed up at home, and Dad's grounded me. Not much else to do but read. Not so bad. You should try it some time."

She giggled, then smiled and wrinkled her nose, but to me she looked like Miss Piggy. She seemed to be waiting for something, but I just said, "See you later, Aileen." Her face deflated, and even her puffed and shellacked hair wilted, and she stopped moving. She looked like a child who hadn't gotten her way—lower lip pushed out, eyes reddening with tears. Downright ugly.

There were nice girls and not-so-nice girls. Before I met Becky, I only spent time with the not-so-nice girls. After Becky, I didn't spend much time with girls, or even my guy friends. On the weekends when

I was in eleventh, I was home, and at home I didn't go out with anyone because I was grounded. By senior year Dad relented because we hadn't heard anything about Becky being pregnant, and I was allowed out, but I was in no shape to be on the football team, and I was an outsider by then, anyhow. Jason was fed up with me for always having my nose in a book, and I'd started to dream bigger. Durlin and Ralph stayed close to home and close to me, but guys don't talk about that stuff much. Doesn't mean we aren't old friends, though. They knew something was really wrong, and that it involved Becky, but they didn't try to fork it out of me. They just accepted me and the ways I changed after being grounded. Then, finally, after Dad ended the grounding, we could hang out again together.

We all wanted to come back to live on the island after high school. We couldn't see another life than that, and we couldn't figure out how to make a living except by fishing. Durlin thought he might want to work for the town, and Ralphie, he's an artist. Always has been. He can paint extraordinary, detailed pictures of the sea and boats, and he thought he might be able to make a living fishing and painting. We all knew we'd have to do a few things simultaneously to survive and raise families, and we all wanted families. Maybe it's like the weather—we've got four seasons, and we like the changes. So we work the same way. A lot of that has changed now, though, with all the fishing regulations, and the fish gone.

Ralphie's father and his father before him were groundfishermen. Way back, his family fished cod from a small boat and used hooks and lines. There were so many cod then that once they got the boat into a school of fish, men just threw the lines in and drew them out in a continuous furious motion, and the fish fell into the boat, jumping and thrashing around. His family did so well they bought bigger boats, and his grandfather bought one of the first diesel-powered boats in the late 1920s. By the 1930s, fishermen were landing a lot of fish. Thank heaven for the Catholics and the invention of fish sticks.

During World War II, there were so many guys from Maine fighting that there weren't so many out fishing, but then after the war, the new technology from chasing submarines was adapted to finding fish. During the war, meat was so high that many people ate more fish, so there was a good market. And refrigeration meant the fishermen could go after halibut and the smaller flounder that don't salt well. So after the war, the fishermen went back to work in bigger boats with better gear, and better ways to locate fish. Then the government got worried when the haddock about disappeared and began thinking about regulating the nets. Some people said the mesh was too small, and the little fish couldn't get out and grow big enough to justify catching, but the government didn't get around to regulating that for another twenty years. Probably would have been better if they'd done it earlier. Lots of politics and power behind the decision not to do anything, so that's not new either. Got me asking what was true, though.

Going to college—that was gut-wrenching. I was the only one from the island who went, though Durlin managed to go to night school a few years later. Mumma and Dad were terrified, and that made me scared. We didn't know what to bring; we saw other kids and their parents laughing and hauling in baskets and boxes of stuff to decorate their rooms—furniture even—and I felt like a poor dumb hick. First time I saw the tiny room I was going to share with a stranger, I wanted out before I'd even stepped in. It was painted beige, a spare rectangle with two skinny, lumpy beds, two bureaus, two desks, and a closet. It was hard to move around. There was one window, and my roommate, Gus, had already claimed the bed next to it. I wondered how I was going to breathe.

The University of Maine Orono was my doorway to other ways of living and thinking. I took the freshman classes in a daze, awed by the size of everything and the number of people. I was in a dorm with a lot of other kids, most from Maine, but also some from out of state. I met a kid named Forest—liked him and his name right off. It seemed a Maine kind of name, but it turned out he was from Connecticut. His grandparents had moved there from Hancock, Maine, during World War II to work in the munitions industry, and stayed.

Forest wasn't so great at academics that he could scramble into a better college, so when UMO accepted him, his family was relieved and said he was just going home. I went to visit him a couple of times in Stamford, Connecticut, and he came to see me. The city mouse and the country mouse; that was us. I took him fishing and snowmobiling around the island. He took me to a dance and a couple of movies, and just driving around. We went into New York City, but it was so busy, dirty, and noisy I didn't like it much.

Forest told me he wanted to be an investment banker when he graduated, but I didn't have a clue what he meant. I asked him why, and he told me he wanted to make a lot of money, have a gorgeous, blonde "trophy wife," 2.4 children, a fancy house, and a Porsche. I knew he was joking, but also that it wasn't totally a joke. "What do you want?" he asked.

"Me. I want—well I want to live on the island. That's home. I want to be with my family—my whole family. City people think we country people never have an original thought or read a book, but that's not the way it is. I can live on Islesford and have a good life if I find the right wife. Two-point-four kids? I'll settle for two. But I don't want to work in an office chained to a phone. I want to be on the water. I want to fish, but I want to know about the world, not be closed in like some island people. It's tough to figure out how to do that."

'Course fishing now really means setting traps for lobsters, but the language tells the story—we still go fishing, just like our great-great-grandfathers did, and even our grandfathers. Trouble is, now there isn't much to catch except lobster. Even though the cod bounty ended in 1866 because Midwest farmers and others not eligible for the bounty complained, the fishery expanded. To qualify for the bounty, the captains had to keep those log books, and I read some of them when I was at Maine Maritime. They recorded huge quantities of fish—sometimes whole schools were harvested. The bounty had favored fishermen with larger boats, so after the Civil War there were fewer boats overall, but larger ones that were better equipped to catch hake and haddock, cusk, pollock, halibut, and flounder.

Everyone loved flounder. To me flounders are damn ugly fish with their eyes squished onto a flat face, but they taste good. People loved them to death. That's what Grampie told me to explain why we hardly ever find them anymore. Now I worry that we're loving the other fish to death as well. Using long lines with 600 or so hooks meant fishermen had to have a lot more bait, and that put pressure on the little fish. Using gill nets and purse seiners, as well as the old weirs, allowed fewer people and boats to catch more fish.

By 1880 or so, the cod were getting scarce. They'd moved offshore, and the fishermen had to follow them. Only big boats could do that.

And in the late 1800s the rusticators started arriving—that's what people called the first tourists. They weren't so damn rustic, staying in the fancy hotels that got built in Bar Harbor, but that's how they saw themselves, and perhaps in comparison to the way they lived at home in New York, Boston, and Philadelphia, they were rusticating. They'd fish off the docks and catch fish, including flounder. Made them happy I guess, and like the people in the party boats that fished for cod in the '50s, they had their photographs taken on the dock, and someone to dump out the fish afterwards. Damn waste.

The nets and the draggers—gill nets, purse seines, beam trawls, and otter trawls—methodically scooped up everything in their paths. They caught hundreds of thousands of juvenile cod, and some haddock, many too young to breed, too small to eat until someone gave them a new name: scrod. Scrod fit neatly on a plate, but eating them is like eating our seed corn.

After a while I got used to college, and Gus and I got used to each other. We weren't ever really friends, but we got along, and then next year I roomed with Forest. We had a big room with two windows and some nooks and crannies, so you didn't feel like you were living in a box. We painted two walls deep green for him, and two walls ocean blue for me. I'm not sure we were supposed to do that, but we did. And I began to figure out what I was going to do with my life.

Fishing's gotten worse, a lot worse. That's where I thought I could do something to make a difference, by trying to understand what's happening. What's changing the way we've lived for so long, that built our communities and fueled them? What are we going to do? What am I going to do? And for Christ's sake, why is she here?

The hand-line cod fishery.

CHAPTER THREE

At the end of my sophomore year at UMO, when I met Professor Jim Acheson, I started answering how I could earn a living, learn about the world, and stay home in Maine. He was doing research on lobsters, and he put an announcement in the college newspaper looking for people to help him that summer with a study of the fisheries. I volunteered.

Professor Acheson, now my friend Jim, has done more to make sense out of lobstering than anyone. He's an anthropologist studying behavior, not just of fishermen, but also of the fish and lobsters, and how that affects fishing. Turns out that there's a lot more to fishing than just fish. But that was way ahead of me when I was in school on the island.

There were nine of us kids in the Islesford school those years, so we were all in one classroom, and I was lucky to have three other boys close to my own age. School was just an extension of our family because we knew everyone on the island, and maybe even more important, everyone knew us. When we decided to make wine with a pumpkin Ralph found in a field, there wasn't much chance it would be a secret for long. Not with Jenny, Ralph's sister, in the same school. Of course, everyone knew when the pumpkin blew up and splattered stinking rind and decayed pulp on Mrs. Jones' laundry that was hanging on the line. We spent the weekend cleaning up and several other weekends doing chores for Mrs. Jones.

After school we'd go hang out in a dinghy, rowing around the harbor, out to the point, or over to Great Cranberry when we got older. Durlin got sweet on one of the Mackel girls on Great Cranberry, and we'd row over there and pretend we were hunting for crabs at low tide until she happened to come along the beach. Then they would sit down near a tide pool and flirt and giggle while Ralph, Jason, and I pretended not to watch.

Summers, even when I was little, I worked on Grampie's boats. That's where I learned about summer people. Most of them either paid no attention to me or were at least polite. Some were even friendly. Mr. Baker used to ask me about school and say it was really—I remember he said *really*, not *real*, like everyone else—important that I study hard. He never told me why, though, and I didn't have any idea how knowing that the Ancient Greeks fought at Thermopylae or the Egyptian slaves built pyramids might help me fish. We did like learning about embalming, though. We thought the photographs of mummies and alabaster jars for hearts and livers were pretty gory and, therefore, interesting.

I learned how to fish from Uncle John, one of my father's brothers, and from my dad, of course. Uncle John didn't have any sons, so he borrowed me sometimes from Dad on weekends. Not that I could do much that was useful at first, but as I got older, I learned to bait the traps and helped haul and clean them. I loved the swish of the water washing out of the traps as we hoisted them from the ocean, the smell of what came out of the sea, and the surprise. Uncle John was an enthusiastic bear of a man, and always excited about what was in the trap. "Goree— we got a big one. Look at the size of that mutha—and mother she is!" He'd measure, though he didn't need to do that to know we'd caught a breeder and she had to be clipped and put back to set her eggs. One day he caught a blue lobster and gave it to the Oceanarium to show off to the summer people. Beautiful creature.

I fished with Uncle John from when I was a fingerling myself, probably only seven, maybe eight, years old. I didn't go out often because I had school, but I loved his stories because he was so interested in everything. Opinionated, but enthusiastic. He asked questions even back then about why the fishery was changing. He knew from older fishermen that there had been twice as many men fishing at the end of the 1800s as there were by the 1920s. Sure, some guys worked on the shore fishery using weirs and traps for herring and other fish, but the fishery wasn't sustaining as many families as it had, and the groundfish were farther offshore. Shore fishermen also work from small boats, and following the groundfish farther out got too dangerous. We lost men to the sea, and that hurts the whole community. Most people had to change to lobstering, and Uncle John wondered about how that would affect us.

Groundfish are exactly what the name sounds like—the fish that live close to the bottom or the ground. We don't think of the bottom of the ocean as ground, but that is, of course, what it is. And the fish weren't there. Adapting to any change is hard. You hear that and you say, "Well, I can change." But think about it—what your parents and grandparents did doesn't work anymore. What you've known all your life doesn't work, and what you thought you would do when you raised your own family doesn't work. It's unnerving because you don't know what will work or what is right. Overfishing's killed the fish, they aren't coming back; or the fish just migrated, they'll be back next season.

A fisherman has to learn the habits and habitat of the fish he's hunting, the seasons and the weather, just like a farmer has to know his land, or a hunter the woods and the ways in which animals use it. For a fisherman, it's that much tougher because he can't see the environment where creatures are living and hiding. Some of the new technology helps him—he can scan the bottom and read the nooks and crannies— but he can't see it unless he scubas.

"Can't be good for anyone just to fish for one kind of critter," Uncle John told me. "Used to go after a little bit here and a little bit there. Scallops and shrimp in winter, lobster in the summer, and the fish. That's better for the fish too. Gives 'em a break from being hunted and caught." There were so many kinds of fish to catch, he said, from some you've never heard of to alewives, salmon, and eels. "Never liked catching an eel. Slimy sucker. But to go from catching one fish at a time to six hundred on a long line, to six thousand in a trawl or sixty thousand in a purse seine? Something's got to give. We're some lucky we got lobsters."

He told me about the otter trawls that came in about the twenties. The otter trawl's an efficient killing machine. It looks like an enormous manta ray with wings for balance and a huge mouth scooping whole schools of fish and everything else around them. When guys haul in the net, there are a lot of fish they don't want, and they throw them back. I guess that makes good food for gulls, terns, and other predators, but most of those fish are so bruised they die. Just like when men used gaffs to catch mackerel. There'd be schools of mackerel so thick and so long that they could just jab away, hauling in one or two fish with each punch of the gaff into the water. But they also injured and bruised many fish that later died. Fishermen knew that was wasteful, and that practice ended soon after 1850. Maimed too many fish. Fishermen knew even then the stocks were being depleted and people were the cause. John said guys were still talking about the otter trawl that caught 10,000 pounds of flounder in 1919 in one sweep because now people catch so few of them.

Uncle John had been fishing since he was a kid, and he'd lived through the changes. One thing he got really upset by was the way the "newfangled" machines had made fishing too easy. "Used to be we knew the map of the ocean in our heads. We had our marks. Guys would pass the marks along to their sons, and families would pass along the tradition of where to set traps. One of my great-uncle's favorite marks was just off the end of the Coast Guard dock in Southwest. He was sweet on a girl who lived on Clark Point Road, and he'd lay a set of traps around there. Did really well. Married her too."

Back then, he told me, the Eastern and Western Ways were both good places to find cod, haddock, you name it. You could catch haddock and other big fish right off Weaver's Ledge in Bass Harbor, but not now. The fish got a break during World War II. As I've said, men were off fighting, but also because there were Nazi subs working the waters. No one wanted to meet up with one of them. There was a good market for fish, though, because the beef went to the troops; there just weren't as many people fishing.

What makes John so mad today is he thinks the balance is off—unsustainable because anyone can point a sonic fish finder at the ocean and find fish. He thinks using sonar is like cheating and there's no skill to using it. Of course, after the war, fishing really picked up—the men were back, and the trawls and fish finders meant there was no place for the fish to hide. The trawls just vacuumed them up. Back then most of the fish went through wharves like Beal's in Southwest or Stanley's in Manset. Most of it was kept fresh, with just a portion being salted for locals who still liked their salt cod. Now all the fish goes to Portland.

John's first paid job in the fisheries was cleaning out the oak barrels in which the fish were stored. Of course, the wharf owned the barrels—ten-bushel oak barrels that had been shipped from Argentina full with hides. They smelled gut-wrenching awful by mid-summer. It's a wonder John kept going—but then a lot of the kids were washing out the barrels, so there was fun in that. He said they stored all kinds of fish, but haddock was more popular with locals than cod because it had fewer worms.

Other kids worked baiting the long lines. There were 600 or more hooks on each line, sometimes up to a thousand, and you had to run the hook through the eye—mostly they used herring then—then curve it around back onto the hook. I'm glad I never had to do it. Working on the ferry was a lot cleaner.

I learned from him that we had to be careful about where we fished. Uncle John is an Islesford lobsterman. Lobstermen belong to a family and community, almost always centered around the harbor they live nearest. Fishermen from each harbor control their territory. Of course, the state doesn't recognize these territories, but the fishermen do, and that's what counts. Jim Acheson calls these groups "gangs," but we don't, we're just guys who fish together and share the same territory. Guys from Cranberry fished a big area extending around the island and toward Mount Desert, as well as beyond the Cranberries toward Baker's and farther. We each had our grounds within it that we liked. We tried to get our own traps out first, without looking like we were racing each other at the beginning of the season to what we thought were the best spots.

I've never been a high-liner—a top fisherman—but Ralph was. We've competed hard all our lives, though, and now too many times he gets to moon me on the way home to show he's got crates full of lobsters when I don't. Trick is to do it without anyone else seeing. Lobstermen learn the culture of their gang. What's acceptable behavior, how to help each other out even when we're competing—that's why we keep our radios on the same frequency, so we hear each other. Older men teach the younger ones, and we share tips about equipment, where the lobster are, what we're finding. Most important, perhaps, we've created a sustainable fishery by monitoring ourselves and throwing back lobsters that are too large because they are breeders, or too small. And we still moon each other, and joke, and some guys drink too much.

We measure ourselves against each other, too, because we're the ones who know each other. How are we doing, who is top? There's no point comparing yourself and how you're fishing with someone who's going after shrimp, crab, or groundfish, because they're working totally different conditions with different challenges. Of course, some guys work the different fisheries at different times of the year, but the licensing is tough.

We protect our territory because we have to, and sometimes there's trouble. Jim calls these skirmishes "lobster gang wars," or just "lobster wars," because we all had our own turf handed down over the generations, and protecting it can get ugly. Sometimes guys from other places try to push into our territory. First we just snag a buoy with our gaff and retie it backwards as a warning. Next step is to haul a trap and tear off the door, or throw out the bait bag before throwing it back. Last step is to cut the rope to the buoy so the trap sinks. That usually works, but if someone from out of our gang persists in fishing our territory, it can be worse. If someone from another gang set traps where he thinks our fishermen won't notice, we have to push him back.

A few years back, a guy from another gang fished our turf out of a black boat with no lights. Sometimes he'd fish at night in the dark, and the guys got suspicious that he was lifting their traps when they weren't looking. We warned him, but he kept trying to fool with us. They set a trap for him—boats out at night with no running lights on and no radio calling between them. They just waited. Seems he was scooting around the coves out of sight of the villages and taking just a few lobsters from each trap. You don't want to know what they did with him, but he won't be trying that again. Sometimes summer people think they'll just put out a few traps for the fun of it. Guess it makes them feel cool. For the fishermen though, they're just a nuisance.

When I was a kid, there were summer people on the ferries who made me feel like a piece of dirt or worse, as if I didn't even exist. Sometimes it was kids, particularly girls, who just ignored us. They had a way of looking down at us, even if we were taller. Amazing you can do that. How do they learn to act snooty? Do summer people have classes for that?

It got to be a joke with us. Jason might have looked like a wet rat, but Ralph wasn't bad looking. He had some French Canadian blood on his mother's side and could speak some French, so when there were French-speaking tourists on board, he could translate what they were saying, though they didn't suspect he could understand them. That's how I got picked for the dare. In early summer just after my ninth-grade year, two French girls about sixteen came to stay in Islesford for a week with one of the summer families. Long blond hair and blue eyes, flirty little short dresses, very sexy. They moved differently than island girls, self-conscious—not in a bad sense—just conscious of themselves, swaying as they walked, bouncing, sitting on the rocks with their dresses pulled up much farther than any respectable island girl would have done. Ralph could understand them, but he didn't let on to them at first.

"Mais il et le plus beau. Ce jeune homme avec les yeux tres bleus." Ralph said they were talking about me and saying I was good looking and had very blue eyes. After that the guys called me Blue Eyes, and the dare was which of us could get one of the French girls to speak with us. So one day we just waited for them outside the store where they went to get ice cream every afternoon. We followed them as they walked down Coast Guard Road toward the beach and tried talking to them. We weren't very cool, though. Ralph said, "Hi, Frenchie, you sure are pretty."

Jason piped in, "I like the way you walk, Madmwoselle."

The girls giggled, and Ralph whispered what they were saying to each other, that they'd lead us along for a bit. We knew they could speak some English, that was why they were there, but they pretended their English was really bad. They did let us talk to them, though, and over the week they were there, we got to do a lot more. They said at home they were good Catholic girls and never did anything with boys, but they were *en vacances* and exploring America and its beautiful young men. We had a little mutual exploration.

After the French girls left, Jason, Ralph, Durlin, and I were sitting around the harbor one night pretty bored. None of the island girls looked exciting; besides, as I said, they were more like our sisters. There had been a couple of summer girls on the ferry that day with their families. One of them seemed like she was going to fall over the transom when she was getting on the ferry, so I grabbed her hand and arm to steady her and she wrenched it away and snarled, "Get your dirty, disgusting hands off me!" and then went over to her father, who complained to Grampie that I was a "young ruffian." The girl stood there with her hands on her hips, smirking at me. Later Grampie told me it was just her crazy way of flirting, but I figured she had done it to get me in trouble. Grampie assured her father that his "hand" was just concerned she might trip, but she made me feel worse'n dirt.

So after supper Ralph, Durlin, Jason, and I met in the harbor and hung out for a while. I remember the sounds of slapping lines and the smell of fiberglass from repairs someone was making to a dinghy. Some guys say they work in fiberglass just for the smell—gets them high—but

I don't know. So we're joking around about summer people and how stupid and impossible some of them are. Jason said, "So could you get someone from the mainland to come over here—a summer girl? I bet even you, Blue Eyes, even you couldn't make that happen."

"What's it worth to you?"

"Hell, if you're up to it," he said, his rat smile splitting his face and bearing down on the word up. "If you're the man you think you are, no problem right? Fifty bucks. I'll bet you fifty bucks."

That was a powerful lot of money to me then, but his greasy smirk got under my skin and I said, "No problem, rat shit. I'll bet you fifty dollars I can get a summer girl to come over from the mainland just to be with yours truly, your resident heart throb."

Ralph and Durlin were trying to warn me off by raising their eyes and shaking their heads, but I wanted to grind Jason into slime. I knew fifty dollars was even more money for him than for me, so I took him on. That night at home I knew I'd made a huge mistake. I'd risked a week's wages and my pride.

Atlantic herring

CHAPTER FOUR

Sometimes you know that you just connected to something important—a person, a thought, something someone says or does, a photograph that etches itself into your head. Becky was that for me and more, and then there was the bet. I'd tried all summer to see her again. Like I said, every time I heard Grampie had a charter out of Northeast, I volunteered. At first he thought I was just some eager to make money, and that was part of it, but not the important part. I remember standing on the bow of the *Sea Princess* while we powered over to Northeast that day in early August. We were a little late because someone had forgotten to wash the deck and make things ready for the summer people, so Grampie was racing through the harbor. When we slowed down, I skimmed over the people standing on the dock with their picnic gear.

Always amazed me how much stuff summer people thought they needed for an afternoon. Boxes of food from the Pine Tree Market, coolers of wine, beer, and sodas, chairs, bags of extra clothes, and towels, blankets, more luggage than my whole family would take for a week. I looked around the dock, but I didn't see her. Tried to pretend I wasn't looking, but Grampie had a funny smile on his face. I think by then he knew I was sweet on her or something was going on because I'd asked to go on the picnic charters so many times.

After I saw her, I told my cousin Bud, who was the other hand that day, that I wanted to row her to the island later. I gave him a dollar and promised to help him bait the bags for his father's traps if we accidentally arranged it that she and I were left on the *Princess* and I had to row her to Baker Island. Somehow it worked. I helped her into the boat. I can feel her hand still. It wasn't soft and mushy like some girls'. There were bones in that hand and some strength, but it wasn't rough like my mother's. It fit in mine, and I held it for longer than I needed to guide her into the dinghy.

When we were on the *Princess* going over to Baker's, she told me that she wasn't good at rowing. Seemed odd to me at first that she wouldn't know something so simple, but then I thought, Where is she going to row in New York City? I knew by then I liked her. I got that same queasy feeling in my gut when I looked at pictures in the dirty magazines Jason kept in an old bait box in the shed near his house. He'd gotten them from his older brother who was in the Navy and sent them as a present when Jason turned fifteen. Certainly were second- hand, but they were new to us. Anyhow—that feeling of being drawn in, wanting more, but not knowing what I wanted. Trying to take her clothes off in my mind. Fit her into one of those bathing suits the girls seemed to be falling out of in the magazines. It really didn't work. She was stacked, but so proper, at least at first. I couldn't figure out what pulled me in—except that she was very pretty, and she didn't know it. She wasn't cold and snooty like other summer girls. She was even a little shy. That helped. So I just barged ahead—I knew she was my best chance of winning the bet, and besides I liked her.

"What's hard about rowing?" I asked her as I rowed us over to Baker's from the *Princess*. I was thinking I might be able to get her alone and show her how to row, maybe hold her hand again. When she looked up at me, I felt as if she was testing me, but for what I couldn't figure. Looking so deeply into me that her eyes felt like drills. I looked at myself through those eyes for what seemed a long time. I couldn't see what she saw in me. A fisherman's kid and a ferry hand. I wondered if I smelled like bait and lobsters. I felt very small, caught in that stare. And then she started talking, and the words poured out of her like I'd pulled the plug from a bait barrel. Sadness and fear mixing with the words, a silver torrent of words, and listening to her, I wanted to pull her against me and take away that sadness.

She seemed so lost and alone, so sad, and she made me feel special. Special that she trusted me with her sadness and with herself in a way no girl ever had. Like a friend—something deeper than sex. She told me her sister had drowned, and she didn't know how to swim. How could she learn to swim when it made her feel as if she was drowning? I understood that, and I knew she was ashamed and felt guilty. I wanted to help her come through that fear. Maybe that sounds silly. When I think back on it, I think it was the first real connection I made with a girl. The first time I saw one of them as a real person.

I thought about what Grampie told me when I was trying to learn to dock a dinghy. Guess I was no more than five, and doing it by myself scared me. I knew people would be watching. First Grampie showed me what to do by putting out buoys, and I had to row the dinghy between them in whatever pattern he called out to me. When I'd done that a few times without hitting any of them, he said I was ready to try docking at the float in the harbor. I tried to look him in the face and feel brave, but I was scared so bad I could only look at my feet and twist the piece of rope in my hands. Grampie said, "What's eatin' your breakfast?" so finally I looked up and he smiled at me. He always melted me with that smile.

"I'm scared," I answered because I trusted him not to laugh at me. "Scared people will be looking, and I'll smash up against the float, and they'll all laugh at me in school."

"I know that, Chummy," he said. "But you've paid attention. You've practiced, and it's in your blood. I've been watching you, and I know you can do it now. And always remember, even a seal pup has to learn to swim." I've thought about that many times. It's in their nature to swim, but there's still things they have to learn about judging the current, and their own strength. How to swim fast enough to evade a predator, how to catch a cod, or keep up with their mother.

"Even a seal pup," I told her then, "has to learn how to swim." It seemed to help. She smiled, and I felt as if I was king of the world. Or at least that dinghy.

When we got to Baker's, she asked me if I wanted to eat lunch with her. Amazing, that. She had no sense of how people would react, but I knew. I knew that snotty pair of Johnson kids would make us both feel like dirt, so I told her no and went to sit with Grampie and Bud. I watched her eat and then wander off by herself. I thought I'd slip the other way down the beach so no one would suspect, and then head across the dunes to catch up with her. I told Bud I was going to take a piss, and he winked. Once I got around the arm of the beach, I turned into the dunes, scaring up a family of spruce grouse. That almost stopped me. There aren't so many of them left, maybe because they're damn dumb and trusting. You can almost reach out and catch them, but I had a mission. I was on another hunt.

When I walked out on the rocks of the shore, I saw her about fifty yards ahead, just standing on one of the table rocks. Big slabs of pink granite, like a giant hand had placed furniture for people to enjoy. She was dancing, and I watched her body moving to a rhythm only she could hear. When I got close, I heard her singing and I almost burst into laughter. I watched her body undulating, moving fast and slow, and watching, well—I got a hard on. That was a problem.

Whenever that happened, I thought about putting my hands in the slimy cold bait buckets to pull out the chum. It's totally disgusting, even if you remember to put on rubber gloves. By the time I got close enough to call out to her, I was OK, but I probably looked red as the watermelon her parents were eating at the picnic.

I startled her, and she got huffy when I offered her a hand getting down from the rock. She jumped, and I wanted to catch her and hold her, but she was stubborn and tough. I told her Grammie would say she looked like a pig on ice, and I was relieved when she laughed. I guess she could have been some ticked off. We started talking and then walked a bit, and I pointed out the crabs and other critters in the tide pools. That's when I asked her if she wanted me to teach her rowing. She said yes, and now I was sure I could get her to come to Islesford, but a feeling that wasn't what I really wanted was tugging at me. I didn't want her to come so I could win the bet. I just wanted her.

She rowed while I talked and watched. She was clueless at first, but she paid attention and learned quickly. She couldn't make a landing against the *Sea Princess*, and I got so frustrated that I put my hands over hers on the oars. That changed everything. I never felt such a wave of—what—emotion, hormones, lust, love? I know she felt it too, and we crashed into the *Princess*. Grampie must have heard the noise, but not seen the crash, and thank God we didn't do any damage. He never mentioned it to me. I made her try again, and when she succeeded, I felt such a rush of adrenaline that I shivered.

And she did come to my island. She came for my birthday picnic. I don't know what she expected—that we lived in a bait shack? I met her at the Northeast Harbor dock and brought her over on the ferry. Then we followed the path from the dock to Grampie's house, and she seemed surprised we had houses together, the whole family. All she could think of was one of those summer places with the guest houses so's people don't have to spend much time together. Grampie took us into his library, and I thought her jaw would fall off when she saw the titles of classical books. Then she pulled out a book in Greek and I told her Grampie could read it, but I couldn't.

Funny how summer people always think they're smarter and better-read than we are, but that isn't always true. Grampie'd read every book in his library, and he told me that Mainers used to have the highest literacy rate in the United States, particularly the women. They spent so much time alone with their men gone to sea. Some men didn't want their wives reading, so the women had to hide their books when the men came back, but not our family.

She drew me a step into her world, as I drew her into mine. She told me that her father had said she would be like an anthropologist exploring a different culture if she came to my world. That shamed me and made me angry, but I realized pretty soon he was right. We came from two different worlds, worlds apart, even though we shared the same islands. I learned that when I asked her to the movies after she came to Islesford. I was really hungry for her, not just because I wanted to hold her, to kiss her, but because I wanted everything about her. I wanted to drink her in, watch her, listen to her, and she seemed to want the same from me. We were two kids who had each crossed half the bridge between our worlds and now stood in the middle.

I knew even better than she did that it couldn't work. Her father was a good man, but her mother was a typical summer person—scared her daughter would somehow be damaged by association with me. Like some horrible cloud of contagion—*Mainia*—would infect her, and no decent guy from her own world would ever want her. Seemed to me Becky saw through the guys from her world who were so full of themselves.

I made a date with her for Friday night, but then Grampie told me I had to fill in for someone, so I was out on the boat the whole day. I rushed home and cleaned up really carefully. Mumma had pressed all my clothes. I looked good, even though I'm the one saying it. Walking to the dock to get the ferry was a gauntlet—the guys teased me, and Ralph imitated a summer girl being impressed. He sashayed around wiggling his hips and saying, "Don't you look divine. I could just eat you up." I told him that's what I was hoping, and he was too jealous to respond, so he mooned me again, and I told him I was sick of seeing his scrawny ass. I just wanted to see Becky and spend time with her.

When I watched her come down the stairs in a fancy blue party kind of dress, I thought I'd made a huge mistake. I didn't know what to say because we were just going to the movies, and then she looked at me and I knew something else was wrong. I thought it was me that was all wrong, but it was the worlds we lived in, and her mother. She said her mother told her she couldn't go out with me because she had to go to dinner at the Inn with her parents' fancy friends, and because what would people think? The first person who asked her out on a real date was the son of a fisherman? I wasn't from the Main Line, just Maine. Well, I wasn't just the son of a fisherman— Dad helped run the ferry— but whatever. It's what her mother thought. Guess she didn't know fishermen can make a lot of money.

When I heard that, I wanted to get out of her house faster than mackerel chased by seals. I wheeled around and stumbled out the door, but she caught me and when I looked in her eyes I knew she cared about me too. We kissed. My head spun and we both sat down heavily on the bench outside her door. I don't think either of us could stand up. Then we heard her parents in the hall, and she had to go, and I was scared that would be the last I saw of her ever.

I knew she and her family were leaving in the next few days, and I tried to find a way to get back to her, but by then Dad and Mumma were worried too. They sensed that my flirtation was turning into something else, and that there was no way I wasn't going to get hurt. The old fear probably got them too—that I'd leave. Why is it we don't see we have something worth living for right where we are—that we don't have to leave our home to do a job that's worth doing, or to live a life worth living? Sometimes I've felt as if I let myself down, or I wasn't good enough because I didn't go away and stay away. I came back. Most of the time, however, I'm glad of it.

Mumma and Dad tried to distract me with extra chores and getting ready to go back to school to start tenth grade, but they knew I was moping around because she'd gone. Sometimes Dad would tease me about my summer girl, but Mumma knew it wasn't something I wanted to joke about.

I was almost glad when school started. I was going to stay again with Aunt Cissy and Uncle Albert in Northeast Harbor. Living most of the week away at their house seemed sort of like going to the boarding school where Becky was, the one her dad went to, because I wasn't at home except on the weekends.

Our grammar school on the island is small, usually about ten kids then, though now we're lucky to even have five because it's so hard for young families to find housing. We hired a teacher a few years back who had three kids, and we built an apartment for them in the attic over the school. That almost doubled the number of students. When I was a kid, it was still a small enough school that we knew each other, knew each other's families, and the teachers knew each of us so well they could tell in a minute if something was wrong. We just had the one main teacher, but special teachers for art and music would come out to our island once a week. Mr. Ellis, the art teacher and I got along really well.

Mount Desert High School took kids from all the villages in that town, including Northeast Harbor, Seal Harbor, Somesville, and Pretty Marsh, so it was much bigger, and there were about forty students in my class alone. Some of the mainland kids, like the ones from Pretty Marsh, spent a lot of time in a bus. That first year had been really tough for us island kids being away from everything familiar. It was so much harder for Mumma and Dad or any of the island parents to come over for special events, games, or Parents' Nights. We missed having them cheering us on. Aunt Cissy and Uncle Albert tried to fill in, but still I felt lonely and distant. I went home, of course, on weekends, and sometimes Wednesday nights as well, if the weather was calm and I didn't have a game or something that kept me at school.

A lot of our guys, the Backsiders, looked forward to dropping out of school at sixteen. There didn't seem much point in staying. Hell, we thought, you don't need algebra or European history to know where the fishing's good or when the tide's going out. Of course, now the technology's taken over what we used to learn from our granddads, dads, and other fishermen. You need a degree, and an advanced one like I got at Maine Maritime's a real advantage, to run a boat and find fish or even lobsters. There are a lot more complications, even now when the distant fleets can't fish our waters. Government regulations, overfishing, changes in the water and the climate. It all adds up.

Years ago, about 1975 I think it was, a Russian factory ship, a huge trawler, chased mackerel into Somes Sound. If they'd done that in the winter they might have gotten away with it. No laws would have stopped them or the hundreds of other foreign boats that sucked up our fish in the Gulf of Maine and the Georges Bank. This captain chose to fish the Sound in August. That was just numb.

Factory ships as big as football fields could haul huge trawl nets, pull eighty miles or so of hooked long lines, or set out forty-mile drift nets. Pairs of them could trawl together with enormous nets and work twenty-four hours a day—catching and processing—that's illegal now. But imagine a ship that filled the view of Somes Sounds from the porches of the big houses on the shore with its rusting hulk, and the noses of summer people with the smell of rotting fish, leaking oil, and unwashed sailors. There was a lot of money and power looking at that trawler. I bet some of the summer residents pushed for what became the Magnuson-Stevens Act that passed in 1976 and set a 200-mile limit off US coasts to keep the foreign fleet away and protect our fish and fishermen.

Magnuson-Stevens got rid of the foreign factory ships, but then the government invested millions in helping local fishermen buy specialized gear and bigger boats. Doubled the groundfish trawl fleet between 1976 and 1984. When you think about what's happening now and the money the government is spending to buy back boats and get guys out of fishing, it seems damn dumb. I'm grateful for Magnuson-Stevens—we all are—but now, of course, as I said, we've created other problems.

I was planning to drop out of school at sixteen. Jason and I talked about it just about every time we left Miss Shortich's class after doing her work sheets. That woman had an endless supply of worksheets. Worksheets for commas and adjectives, for nouns and pronouns, for every part of speech you could imagine, and a lot you couldn't: run-on sentences, dangling modifiers, coordinate adjectives. If I ever finished one early, she had another one to stuff at me, so I figured out fast that being slow was much less work. I don't know how that woman could make learning to write and read so numbingly boring. Why do they teach teachers to be that way?

Mr. Henry now, he was the natural science and biology teacher. He had us studying our own environment and comparing it to places we'd never seen. How is Northeast Harbor like—just pick the place it seems most unlike—the Kalahari Desert, for instance, and he'd help us find something they had in common. We went on field trips, sometimes down to the ocean or in the national park, but mostly just around the school to do things like catch caterpillars and let them hatch into butterflies. We studied what they ate, then fed them the right plants, and one day we walked into the classroom and a lot of them had shed their chrysalises and were flying around the room. It was beautiful. Mr. Henry opened the door that went directly out onto the playground, and the butterflies went fluttering out and onto the plants and nectar we'd put out for them. That was a lesson we remembered. Miss Shortich died a few years back, and I know it's not a kind thought, but I hope she was buried with stacks of worksheets to keep her busy wherever she went next.

I was pretty miserable that first month of tenth grade thinking about Becky. Missing her, wishing we'd had more time to get to know each other. I'd lay awake at night thinking of her, of kissing her and holding her, then getting pissed off at her stuck-up parents. One Saturday morning in early October, when I was home for the weekend, Uncle Clem came in while we were having breakfast and I was telling Mumma and Dad about my week. "I have some real bad news for you," he said. We all knew Uncle Clem could be dramatic. Everything was always the worst thing that ever happened. His face would droop like a Basset Hound's, and he'd say, "We got a real bad problem with the boat. Goin' to be real expensive this time."

Dad would look at him and say, "What is it this time, Clem? A tisket a tasket, another torn gasket?"

Or something like that, and the corners of Clem's mouth would drag down to his ears and he'd say, "Nope this is a big one. The cowling come loose off the engine. I might be able to duct tape it for now, but it's going to be real big when we have to replace it."

Dad would say, "Good enough," and turn back to read his paper.

This time Uncle Clem spread the paper on the table. It took me a minute to understand why. Then there it was, an obituary. "Samuel Granger, of New York City, summer resident of Northeast Harbor, died suddenly of a heart attack as he was leaving for Paris on a business trip."

"I don't understand," I said nervously. But I did, I knew it meant Becky's father had died while she was in school away from her mother and the rest of her family. I pictured her standing in the principal's office—later I learned it was the headmistress's office—being told that he died. I wondered if she cried, but I guessed that the icy calm that froze her when something hurt had encased her. I wished I was there to hold her and let her cry, but then that feeling got mixed up with just wanting to hold her.

It didn't seem right to think of her that way just after her dad died. I thought I should think about her, how sad she must be, how much she loved her dad, and how I would feel if my father died, and how miserable my mother would be. I thought about her family and hoped it was as big as my family and that there would always be people with her and her mother. I wondered if her little brother would miss his father, or if he was too young to realize what had happened and wouldn't even be able to remember him when he got older. I wondered if her mother would ever marry again, and how Becky would feel, but mostly I just thought about holding her and then kissing her under that light outside her parents' rented summer cottage.

I tried to find her. I went to the library and talked to the woman at the front desk, but when I told her I was trying to find Miss Becky Granger to tell her how sorry I was that her father died, the woman looked at me as if she was thinking, Why would Miss Becky Granger ever want to hear from you? I turned around and left. Dad and Mumma said they would find out, but I don't think they did much asking. They didn't want me to get more involved with Becky. I channeled a lot of my worries and energies into football and basketball that year, and then finally it was summer again.

I wondered if she might come back, wondered about their land, what was happening to it. Uncle Clem saw a For Sale sign on it in June, so I knew they were trying to sell it, and I figured that meant they wouldn't be back. I'd forced myself not to think about her and had almost forgotten about her, almost, when we were running the ferry into Northeast the next summer in late August. It was some foggy, so thick I could hardly see the rope in my hand. We had to go very slowly, and the clouds of fog drifted back and forth, hiding the dock sometimes, then drawing back so I could see it. I had a vision of Becky standing by the railing, and it totally pissed me off that I was still thinking about her. The shafts of those thoughts hurt, they actually hurt. I'd tried to push them so deeply into me that I could no longer feel them, but that was foolish. It didn't work, and there she was and my chest was aching. Next minute there she wasn't as the fog rolled over the dock. I knew it wasn't her standing on the dock, but probably some old lady, like the times, so many times, I thought I saw her ahead of me on the street, or going into the library, or down by the dock. Got so I didn't trust my eyes or my mind. I was determined not to let her take me over, so I shut myself off from her. Or hoped I had.

I got ready to jump off the boat and throw the rope over the cleat on the dock, but then the fog rolled away and there she was. It wasn't just an old lady standing there; it was Becky. I had the feeling she wanted to get away from me, and I almost wanted to disappear myself, but her shyness and hesitation made me wave to her. My heart dropped into my gut, and I wanted to shout, "Stay there; I love you," but all I managed was, "Wait, I'll be right there." I wanted to fly up the ramp, to take her in my arms and swing her around, hold her close to me and kiss her all simultaneously, but I forced myself to walk slowly until I stood next to her.

She looked at me with wide open eyes, and then she looked down and I knew she was starting to cry. I held out my hands and she took them in hers. I folded her into my arms and held her against my chest, and she cried. It seemed it was the first time she cried after her father died, and I knew she was letting go of some of the pain. I guess most of it will never go, will always be in her heart, losing her sister and father, but I could feel that pain ebbing out of her.

Girls do look like hell when they cry. Her eyes turned red, then her nose. She needed a handkerchief; I gave her mine. She was a bubbling mess of snot and tears, and I loved her even more because I knew I could take away some of the pain, and I understood her and loved her even when she was a mess. I led her over to a fallen log that had gotten wedged in the cleft of some boulders and made a good bench. I held her and we talked, or rather, I listened.

That week changed my life. I could never have anticipated all the ways it would change me, and if I had, I might have run from it, hidden myself away in my room on the island, never gone to meet her, never gotten off the ferry, never held out my hands to her. I was never the same again.

When I stood next to her, I felt an electrical force surrounding us like an envelope or a shield—I don't know what the hell to call it, but it was a field of energy around us that others felt as well. I know they did. I would be standing next to her feeling as if my body and hers were one. It wasn't even a sexual thing, at least not all the time, it was more a feeling that this is my other self, this is my friend, this who I am meant to love, to protect, and to cherish.

We talked. We kissed. We figured out how to avoid her mother. Thank God for sending Becky's friend Monica. If you ever want a co-conspirator, find Monica, or someone like her, though maybe there isn't anyone like Monica except Monica. That woman's got more balls than a baseball team. She can get a guy to do anything for her, and she loved Becky as much as I did. She picked up a guy and had a convenient flirtation with him just so she and Becky could meet at the ice cream shop to go to the movie. We'd accidentally show up there too, after I got off work, the other guy and I, then pair up with the girls and go to the back row of the balcony. We didn't watch much of the movie, but that didn't matter because we saw the same film three times. Becky's mother never figured that out because she'd just met a guy named Taylor and was more interested in him than in whatever her daughter might be doing.

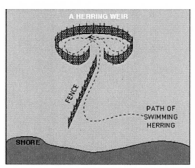

A fish weir

CHAPTER FIVE

Our last night, the last Sunday before Becky and her mother and brother were going back to New York, I asked her for a boat ride and a picnic. I thought we'd go over to the beach at Frenchman's Cove. I imagined us going up the Sound in Grampie's small power boat, then eating a picnic Mumma would make, and talking under the stars and, yes, making out. Imagined that a lot.

Becky told her mother she was going on a picnic with Monica. When I got to the dock to pick her up, Becky asked if we could go to her family's land instead of Frenchman's Cove. She hadn't been there during the ten days they were in Northeast, and she was scared to see it again, but she said she thought she could bear it if I was there with her. No way was I turning that down. She knew her father had loved that land, and she loved it, and now he was gone and the land soon would be gone as well. I felt honored to take her there—that she would ask me to do something so special to her, that she trusted me. That was a gift. I knew it would take a little longer to get to the end of the Sound than to Frenchman's Cove, but I had a full tank of gas, and if I pushed the engine we'd get there soon enough to do all the other things I imagined.

It all started well. We couldn't talk going up the Sound because we were traveling fast and the engine pushing against the water hard was too noisy, but she sat right next to me, and I could feel the warmth of her leg next to mine. When we got to her father's land, she wanted to walk around, to see the places she loved, the ones that were special to her. There was a place they had picnics in the woods, and a ledge that seemed molded to her body where she said she used to lie down to read. She checked out all these spots and I followed behind her; when she finished, I told her she was like a dog making its rounds. She had a laugh at that one. I liked that she laughed at my jokes. If you can't laugh, what's the fun?

We walked over the rocks to the cove where we thought we'd eat, and as we were walking along, she said she wished she'd learned to swim before her father died because he always wanted her to. She told me every time she tried, she could feel the water coming over her head and see her sister floating over the dam. She said her chest would freeze and she couldn't breathe, and her panic made it impossible for her to listen to whoever was trying to teach her. I said I could teach her, and I knew I could if I could get her to relax. I'd taught her to row, so I just kept reminding her that I was a good teacher. I was excited to think about seeing her in her underwear because that's all we had to wear. I hadn't even imagined us going that far and yet there she was, walking into the woods to take off her clothes!

I promised not to look, but I did anyhow. She walked out slowly, peering around, but she didn't see me. The rising moon made her skin glow like gold, and her hair trailed over her shoulders. I'd seen summer girls in their skimpy bathing suits strutting around when we took them on picnics. Island girls wore one-piece baggy bathing suits, but girls from away seemed to feel at ease almost naked. At least some of them. Not Becky. Becky walked quickly to hide herself in the water, which gave me the courage to walk out next to her. I was glad I could hide too, and her shyness helped me feel as if I knew what I was doing. I didn't, but I heard Grampie in my head telling me to relax, so I got her to calm down.

I taught her to float. I bet I was even more excited than she was when she did, but I knew I had to be calm. I had to be in charge to give her confidence. I can feel her body slipping through my hands as she swam on her own, soft as a mackerel going through the water. I can feel the muscles and skin sliding away like a long caress, but then she was screaming that the water was over her head and she was drowning. "Becky Granger, you stop that right now," I said. "You swim back to me. I can come get you any time." And she swam. Do you know how proud I was of her then? I couldn't believe it, and we had done it together. She came right up next to me, put her hands around my neck, and kissed me just over my collar bone. That's a special place for me, innocent and sexy all at the same time. I tipped her head up and kissed her. It was a kiss that has lived in me for thirty-seven years.

We walked out of the water clutching each other and over to the picnic blanket. I ran my hands up and down her body, and I could feel the muscles in her back quivering and her whole body pressing against me. I guess the hormones took over in both of us. I eased her onto the blanket. This I'd imagined. Pine needles for a mattress, blanket over the needles, long kisses. Maybe I'd put my hand on her breast. Most likely she'd be wearing a heavy sweater and she'd push my hand away. I never imagined lying next to her, kissing with passion I'd never felt before, twining ourselves around each other, our wet bodies so close the little bit of clothing we wore seemed foolish, unnecessary. I slipped her clothes off, but I don't remember doing it. I just wanted to be closer to her, and I kissed her and caressed her; my hands couldn't get enough of her, or my mouth. I explored her and all I could think of was loving her completely. I told her I loved her, and I did, and she said she loved me too, loved me more than herself even. Then suddenly it was all gone. I loved her too much to make love to her. Maybe that doesn't make sense, but I knew we weren't supposed to be doing this. My body was on fire, but my mind said no, and I sat back away from her and told her I was sorry, I couldn't do this to her. She was special, she was someone I wanted to protect, and a feeling of tenderness more powerful than lust took me over.

I thought she would sit up too and I'd wrap her in the blanket. I wished that she smoked and we could share a cigarette. I was still het up, but I thought she would be glad I'd backed off, relieved, but she wasn't. It was as if I'd let loose a demon. She kissed my neck, stroked my chest, and there was a desperate energy in her fingers that drove me crazy. The hormones took me over again, and I made love, or something, with her. I don't know what to call it. I knew the grief had driven her crazy, somehow I knew that. I knew I was filling a deep emptiness inside her that she didn't understand herself. As soon as we were finished, though, I thought she would be hurt and even angrier with me than I was with myself. I give myself some credit for understanding that, but I knew it was over. She didn't really love me; she was just vulnerable and overcome by sadness at losing her father.

And then she leaned over and bit me hard on the neck. It shocked me and it hurt. I wanted to slap her. I pushed away and rubbed my neck and thought, This is getting weird. It was weird, and as I got older the mark still stained my neck like red dust, reminding me that she had loved me, loved me so much that she marked me, marked me as her own, for always.

I couldn't talk to her then. I was numb. I stumbled through putting our gear in the boat, rowing the dinghy out to the power boat, and then flying down the Sound. Thank God and Grampie that I've spent my life in boats. I didn't have to think, just watched for buoys and followed the stream of moonlight on the Sound, docked at the Inn, and walked behind her as she walked ahead of me. Didn't say a word, my heart and gut strangled in knots of fear and sadness, missing her already, knowing I'd never see her again. I couldn't bear to look at her, waves of shame and sadness flowing over me again and again, and when she turned toward me, I turned away. I'm not proud of that, and I must have hurt her even worse, but I couldn't bear to look at her. I've tried so many times since then to see what she looked like that I half believe the images of her in my mind are real.

She'd just started attending the boarding school her father went to. That's where she was when he died, and when I saw her that summer, she told me it was horrible being the new girl who'd just lost her father. People didn't know how to talk to her, even the teachers. People talked at her instead of listening to her. Maybe it's too frightening to listen to such pain, knowing there is nothing you can do to make it better. Her friend Monica made it better, and I hope I did too, just by listening to her when I saw her, but after? After what happened, there was nothing I could do. I didn't know her address. Funny we didn't think of that. I did know her phone number, but I didn't think I could call—I might get her mother, and even if I got Becky. I didn't know what to say, not with her being so far away after she and her mother and brother went back to New York, and not how it ended.

And then, as I told you, Dad found out what had happened and grounded me. Eventually I got so I could study and care about books, and not assume because I was an island kid that I'd drop out at sixteen and work on the boats. Now here she was, back on her island after all that time. It made no sense to me. What was she looking for, or who? I wondered if it was me, wondered how I could bear seeing her again.

Right after I graduated from UMO in 1964, I joined the Coast Guard. I decided not to enlist in the Navy, which would have been the natural choice, I suppose, but I've spent a lot of time in small boats. I know people who criticize the Coast Guard, but I think the bravest of the brave serve there. Imagine hooking yourself to the end of a big fish line, swinging out of a helicopter, hovering over a disabled boat at the mercy of wind and ocean to pluck the crew off a deck that's pitching and yawing, or grab someone out of the waves who's clawing at you in panic. I'd seen them do that, so joining up made sense to me. Made sense too that I'd learn more about being a captain of a small boat in the Coast Guard than in the Navy. I wanted experience on small boats, and Jim thought I'd get it there.

He was right again, though not in the ways he predicted, and then there was the war. I didn't exactly oppose it, but I didn't understand how forcibly pacifying a country was going to help it or why the Vietnamese would throw away three thousand years of their culture to eat hot dogs and hamburgers. I wasn't sure of anything, of course, but I didn't feel as gung-ho about fighting that war as some of my friends. I thought I'd found a way to support my country and coastal fishermen by joining the Coast Guard, and I was proud of the work I was learning to do. Then the Army and Navy asked for Coast Guard support in 'Nam, and on April 29, 1965, President Johnson authorized the Coast Guard to operate there under the Navy.

It was a surprise to those of us serving aboard the US Coast Guard Cutter *Point Banks*. We'd just pulled into our home port, Woods Hole, Massachusetts, after two weeks at sea. Not an easy tour either, as we'd rescued the icebreaker *Atka* and escorted her back to port, then dealt with bad weather until the last day of the tour—April 29, 1965. We were looking forward to a seven-day liberty, and I was headed up to Maine for a couple of days, but while we were getting ready for leave, we got the news. Our ship had been assigned to Coast Guard Squadron One to support Operation Market Time, and along with sixteen other Point class cutters, we would fly out soon to California to start training while the *Banks* got refitted and shipped west. We heard there was one guy on another cutter who was supposed to get married the next day, and I bet he, even more than the rest of us, was in shock. Some guys were excited, others worried about leaving their families, but I doubt any of us would have asked to be relieved of duty. We thought we were needed.

The *Banks* was an 82-footer and could move out at 17 knots. Usually we had eight men, but in preparation for service in Vietnam, the ships were adapted to accommodate two more officers and a Vietnamese liaison, and we got a larger food locker so we could stay at sea longer. The mounted machine gun on the fo'c'sle was replaced with a combination over-under "piggyback" .50 caliber machine gun/81 mm trigger-fired mortar that the Coast Guard had developed for use in Vietnam, and four .50 caliber machine gun stands were installed aft of the deckhouse. A new steel frame welded to the deck could stock 5000 rounds of machine gun ammunition, and the old girl got fresh paint below the gunwales. Just as the ship had to get prepared, so did the men. I thought that was the worst. Training to avoid dying. Later I learned the worst was what we didn't learn to deal with—watching a buddy die.

We never got leave to say goodbye to our families. We had just docked at Woods Hole when we got orders to fly to Alameda, California. Our captain, Senior Chief Boatswain's Mate Bernard Webber, did the best he could to look out for us. He was furious we'd lost a well-deserved leave, but he got permission for a two-day leave in Boston, with the understanding we'd fly out from there. There wasn't time to get up to Maine and back to see my family, but I could at least talk with them. Dad took it pretty well, but I could hear my mother crying in the background even through the static on the phone. The thought that I might never see her or Islesford again choked me, but maybe it was harder on the men who actually had to kiss their wives, children, and parents goodbye. At least I didn't have to watch anyone crying, or fight back tears they could see.

The *Banks* got loaded aboard a freighter, along with other cutters, and shipped as deck cargo to Subic Bay in the Philippines. I was sorry not to be one of the two men sent to accompany her, but I was going to go through five weeks of training at Alameda Naval Base in California. We were heading into a different sort of action than shepherding ships and crew around the coast of New England, and we knew our world was about to change.

I had never experienced anything like that kind of training—certainly not when I joined the Coast Guard. Being stripped of everything you think you know, every shred of evidence that you're important to anyone, that you're capable, that you're a human being, a man. I felt hollowed out, even though I knew, I really knew, they were just reducing us to blanks so they could carve us to their specifications. Still, it was hard to remember that I was who I was, not their version of me. Of course, we got physicals, and shots, lots of those—I got twelve in one day and couldn't move my arms after the typhoid shot.

What I hated most was being briefed on making a will and setting up powers of attorney. Those lectures pulled me between duty and home—

wanting to leave and wanting to stay. We had refresher training in nuclear, biological, and chemical warfare, and a damage control exercise in which we almost drowned trying to stop the "ship" we were on from sinking. One guy was so exhausted and stressed that he started giggling uncontrollably. Not a good idea. We never saw him again.

The next stop was Treasure Island, a misnomer that. We had lectures on Vietnamese culture and history, the communist aggression, and on why we had to fight. The real stuff began when we moved to Camp Pendleton, the nearby Marine Corps base. We hiked, and hiked some more, each time carrying more than the last. We learned to shoot pistols, rifles, shotguns, and machine guns, which was easier for guys from rural places like Maine than the guys from suburbia and the city. We've handled guns since we were kids, though not machine guns, and never grenades. I wasn't in bad shape, or didn't think I'd been, but I started taking pride in being able to hike long distances with a lot of weight. Just as I was beginning to feel I had everything under control, there was the grand finale.

Survival week. I lost twelve pounds; other guys lost more. There were times I was terrified and thought I would pass out, but I kept telling myself this was preparing me for the real thing—for 'Nam. The only shelter we had was what we could make from shreds of parachutes. The first day we lived off what we could catch with our bare hands along the shore. I knew we could eat seaweed, but most guys threw it up if they ever even got it down. Urchin roe is OK too, though I like it with a squeeze of lime, and there were clams you could dig for at low tide. I taught some guys to dig them out with their toes if we waded out into deeper water. One of the guys from the woods of northern Maine caught a rabbit that was released for us. The game that lived there had long been eaten or left for safer places. This poor little thing had never lived in the wild and thought we were bringing it food instead of the other way around. At night we had to guard against attacks by guys playing guerrilla, so we were sleep-and food-deprived. On the fourth day we were broken into small groups, each given a compass and a topo map, and told to get the hell off to the next campsite—another full day's march over trackless terrain.

We were so beat we were mindless, and then came the real test: avoiding capture, resisting interrogation. We weren't allowed campfires, and it got cold at night. There was nothing to eat. The next morning we thought it couldn't get worse, but we were wrong. They told us we had three hours to make it to "Freedom Village" by getting through a one-mile sector stalked by the enemy. Our reward if we made it—some fresh fruit and an hour of rest. That sounded like a pot of gold and a room full of Playboy Bunnies—not that any of us had the energy to enjoy that.

Very few of us made it, but I was proud that in our group of over a hundred Navy sailors and fifteen Coast Guardsmen, several of our guys got to Freedom Village. I did not. I was creeping through a thicket of brush, making too much noise, I knew, but as quietly as I could, when a grim-faced "enemy" stuck a rifle in my chest and said, "You're mine, maggot." The next few days were hell, but I kept focused on what I needed to learn so I could deal with what might happen in 'Nam. We were stripped to our underpants, herded into a compound, and forced to kneel while someone soaked us with cold water. We were slapped, hooded, and pushed into small boxes where some guys with claustrophobia started screaming they had to get out.

Inside the box, I took off my hood, but sweat was streaming down my legs and I got dizzy from the heat and loss of fluid. We could hear guys whimpering about being beaten and the US using chemical weapons. I guessed they were acting for our benefit, but my mind was so warped I wasn't sure. Then someone told me to put on my hood, yanked me out of the box, and pushed me into another box, where I had to kneel so circulation was soon cut off to my feet. Suddenly the hood was yanked off and I stared into bright lights, blinking, seeing nothing, hearing only a harsh voice yelling questions. I repeated my name, rank, serial number, date of birth, and religion. Again and again. When I wouldn't break, they put me back into the box.

Sometimes the thought that if I just give them what they want they'll stop crept into my head, but I didn't want to give in. I knew what I was experiencing was tough, but that I was basically safe if uncomfortable. This was play-acting. This was training, and they couldn't really hurt me; if they did, they would have to take care of me. The Cong could hurt me, and they didn't have do anything to help me. That helped, and I didn't break. I'm proud of that. God knows what I would have done if it had been real. Finally, they let me and all the other men who had "passed" out of our boxes. I heard later that the guys who didn't pass went through much worse. We marched to a mess hall to eat oatmeal and an apple, which was about all we could stomach. We were glad it was over, but some guys said they didn't want anything more to do with the sadistic SOBs who had tormented them for a week; they enjoyed their work too much. I felt strangely grateful to them, however, and I respected them for doing a difficult job, and doing it well.

We regrouped and then got sent to Subic Bay, the naval base in the Philippines. Olongapo, the town just outside the gate to the base, was a miserable clutter of bars and whorehouses, and known politely as the armpit of the P.I. I liked the pachinko parlors and playing the guys for beers, and to me it seemed like paradise after Treasure Island. We settled quickly into the drab barracks at the base, working fifteen-hour days on the cutters, adding communications gear and floodlights, fitting the stands with machine guns, and filling the boxes with ammunition. We had gunnery exercises, emergency drills, and drills for night boarding.

We were assigned to Division 11 of Squadron One and would be based at An Thoi, a small village on the southern tip of Phú Quôc Island, along with eight other cutters. They warned us that only the immediate area around the base was safe; the rest of the island was in the hands of the Vietcong. That made me feel trapped even before we left Subic. After we completed sea trials, we chugged out of Subic on July 17, 1965, escorted by the *USS Floyd County*. We crossed the South China Sea, eight white ships gathering around the skirt of our gray lady, a destroyer.

We had a particularly rough crossing, too rough to take a shower without getting bounced around the narrow cubicle. Fuel oil from a loose injector adapter diluted the lube oil in one of our main engines and stalled us for a while, but our engineers got it back working, even in the rough seas. I don't know how the engine room crew functions at all when the heat reaches 140 Fahrenheit, but they do. Fortunately, we didn't delay the squadron and, after crossing, getting to 'Nam was almost welcome.

August 1st we arrived in Phú Quôc and started patrolling the Gulf of Thailand near the Cà Mau peninsula. Our duty was to board Vietnamese junks and search for contraband. No way to make friends on that job. People resented us for being there, even if we were trying to protect them. When we found arms being smuggled into Vietnam, of course, it was much more dangerous and harder than when we didn't. Worse was when we needed to support ARVN or our own troops on the shore, or rescue them from the Vietcong. That didn't happen often, but evacuating men from the shore could be a real mess.

Most of the time we stopped boats that were doing legitimate work; at least we thought they were. But you couldn't trust anyone, and boarding a boat with people glaring and screaming at you was always tense. We had a Vietnamese liaison officer who did the talking, but it's unnerving listening to a language you can't understand. You can feel the anger and hate, feel the tensions and fear, and you wonder if in the next moment someone will break and attack with the long knife or machete that's stuck in his pants.

In June 1966 a North Vietnamese officer with the Viet Cong on the Cà Mau Peninsula defected and told the Navy that between 1963 and 1965 trawlers had reached shore forty-two times: twenty in 1963, fifteen in 1964, and only seven in 1965. The junks or trawlers were armed with heavy Soviet machine guns, similar to our .50 caliber machine guns, but larger, so they were formidable. Each ship carried enough munitions to arm Viet Cong battalions for months, and our commander estimated that in 1965 the Viet Cong were getting seventy percent of their supplies by sea on these ships. Our job was to stop them from getting through and resupplying the Cong, and the defector told us we were doing that job well.

A job well done. Hard to leave it at that. I can feel the anxiety fluttering my chest whenever I think about 'Nam. It's easier to write about it than to talk about it. Hard even to write about it, so I hide in details. Is that what we do—hide from our hearts in details that really don't mean a damn? Hard not to hide when you've got your whole world telling you to be a man and shut up. Hard when there's no woman in your life to listen.

Atlantic Sturgeon

CHAPTER SIX

In 1968, when I was in my first year at Maine Maritime, I met the woman I would marry, Abby, at a dance at the Grange Hall in Bar Harbor. I noticed her right away when she came in with her friends because she wasn't flirty like they were. She stood about five foot five, with long, dark, curling hair that framed her face, deep brown eyes, cute dimples, and a body that curved in all the right places. She seemed to ignore the boys, and she particularly ignored me. I watched her leaning back against the wall of the Grange surveying the dancers, but not seeming to care if she danced or didn't. I thought that took a lot of confidence, and that made her interesting.

I didn't feel the overpowering attraction to her that I'd felt with Becky, but by then I didn't expect it. I was twenty-five, just back from 'Nam, trying to find something normal again, and feeling like an old man. I'd had enough excitement running rivers in small boats, pulling guys out of the water when their planes went down, and standing down the junks that crept along the shore in the dark.

At the very end of the dance, I walked over slowly, and she looked me straight on and smiled, just a small smile, but it seemed to say, "I've been waiting for you, wondering when you were coming over." I took her in my arms, and she fit. We danced a slow dance quite close, and then the lights went on bright and it was time to go. I knew I had to do something quickly if I wanted to see her again, so I asked her if she wanted to go to see a movie some time. She said she would, but she was finishing her teaching degree at UMO and was just in Bar Harbor for the weekend visiting her friends. I said I'd come up to Bangor. That surprised us both.

When I saw her walking toward me to meet at the movie theater, I didn't feel the gut rush, but I figured that sort of emotional high was over. It was time to get to the work of being married and raising kids; besides, we got along well. Abby was smart, funny, loved kids, and cared about books and education. She understood that I did too, though not why. She was proud of me for getting through college before the war, and getting into MMA, and I was proud of her for earning a degree in teaching, and we had UMO in common. We went to Black Bears' games and she even enjoyed them. I knew she would be a terrific mother, and I thought I loved her enough to make a good life together.

We got married the next summer out on Brant's Island, where she was from, and then we lived in student housing in Castine while I went to MMA. Because I'd served in the Coast Guard, I got some credits, and in a year and a half I had my captain's license and an MA in marine biology. I didn't know what that might lead to, but I wanted to work on the sea and try to understand what was happening with the fisheries. There were terrible tensions. Some said the fishing was doomed by government regulations that were killing a way of life. Others said the fishermen were killing their own livelihoods by overfishing. Hard to know even now who's right, probably both, but I wanted to find out.

After Magnuson-Stevens passed in 1976, so many American fishermen went out for cod in bigger boats with better gear that the catch increased significantly. The percentage of fish caught was higher, which masked the reality that there were fewer fish, and the trawls caught fish of all sizes and ages, including those too young to spawn. The government began to realize it had made a mistake in subsidizing the American fishing fleet and started to regulate fishing. Ralph and I still argue about this.

"Dammit," he'll say. "Whose side are you on? The government's? Regulators are killing the fishery and killing us."

"I'm just trying to figure out what's happening, Ralphie."

"You're turning into a gosh-darned liberal pushing government interference. Getting barmy."

"I just want to know where the fish are going, and how we can keep a sustainable fishery."

"*Sustainable's* just one of your fancy words for killing the fishery. You're cracked on this one. The fish are just migrating. Damn foreign boats scooped most of them up, and the rest got scared and hightailed it. They'll be back. We don't need regulators or more regulations."

He was right, to a point. Up until Magnuson-Stevens, foreign factory ships were hauling off whole schools of fish, and by 1974 researchers found the fish stocks had plummeted to the lowest levels ever recorded.

Everyone blamed the foreign boats, but there were other problems. The new law helped, but it wasn't just the otter trawls and the fish-finders that doomed the cod. The fish they ate, like the pogies, sardines and alewives, were getting scarcer too.

The pogies were fished out for oil, fertilizer, and pet food, and the alewives couldn't spawn in the polluted estuaries, or get over the river dams built to produce electricity. With fewer small fish to eat, the groundfish weren't brought close to shore. At first, that wasn't clear to fishermen around here, because the sardine plant in Bass Harbor just tossed the guts and other waste into the water outside the harbor. That meant cod swam close to shore to eat the offal, but one by one the sardine canneries along the coast of Maine closed for lack of fish. Some people, including me, were worried. I wanted to understand what was happening to the ocean, to my island, my friends, to our way of life, and to my family. That's what drew me to do more research.

We understand so little about the ocean. When you look out at the ocean, what do you see? The surface. An endless interweaving of blues and greens, grays on a stormy day, distant horizon, clouds, seabirds soaring and diving, maybe some boats, and if you're very lucky a fish, seal, porpoise, or dolphin cresting out of the water. We see islands that seem to float on the water, but they are the tops of drowned mountains. Beneath the surface there are deep cold basins where no light penetrates, but there are also channels and shallow banks that funnel water throughout the Gulf of Maine, creating rich, hidden worlds for fish.

If you stand on the shore near a tide pool, you glimpse the richness of life in the water. Skittering minnows, periwinkles, mussels, and— sometimes near docks—schools of mackerel slashing through the water in tight formations. You see the play of season, weather, wind, and waves, but most of the time you see the ocean as it relates to you, to how it makes you feel—cleansed, freed by the seemingly limitless expanse, reconnected to nature, relaxed even. What you don't see is everything beneath the surface. Fishermen look at the surface of the ocean differently. We see the worlds below. We learn to read the patterns in the water, just as hunters read the land.

The Gulf of Maine and the Georges Bank are some of the most extraordinarily productive fishing grounds in the world. The whole area, including the Gulf of Maine, Georges Bank, and the Bay of Fundy, is often thought of as a "sea within a sea." Bounded on the north by the Scotian Shelf, and on the south by Cape Cod, which juts into the ocean and interrupts the passage of water, the sunken land contains diverse habitats. Above it rises the water column, just as the air rises above the land we walk on, providing a range of habitats. It is an incredibly diverse, ever changing—fluid, of course—environment.

Look at a map of the currents in the Gulf of Maine, and you'll see arrows indicating the flow of water, gyres traveling in different directions. Water of different temperatures and salinity is constantly meeting and mixing inorganic nutrients, as well as deposits of organic nutrients. Where this occurs along the boundaries of different water masses, plankton and zooplankton flourish and attract dense schools of oceangoing fish, including herring and mackerel. The plankton feed the little fish, which then feed birds, mammals, and the large predacious fish.

The rocky coast of Maine exists on display for a photographer's camera, as well as out of sight, and the Gulf of Maine, particularly coastal Maine and Nova Scotia, has more rocky habitat than other place along the Atlantic Coast. There is nearly ten times more seaweed growing on these rocks than in the nearby ocean, and many creatures eat, hide, and make their homes in seaweed. Salt marshes and estuaries are nurseries for many larger fish, and home for smaller ones, and they also absorb vast quantities of carbon dioxide. Seagrass and kelp beds provide other environments, and beds of shellfish absorb nutrients from the water that are then transferred to their predators, including us. There's also sandy habitat on the ocean floor, and muddy bottom in calm intertidal areas where fine sediments have settled, which we know as tidal flats. These areas are important to the fish we eat and, therefore, to us.

The estuarine and marine water of the Gulf of Maine forms the water column, which is, of course, three-dimensional and contains distinct levels and boundaries, visible and invisible, separated by temperature, salinity, and density. The water column in the Gulf of Maine is rich and diverse, and areas where the water surges upwards, bringing nutrients to the surface, are particularly rich.

Ralphie tells me that fishermen don't need to go to school to learn these things. We see them. But I think he's wrong. We do see them, but we don't always understand them. How can we protect the ocean and the fish if we don't understand what's going on?

Abby asked me once to talk to her class about fish when she was teaching in Bucksport. Key word there is "once." I was so proud of what I'd learned that I just spewed out terms: demersal, benthic, benthopelagic, pelagic, catadromous, anadromous. Bored the kids silly. Abby saw they were fidgeting and tickling each other, so she said, "Let's pretend we are all fish in the ocean. I'll give each of you the name of a fish. She passed out cards she wrote on hastily with the names of benthic groundfish, like flounder and halibut; benthopelagic fish, including cod, haddock and hake; and the pelagic tuna and swordfish. She instructed me to write on the board which level of the water column the different fish live in and told the children to "pretend you are the fish of that type. Figure out where you are in the water column and a way to show us where you live."

That took a while, but the kids sorted themselves into different types of fish. The kids playing flounder and halibut lay on the floor and wriggled, while the cod, hake, and haddock each found a chair, lay down across it, then kicked their feet and waved their arms. The kids representing tuna and swordfish made drawings of fish that they held above their heads as they cruised around the room.

Then Abby said, "Now Tina and Georgie, you get to be fishermen." She gave each of them the end of a volleyball net she used at recess and told them to catch the fish. Tina and Georgie huddled, then suddenly spread out the net and ran around the "fish." They caught all the cod, hake, and haddock, but they couldn't net the flatfish, and some of the pelagic fish were too high in water for the net. Then Abby put some crates and boxes around the floor where the fish could "hide." George and Tina soon figured out they could "scare" the flatfish with a broom they swept along the floor, and this time all the groundfish were netted. In the process, they messed up the boxes and crates that were the bottom habitat, so it was a perfect demonstration of what happens with a trawl net and a rocker. They caught all the fish except for one who ran out the door. Wish I could get fishermen to try the same game.

Then Abby asked how we could protect the bottom of the ocean and the fish too young to spawn. One boy said the small fish get through the holes in the net, but I told them that as the net moves quickly through the water they get tired, then jam up against the back of the net. Many young fish don't get through the blocked mesh and end up bruised and too damaged to live, even if they do get thrown back as too small to sell. No one had any idea about how to protect the habitat except to stop trawling the bottom.

When I was growing up, I expected to go out on the larger boats to fish when I was a man, not to study why there weren't as many fish, but that's what happened. The more I learned, the more I worried. Ask a lobsterman about the condition of the fishery, and he will always say there are more baby cod and flounder in his lobster traps than he's ever seen, but I think fishermen have been saying that for decades. It's that baseline problem again—we're only judging the present against a generation or two, and that's only forty years or so. Maybe we're just seeing what we want to see, what we hope is happening. The fish are just going away for a bit, and soon they'll be back.

Problem is that what was normal forty years ago isn't what was normal eighty years ago, or a hundred and sixty, let alone what it was like in the late 1400s. That's when John Cabot sailed to New Found Land and came across Basque fishermen who'd been working the Grand Banks for over four hundred years, hiding the secret of the riches of the Western Atlantic—enormous schools of cod that made them rich and fed Europe.

First I went out on the big boats for groundfish, but even then I'd be thinking about why we weren't seeing vast schools of cod. I'd listen to the old-timers talk about when they'd throw out long lines and haul them back with a fish on every hook.

In the old days—and that's not so far back—you could drop a line and haul it back in one motion—and when you were in the cod, you always caught one. Hard work, but you didn't even use bait. Just dropped the jig to do its dance, but then the draggers and the gill netters got in the mix. Finally the government started doing systematic research, and I found work on the research boats, as well as keeping my own traps and working sometimes for Grampie and Dad on the ferry. It kept us all going.

Guys were complaining that the fish were moving even farther offshore. By then there were fourteen draggers out of Bar Harbor alone, and about a dozen from Southwest, and Dad and the other fishermen worried that the draggers were mucking up the bottom and destroying the habitat. That was the beginning, and we don't yet know the end.

Of course, it goes back and forth. In the fifties there seemed to be nothing to catch. By 1992, the cod catch peaked at over twenty-one million pounds—five times what it was in 1974. Then in 1993, we saw the cod catch collapse. There were pockets around Mount Desert where you could still find groundfish, but essentially the industry was dead close to shore. That was tough on a lot of guys and their families. We were glad of the lobster, but I'm jumping ahead.

When I was just out of college, and then in 'Nam and at Maine Maritime, I felt a tug, like a hook and line right into my heart, pulling me to Islesford. Grampie was sick, and it was home, but just as strong was the pull away to "make something of myself," and that meant never going home to live. It's a fearful legacy that, being pulled to stay home and then feeling if you do that you've given up and won't ever amount to anything. Ralph said to me once, "What can you think about yourself if you know the cream rises and goes away, but you stay." It's hard to reconcile feeling that you've given up on yourself by living where you really want to be, home, and it's a strong tide that pulls us both ways.

I'm one of the lucky few who's been able to live at home where I want to be, but do something that matters and interests me. Ralph settled for fishing, but now it's lobsters not groundfish, and he paints, but he never got into books. Durlin runs the town, and he feels honored to do that—at least most days—but that's a part-time job, and he picks up construction work because he's a fine carpenter. So they've managed to stay here too, but most can't. And Jason, Jason's just Jason, and he scrabbles together whatever he can, at least when he's not drinking, and he takes disability.

Abby knew something of Becky. We'd only been married a few months when I made a foolish mistake. It was so numb I can't believe I did it, but we were making love and I called her Becky. The name of an old love is not what a new bride wants to hear. Abby sat up, pulled her nightdress down around her and told me I could sleep on the couch or anywhere but in our bed. I let her be, and in the morning I apologized. I pretended Becky was nothing to me, but Abby asked Mumma who Becky was. Mumma never knew how special she was to me, so she tossed her off as a summer flirtation many years before, and that was enough for Abby, for a while at least.

That was a struggling time for us, but good. Abby had a job as an assistant teacher in Bucksport. She was in a tough school—kids of parents in the paper mill weren't too interested in learning much of anything, even if their teacher was young, pretty, and working hard to keep them focused on their schoolwork. It's a mess, really. How do you keep young boys who want to move around from fidgeting? How do you teach middle-aged teachers used to controlling with a whisper how to work with kids who don't care? Kids who are poor. Kids with no expectations of not being poor? A few of the younger people see education as the way out, but most think they're going to fail, so they do.

Abby figured a bunch of kids is like a litter of puppies. They have to squiggle around. She didn't worry about the fidgeting; she just let the kids fidget and walk around the classroom when they needed to, as long as they were doing the work and not bothering other students. She'd find ways to use their interest in anything to help them understand why they needed to read, write, and compute figures. Just like us island kids, most of the mill town kids figured they would have a job when they left school. They'd be working for the mill, or married to someone who did, so school wasn't important to them or their parents, but now some of the mills have closed, and others aren't doing so well.

Abby had some success with her students, but the other teachers got jealous that the kids liked her. They worried that she was able to keep kids interested so they didn't act out, while they could not. One day when the head teacher was sick, Abby took a group of fourth graders on a treasure hunt around the school to see if they could find signs of spring. She'd written funny clues, and the kids loved the game, but she was violating the school policy that kids didn't go on a field trip without permission. A field trip to the land outside the school didn't seem like much of a violation, but the principal told Abby that the kids needed to complete their seat time—that is how much of the day they sit in a seat. Doesn't matter how much they learn. Seems the Department of Education thought kids learn through their butts.

Abby had wanted to stay at the school as a head teacher the next year when one of the older teachers was retiring, but that incident changed her mind. She decided she would rather work in a small school as far from the Department of Education and a superintendent as possible.

Just then the teacher at the school on Little Cranberry said he was leaving, and Abby applied for the job. It helped that her last name was Bunker, and it helped that I was just finishing my degree and could ship out from Islesford as easily as anywhere else. The opportunity pushed us into doing what I'd wanted an excuse to do—move back home, and Abby was happy to have a good job on an island. We moved out to Islesford that summer, and Abby took over as lead teacher and head of the school.

There were six kids, ranging from Tyler Jones in kindergarten to Phoebe Tibbetts in eighth grade. Abby loved them all, and they loved her. She worked up until Christine was born in late June, and until the Christmas break when she was pregnant with Ray a couple of years after that. Lucky Tim arrived on time just after Christmas, and she could take him to school with her. Some of the rules didn't apply, or at least weren't applied in the island schools as they were on the mainland. Abby might have had to leave teaching as soon as she showed, but kids who've grown up in rural places aren't so shocked by the biology behind giving birth as town kids, and no one on the island minded. They liked Abby, and me too, and they didn't want to lose her.

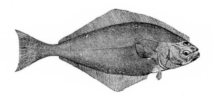

Atlantic halibut, one of several species targeted by long-lines, and an example of a long-line, which could extend for many miles.

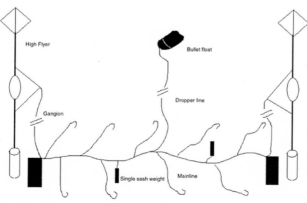

CHAPTER SEVEN

Am I just trying to avoid thinking about Becky? It feels that way, but it's hard now to figure it all out. Abby has been good to me, and good for me. She's a tough little bird. Like with the cancer. When it first showed up, she had to go through chemo, and, my God, she was sick. I'd sit next to her holding the pan, and it felt as if she was throwing her guts up into it. She never complained, just sat quietly in her bed after being sick, and sometimes we talked in ways we never had. That was a blessing, and the last years were good to us both. There were things we had to forgive—forgive in each other and ourselves.

It was a long time before the images from 'Nam left me alone enough to sleep through most of the night, though I suppose they never have and never will completely. My mind is calmer now. I don't see the bad times the way I used to, but I don't like to talk about it.

At night over there, I'd lie in my bunk and think of home. Sometimes I'd think about whom I was going to marry. I figured she must have been born—hell, I was twenty-four, an old man already—so I figured I might even have met her. I'd go down the list of girls I knew, scoring them one by one in my mind. Points for looks. Points for being friendly, good sense of humor, good in the sack, though I didn't have too many candidates I knew much about in that category. Points for being from Maine, though I only knew a few women who weren't. It was a game, and when I got sick of playing it, I thought about Becky. The rest was just prelude to thinking about her, really, a way to postpone the inevitable. She kept me going for a long time, a whole tour of duty in 'Nam. I'd try to remember her head against my shoulder when we were at the movies, or kissing under the light at the house her parents rented, or even that awful last night.

I'd think about heading Grampie's boat down the Sound, wishing the ache in my neck from where she bit me would go away, wishing I could stop the boat, turn around, and put my arms around Becky. Wishing I could hold her and feel her chest moving against mine. I'd think about her body in the moonlight when we went swimming in the cove, the glistening water trickling between her breasts and down her legs, her bra and panties tight against her wet body, transparent as she lay on my arm in the water while she learned to float. My God, what a memory that is.

Sometimes I'd think about the hours upon hours I spent alone at home in my room over the kitchen, the smells of Mumma's chowder or fried shrimp seeping up through the floor boards, or at Aunt Cissy and Uncle Albert's. I could hear kids playing pick-up ball on the field below our house, or in winter sledding and throwing snowballs, their voices high and dry in the pinching air. I longed to be outside with them, even just watching the younger ones. Longed for the bite of snow melting on my face or the roll of the deck of the *Sea Princess* as she butted through the rising sea smoke in the early morning.

Like I've said, the room I had in the back of Aunt Cissy and Uncle Albert's house was away from everyone, and that was worse. No sounds or smells to distract me, nothing but weird red and white wallpaper of two distinct patterns, bought cheap decades ago at the discount shop. Trains and horses each charging off to nowhere in different directions. I'd stare at the ceiling, and then at books, and I got so I was hungering for what was in those books and I studied hard. That's what got me to college, and how I met Jim.

When I got back from 'Nam in early '68, he helped me get into a program at Maine Maritime so I could earn a captain's license and MA in marine biology pretty fast. I had the service to thank for helping pay for it. As I said, I was in my first year when I met Abby, and I knew after the second date she was the woman I was going to marry, the woman who would have my children. I knew she liked me, and I liked being with her. She had ambition and she was smart and funny.

I proposed over a lobster sandwich at Beal's Wharf in Southwest. There was mayonnaise dabbed on her mouth, and when she said yes and we kissed, she tasted like lobster. Seemed a good luck omen, and it was. We've had a good marriage, particularly when I think about all the time I was away on the boats. Even in the troubled times, underlying love and respect—and the kids—held us together.

But I don't want to write much about my children. I think they should tell their own stories, though I hope they don't feel left out of this one.

They were always the center of our lives, mine and Abby's. Sometimes, perhaps, they were too much the focus, and we lost sight of each other.

Ray was angry that I cheated on his mother. He blamed me for leaving her alone because I was out on the water so much. It's a hard line to steer when you've got bills to pay and the only way to pay them is to work away from your family. I don't know what else I could have done except full-time lobstering or working on the ferry. That wasn't me, but it's hard to explain to a child who just wants his daddy to come home every night. Hard to explain that his mother was the one who strayed before I did, hard to say that when you're trying to patch things up, to forgive and forget. We wouldn't do that to the kids—bitch about each other in front of them. I give us credit for that.

Chris understands better than Ray, and I think she forgives us both, but she may have talked more with her mother than Ray and I did. I feel guilty I never sat him down and talked it through. I tried, but we kept falling back into baseball scores—safe ground, but stony. He'd come home for Christmas, but there was always a wall between us, and as he got older and built his own life, that wall got longer and higher.

Ray decided to get as far away from living on this island as he could and still be in Maine. He's in Portland with his partner, Joyce, and their child, Jocelyn. We don't see them as much as I'd like, and sometimes months go by when we haven't even talked. They're busy with their work and friends and a child. Ray says it's hard to get all the way to Islesford, and Joyce doesn't think she'd like living in the country.

We got past that they weren't married, but that was hard too. How can you have a child and not marry her mother? Seems so strange to us, but then a lot of the younger people are doing things that way now. Guess it makes splitting up easier, but what happens when the times are bad and you're tense and bitter, the little angers rise up fast and you think you can't stand it anymore. So you don't. You walk, and just don't come back? I've wanted to do that sometimes. But I didn't. We always forced ourselves to stay together for the kids, at least, but maybe it was also for us. Failing at marriage seems like failing at being your own self.

I thought Abby and I would get old and gray together and that Ray and his wife and daughter and Chris and her husband and kids would be coming over for Sunday dinner like Abby and I went to Mumma and Dad's after we were married and until they died. We went over to

Brant's Island at least once a month to see Abby's folks and her family, but now there's soccer, basketball, and baseball that drag the kids and their parents away most every weekend. Practices and games all the time. Sundays even. The kids have to travel off-island to play, and that makes it hard to go to their games, and the coaches are some eager to have the kids play all weekend. Seems an ego trip to me, and not good for the kids. Young bodies need to spend their energy on growing, and they can get hurt easily. Hard on families too.

But here I am now, and I don't know what to do. I want to clean Becky out of my mind. I wonder why she came back to Northeast. I don't think it's because of me. I don't know if she's married, or has ever been married. I don't know how long she'll be here, or why she's here at all. Of all the places in the world someone like her could go, why did she have to come back to Mount Desert Island? I bet she married a fancy summer guy who made buckets of money and they're just visiting. Maybe they have one of those enormous boats that get in the way of the fishermen because they think they have the right of way, not the little boat. When I'm in a small boat, I steer clear of them because they're so unpredictable. Even some of the men who captain for them forget that small boats have the right of way. Start to feel entitled themselves, or maybe they're just under pressure from the owners. I wonder if these "captains of industry" run their businesses without obeying the rules.

Jason told me in late June that he'd seen Becky when he went to Northeast hoping Katy would let him see his kids. She would have, but they didn't want to see him, which hurt him worse, and he burned in anger. Maybe that's why he called Becky a bitch that day.

There's no one I've been able to talk to about Becky—certainly not Abby or Mumma, or even Ralph or Durlin. I thought about talking to Dad, because he's the only one who knew what happened between us. I don't want to upset him. Besides, he and Mumma have turned the corner into being old, and the last time I tried talking with him about such things, he got upset. Or maybe he just upset me.

I went to sea the next week, so I didn't learn much more from Jason or anyone else, and I was gone for stretches of the summer because Abby was still feeling good. Jim had a grant from UMO to study the scallop catch, and I went out many times with him and by myself to gather data. Great having data you can eat, and Maine scallops are perfect sautéed in a little sea water with garlic. Maine fishermen were making a lot of money from scallops, even more than from lobster. We'd fish too, but it wasn't like the "good old days." The fish were farther offshore, which is difficult for the guys with smaller boats. High waves and bad weather can catch you before you can turn away from it. Lucky the lobster were coming back and a lot of people switched to lobstering.

I came back from the Gulf in late July, and after I'd delivered the monitoring devices and all the slides and data back to Bangor, I went home. First thing after I slung my sea bag onto the Islesford dock, cousin Bud sidled over to me and said, "Remember that summer girl you were sweet on? I think she's living in Northeast now. I heard from your Aunt Cissy that they see her in the market most days. She spends a lot of time in the library too."

"Don't say," I said, trying to sound nonchalant, but I was really thinking, Please don't say anything more about her to me. I don't want to hear. Don't want to think about her.

"Yup," Bud replied. "Cissy told me her friend Alice works up to the real estate office and Mrs. Evans, that's Becky now, she's rented one of Dot Jacobs' new places she fixed up over the winter in her house. *Suites* she calls them. Staying the summer, I heard. Don't suppose you'll meet up with her," he added, raising his eyebrows.

"Bud, why would I want to meet up with her, or she to meet with me?"

"You were awful sweet on each other."

"Bud, that was a lifetime ago. I'm a happily married man."

And I was, though I know Bud was remembering times when it wasn't so good between Abby and me. When she got lonely and she and the music teacher kept each other company. He was single, and she felt like she was as well with me gone so much, but they shouldn't have done what they did. I shouldn't have done what I did, either, carrying on with the new postal clerk. She was just filling in for Bernie, who was tending her father as he was dying, which made it easier because I knew she'd be leaving after a short time. I started seeing her in the late afternoons in the back of Grampie's barn, where there was a room with an old bed. That's all it was for me, sex with someone I didn't care about because I'd been hurt, and I wanted to hurt back.

We thought we kept it a secret, but nothing's a secret here, and not so deep down I wanted people to know. They knew about Abby and the school teacher a long time before I knew, and that made me angry. Jason hinted, but I didn't want to hear him, and finally he just out and told me, "You think you're the man, but the real man is that wimpy music teacher who comes over a couple of days a week. Stays over sometimes when you're away. Says he's just saving on the ferry and they're colleagues. My ass."

Walking into my house, knowing she was in the kitchen, the kids long gone, no one else in the house to hide behind, my gut turning. I'd try to avoid her, to walk out when she walked in, as she walked out when I walked in. We managed to stay civil, but so cold. Cold as a dog on the ice with the wind behind him. Then she got sick. They say stress can make a person sick, and she was from Brant's Island. That's where someone discovered radon was seeping out of the granite into the foundations and poisoning people. That little island had the highest cancer rate in Maine, and Abby was one of the statistics, though she probably didn't show up on any chart because she wasn't living there when she got sick. Still, I think the radon and the stress made her sick.

I don't know which was harder for Dad and Mumma, when they found out I cheated on Abby, or told them she was sick. "It's not supposed to go that way, Son," Dad said to me after Jason tipped him off about my—my, whatever the hell it was. They were standing in the Post Office waiting for the woman who replaced Bernie, while she tended her sick father, to sort the mail. "Gotta speed you up there, deah, so we can get out of here before suppah," Dad said to her. It wasn't kind of him, but he was expecting something special in the mail, a check, I think, and he was a little tougher than usual.

Dad told me later that they could hear one of the mail sacks drop onto the floor, and envelopes sliding off the counter. Then Jason said, "Well, you got her as flustered as your son does, I bet."

Dad didn't like or trust Jason. He knew he was the source of a lot of the trouble I got into as a kid, but he couldn't dismiss the accusation in Jason's sneering comment. He asked a friend what he could make of what Jason had said, and the guy was a good enough friend to tell Dad straight that I was playing around. Told him where too. The next time I met her in Grampie's shed, the bed had been cleared out and there were some reeking old bait barrels in its place. I got the hint.

The next time I saw Dad, I told him I was sorry. We didn't usually talk about stuff like that—emotional things that hurt deep but you could coat them over most of the time. "Ben," he said. "If you love someone, you've just got to accept that there are good times and bad. There are times you can't wait to get home and put your arms around her, and you don't care about spending the day freezing outside, or the boat engine just blew, or you're sick to death of summer people and being polite. You just want to be with her. And there are times when the wind's in your face and everything she does sets you off. You get home and the first thing she says is, 'Take the trash to the dump.' Even before you sit down after a long day on your feet. She's right, of course, but damn, it's not what you want to hear. Or you walk in the door and all she wants to talk about is her day—diapers, crying kids— or give you all the gossip you don't care to hear. So you've got to wait and let her get it out, and then take your time to appreciate the smell of what she's cooking for you, even if it's the last thing you want to eat. And finally, you get to tell her about the guy on the ferry who pissed you off, or how the price of lobster is falling, or what a horse's ass someone is who can't get you a part for the boat, or state regulations. That was always good for a rant. And finally, when you're both all done getting rid of the day, you go upstairs and go to bed. And that's the best."

"I know, Dad. But Abby played around with the music teacher. That hurt me. I know I was gone a lot, but how else was I going to support her and the kids? Didn't seem fair.

"Wasn't. Doesn't mean you should do the same thing, though."

That first time she was ill, I tended her best I could, and in doing so I loved her as I never had. I learned her like I've learned a boat, by caring for it and understanding its ways. She had breast cancer, and it was hard for her to admit she was scared I wouldn't want to touch her again. Somehow that scar became a touchstone for me. I helped care for her, and I helped her get well. I'm proud of that, but she felt maimed. To me, though, she became more beautiful as I began to know the woman beneath the scar so intimately.

Dealing with the scar helped me cope with my nightmares. Most people don't think the Coast Guard was even in Vietnam, but it was. As I said, our mission was to intercept supplies, particularly ammunition, keep them from getting into Vietnam, while another Coast Guard detail worked to protect the harbors and oversee unloading of cargo. The Navy didn't have the Coast Guard's experience policing harbors and supervising the unloading, and that's another reason why we got called in.

Some of my buddies from training were posted to Coast Guard Port Security to help police the harbors, which were a crazy mess with little organization or process. They told me they'd seen Vietnamese stevedores throw a canister of napalm or box of ammunition down on the deck so hard it was a wonder they didn't cause a major conflagration. Sometimes there were fires, fires that killed people. Napalm canisters are so thin that if the canister hits a deck, sometimes the stuff oozes out, and it seems to catch on fire by itself. The slightest spark will set it off. The Vietnamese were paid to unload the ships quickly, but the emphasis on speed endangered everyone. When the Coast Guard took over organizing the docks and supervising the unloading of dangerous cargo. Ships' captains were some relieved.

But what haunts me is that I can still see men from *Point Banks* when we encountered heavy fire offshore while on patrol intercepting ammunition smugglers. Our cutter was assisting along the coast of the Cà Mau peninsula when we saw a ghost of a ship in the fog, a large junk with no running lights trying to get close to the shore. We shone our lights on her, illuminating the deck. We could see men taking the wraps off a machine gun and swinging it toward us. Our port gunner blasted away with the fo'c'sle machine gun and sprayed the deck of the junk, and I saw a man explode, almost beautiful in his dying. Sprays of crimson against the blue of his pants and the gray deck.

Then there was fire from shore as well, and John fell in front of me, his teeth knocked back into his throat and a bullet just below his left breast. I caught him in my arms and we fell to the deck. He bled over me and I started to panic that I was going to drown in his blood, suffocate to my own death. I'm not proud of that moment. We didn't have a medic on board, none of our boats did, but Paul had taken a ten-week first aid course when he served in the Air Force, and he took over, stopping the blood and giving John a shot of morphine. Paul saved his life, and I went back to work, but I was shaken to my soul.

The nightmares started when I got home to Maine, but I couldn't talk about them to Abby or anyone else who hadn't been there. There was a priest at the Maritime Academy who understood, and there was another guy who'd been in the Navy and seen action in Vietnam. Sometimes we'd hang out together, but we never really talked. We just talked around it—football, girls, then wives—anything not to remember.

And then much later, Abby got sick. There's something about tending to a woman who's sick, helping her deal with throwing up and getting to the bathroom, holding her when she can't support herself, brushing her teeth—helping her with all the functions of the body and mind as they fail her—something that made me feel safe telling her how vulnerable I was. We shared an intimate understanding of each other and forgave each other for all the hurting. She has more courage than I do, and when I had to hurt her, peeling away the bandages that were stuck to the wound, cleaning around it, or just cleaning her, she never complained. She'd wince, but she never cried out, and I know it was to spare me her pain. I would not have been so brave. In fact, I'm a wretched patient. I complain about everything and feel sorry for myself. Hard to do that now, though.

It started with Abby feeling tired and weak, and then a pain in her stomach and her gut, and then a lump in her left breast, and it seemed to take so long to figure out what she had. There was one nurse at Eastern Maine Medical who helped us, probably more than she should. A large square woman with blond hair and smart blue eyes. She could be wicked funny and when you thought the tension was so thick nothing could cut it, Stacy could. She told me once that Abby was one of the bravest people she had ever cared for. Stacy and Abby would put on their deepest Maine accents and joke around. Stacy's the one who told me Abby didn't have to go through all the tests the first time she got sick, and that they weren't really going to help her. Stacy also told me Abby was so full of grit nothing was going to get her down, but to take the best care of her I could because if she felt loved she could pull through.

People helped. You think people in small towns pull together in a crisis, and they do, but island people know what it is to depend on each other completely. If the ferry breaks or the weather closes in, you don't have a choice. You need help, you ask for it. If someone else needs help, you give it. Polly at the library and Bernie in the Post Office organized the women so Abby always had company if I was gone and always had something to eat in a clean house. Ralph and Durlin asked the men if each of them would take a week to check on the house, and do chores like stacking the wood so when I was home I didn't spend all my time working to catch up. Jason mowed for us, and he did it regularly, which was a surprise for everyone, but mostly him.

On Wednesdays Bessie, the long-term substitute teacher, came over from school with the children. Some of them were scared to see their teacher so sick, but Bessie brought them over on afternoons to show Abby what they'd learned. Bessie had lost her father to cancer, so she knew what we were going through. The kids from school would sing a new song, or show Abby their paintings or the puppets they'd made from dried apples and leftover yarn and scraps of material, or read her the stories they'd written. One of them always wrote about pigs, another about turtles, and a third loved dolphins. Their stories made Abby laugh, and she told me many times those children gave her strength to fight the cancer so she could go back to them.

Amy, the visiting nurse, came over once a week on the *Sunbeam*, the Maine Coast Mission boat that serves the outer islands. If the weather was so foul the boat couldn't leave its base in Northeast Harbor, Amy called and I followed her instructions to change Abby's dressings. The next day the boat could go out, Amy came to check on my handiwork and bring the medications, but you never wanted to run low.

Christine lived on-island with her own family, and she came over every day just after getting her children off to school, and after work as well. She knew how hard I was trying to make Abby comfortable, and also that there were things that she could do and I could not. Like wash and set her mother's hair, what there was of it, and even trim it when it started to grow back and was scraggly.

Ray would come up from Portland on weekends, but he always stayed with Christine. I would have liked him to stay with us, to be under our roof again, but he and his sister had things to talk about, so I guess that was good too. Ray would sit with his mother in her room, telling her stories about his daughter and Joyce, sometimes reading to her, sometimes just talking in a hushed voice about I don't know what. I always felt I was intruding, so I didn't interrupt them.

It was a grim time, but slowly Abby got better, the waxen pallor of her skin began to glow with some color and life, and finally the cancer was in remission. Then we waited through five years of X-rays and more tests, and worrying every time she coughed or sneezed, every time there was a pain in her hip or knee—or worse, her stomach or gut—until she was declared free of the cancer, and we breathed again. I think the whole island breathed again. Abby had started teaching as soon as she could, maybe too soon, at first just a couple of days a week, and then full-time, and we rejoiced.

I've loved her, but in the dark reaches of my heart, I admit I never loved her the way I loved Becky. That was a love that sometimes overwhelmed me. A giddying sort of love that made my pulse run like a fluttering engine. When I was sixteen, I wanted to run up onto the roof of the church—that's the highest building on Little Cranberry—and yell, "I love Becky Granger, even if she is a summer girl!" I settled for carving our initials in the trunk of a tree far back in the woods on Grampie's land. I did it with the knife Becky gave me for my birthday, and I chose the side of the tree that faced the forest, not the path through it, so no one would see it. RG + BB inside a heart with an arrow. Some romantic that, even though the heart was a little rough. And now she's back, and I don't know what she wants, or even what I want. I don't want to hurt Abby or my children and grandchildren, and I don't want to fall in love with her again. That would tear my soul from my body and leave me hanging by the sinews.

I hope she stays in Northeast Harbor.

That winter she did. I'd hear occasionally from someone that the summer girl who visited me on Islesford, now Mrs. Evans, was staying for the winter. Josh runs his boat over in front of the cove where she had moved from the suite in town, and he'd see her in the early mornings, even when it was cold, bundled up and reading on the deck outside her house. Said she waved to him every morning and he got so he looked forward to it. That's my girl, friendly with everyone.

Oh crap. That's an awful way to think. I can't think like that. She's not my girl, and it shouldn't mean a thing to me what she does. She's Mrs. Evans. Doesn't matter that she's divorced.

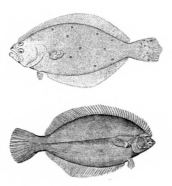

Winter and summer flounder

CHAPTER EIGHT

I t was a long winter. Longer even than usual. The ice shrouded the boats and froze the harbors. Not like the old days when the water froze out to the island and men pushed supplies over tramways set on the ice, but still a cold winter. When you could get out, the seas were rough, and the fishing—that's lobstering—hasn't been so good. I managed to avoid going to Northeast Harbor most of the winter. I did make one trip with Abby to the mainland late that winter, but I convinced her it would be worth going to Ellsworth to shop. She was surprised because I hate shopping, but I told her we'd make a day of it, and I was there to carry parcels and give her a good lunch. Really, I just didn't want to risk being in Northeast and seeing Becky, and besides, so many of the stores are closed there now in the winter; there's not much except the market left for us to shop in. That's true even in summer because the shops that open then seem to sell things just for summer people and tourists. Mostly stuff we don't need and don't want.

I was working on a project with Jim, and that kept my mind off Becky at least some of the time. But what we were finding was discouraging. The research we were doing was telling us what we knew from informal observation. The cod population had changed, at least what was left of it. I think it really always has been different populations. Some schools of cod lived out on the Banks. Then there were local cod that adapted to particular spawning grounds near the river mouths and in estuaries, where they would find herring and pogies. They would also eat anadromous fish, like the alewives that are born in fresh water but live in the oceans until they return to fresh water to spawn. Catadromous fish like eels do the opposite—live in the fresh water, but go back to the salt water to spawn.

We knew these smaller fish had declined drastically, and the cod wouldn't hug the shore as they had because there wasn't enough food.

We'd seen other signs, like puffins flying back home with a herring or two, or even an empty beak instead of a beak full of squirming fish. No way they're going to feed their young on that, and neither are the fishermen. I don't know if there are enough cod to bring back a population. A way of life is changing, not only for the fish and the birds, but for all of us.

Mud month started early that March. The earth showed through patches of snow where the sun hit strong, and the air softened. I can always smell spring before I see it. The air isn't the nose-jabbing cold of winter like dry icicles through to your lungs. There's a softness and redolence in the air, though some of that is simply the compost frozen over the winter starting to thaw. Not much else to do with garbage on an island other than compost what you can. Some places they just toss it over the side, off a cliff, if they've got one. You go out in a boat near those dumps and you see the skeletons of refrigerators, stoves, bureaus, cars even, sitting just below the tide line. We have to haul in everything we use, and everything we don't gets thrown off, buried, or hauled off-island. That's expensive, so we try to use and reuse. You could call us the original recyclers. It's why people keep what seems to be trash—old cars and bait buckets, things to borrow from and patch with. Well, visitors think it's trash, but it's more like a community co-op.

By late April, there's a rush of budding out—flowers, babies, lambs, peas. Life bursts out with a fierceness you don't see other places. Other places can take their time, but here Mother Nature knows she has to get her growing done quick to be ready for winter. Winter can trick you and everything else. The Ice Queen eases her grip slowly, and just when you think she's gone to bed, she reaches out with plunging cold fingers and sends a freeze to remind you who is in charge. By late May, when you can revel in the longer days and the warmer sun, out come the black flies. Now those are buggers.

As winter ended, I began to notice Abby looked tired, the circles under her eyes becoming ash smudges, her walk slower. I tried to ignore it. Sometimes I'd be home when she came back from school, though usually not. One day I saw her drag herself through the door, drop her books on the kitchen table, and lower herself into the chair. Then she put her head in her hands and stared at the table because she didn't think I was home; I walked over and put my arms around her.

"What's going on, dear?"

"I don't know, Ben. I don't know, but something's not good."

My heart dropped into my feet and I looked at her more closely. Age lines had deepened into channels, and her face was luminously pale. "What are you feeling?"

"Oh, I think I'm just tired is all. It's been a long winter."

"When do you see Dr. Jones next?" I asked.

"April fourth," Abby answered softly, and I knew she was scared because her hands were twitching in her lap.

"I'll go with you," I said, and took her hand. I could feel the fear knife through me, and hoped somehow to hide that from her, but she knew me too well. I put my head down to hide the tears that were coming, but she saw through that too and took both my hands in hers. She has small hands, but I could feel the strength in them as they wrapped around my own. Deep sadness that I could not protect her from what was coming overwhelmed me. I cried when I was supposed to be the one doing the comforting, and she sat with me as I knew I was going to sit with her.

"I've had a good life, dear. You've given me a good life. I have you and the children and our grandchildren, and my work and friends. I live in a place I love. What more can life offer than what we've got? And besides, you aren't putting me under quite yet. Let's go for a walk. I love you, dear." We went out to the point where you can see Baker Island and then back through the harbor, not talking much, but feeling the warmth of each other as we held hands in the gentle unison of two people who have walked together over many miles.

It took weeks before the doctor was sure, though he thought the cancer was in her uterus when he told us, "Well, let's be thankful it's not ovarian because that spreads fast. Uterine cancer is much slower, and we can operate." Fortunately, summer was coming. Abby hoped to work until school was finished for the year, though there were many mornings she struggled to get out of bed—she who had always been a morning person and hopped out of bed like the Energizer Bunny to make me coffee and breakfast in the black mornings of winter. She'd decided not to have chemo or an operation until school was over, and that worried me because she was delaying the treatment, but she was determined she would finish the school year and not worry the children.

Just after Memorial Day, I was in the Post Office when I heard Bernie telling Stan that someone was coming to look at Grampie and Grammie's house that was for sale again. Stan's the caretaker for the trust that owns it now. I was glad it was for sale finally after the rich kids who bought it from us decided they wanted to live somewhere else. Good riddance. They trashed it. Bernie keeps the key in case anyone needs to do some work on it, or if a broker wants to show it quickly and can't reach Stan.

"Good enough, I'll try to clean it up a bit," Stan said. "When are they coming?"

"Right now. Next boat."

"Goree, I wish they'd give me warning so's I could make it look a little better. Flies will be crunching under foot like popcorn after the movie. Best I run over and sweep them up. Would be good to get it sold to someone who'd fix it and care for it. Hate to see the old place rotting away."

I slipped out of the Post Office without them seeing me because I didn't want to talk about the house. Losing it to those crazy rich hippies who turned it into God knows what—a meditation room and pot parties was what I heard—that hurt. We couldn't keep it, not with Uncle Clem's granddaughter Sue Ellen so sick, but we lost a part of ourselves when we sold it.

I was heading out for a few days of work for Jim on the herring run, so I wasn't there when Marge took Becky to the house the first time. It was disappointing—the herring just aren't around in the numbers I remember even a few years ago. Pathetic to see the birds working so hard to feed their young, and the seagulls screeching down to peck at the eggs and kill the chicks. Used to be more terns lived on the rocks with the puffins, and they fought off the seagulls. Now they aren't coming back in such numbers, and I think the reason may be that they can't find herring.

When I got back home, Jason made sure to find me where I was standing on the float near the lobster cars. The pens—we call them cars—weren't as full of lobster as I expected they would be in early June. The ones floating next to the dock were half empty. It's a worrying time as the water heats up, slowly encouraging the lobster to shed. After the long winter, fishermen are anxious to get back on the water, but the lobsters are just working their way in from deeper water farther offshore. When the water's warmed, the lobsters shed and then grow into their new shells. Soft-shell lobster, that's the sweetest, but it's hard to ship them, so we keep most for ourselves and local restaurants.

I was thinking about the irony that we compete against our friends, the ones we rely on if we're in trouble on the water, when Jason slapped me on the back. He always slaps a little too hard, and he knows how to slap without leaving a bruise. Ask Katie about that. "Have I got news for you," he cackled.

"Yeah."

"Oh yeah, it's about that…"

I interrupted him because suddenly I knew. I knew he was going to tell me that Becky was the person looking at our old house. It made sense. She was living in Northeast, so she was already here and could see it before the rush of summer people. I felt the news slash into me and turned to Jason.

"Oh, I know Mrs. Evans looked at Grampie's old house."

Jason's face sagged like wet sand and he replied, "So how'd you know?"

"How's Katie doing since her mother died? What's her husband's name?" I asked to throw him off. It was cruel of me, but I had to divert him because I'd been guessing, a guess he had just confirmed.

"Oh, her. I don't keep track of her. Husband's name is Grant—just got made a vice president at the bank. Now don't that beat all. He's got my kids under his thumb, treating them to fancy crap they don't need." He wandered off, as I knew he would, back along the dock up to his battered Chevy truck. The thing sounds like a farting chopper when it takes off 'cause the exhaust pipe rusted off.

I stood by the cars penning the lobsters and watched them lowering and rising in the waves of the incoming tide. The slow hypnotic motion lulled me and let me push away the tension for a bit. Finally I shook myself free and tried to think sensibly. I'm a happily married man, doing what I want to do and where I want to do it. I live on a small island where everyone knows what everyone else does, or thinks he or she does, and I haven't seen this woman for thirty-five years—no, thirty-seven. I don't really know who she was even then, and I certainly don't know who she's become. She doesn't have a husband in tow, but I bet she's looking. I bet she's angry, just another one of the angry divorced summer women who bitch about men.

And then the knowing, the feeling of her against me, the warmth flowed over me, and I rubbed my neck unconscious of what I was doing until the memory of when she bit me forced itself on me. I sat down on the bench and stared at my hands. My hands are brown from the sun, even in winter, up to just past my wrists. I have long fingers, and my hands are strong and clean. Becky looked at my hands hard when I first met her on her family's dock; something surprised her. I watched her watching me, and I knew something was wrong. Then I looked at her hands, the fingers long and thin like razor clam shells tapering to light pink nails with white moons. Again, I saw her looking at my hand when I helped her into the dinghy and rowed her to Baker Island from our power boat.

I'd never thought much about my hands before that, but she made me see the black grime under my nails, the oil stains across my knuckles, and the gray dirt ground in so deep and for so long the pores of my skin didn't want to give it up. She made me want to clean my hands, and I did. It wasn't easy—dirty hands are a badge of honor for a guy and a lobsterman—and I couldn't explain to my friends what I was doing or why. I scarcely understood it myself, but I knew that I wanted to touch her with clean hands.

"You're worse than Mrs. Jenkins with all this washing, Chummy. She must have really scared you in hygiene class. Whatcha 'fraid of a few germs for?"

Now I looked at my hands and wondered who I was. Why had I wanted to be in her world yet stay in my own? Why had I washed my hands for years, even now? I thought about Abby and how she told me a long time ago that she started to love me because I was different from other guys. I wanted to use my mind, be educated, and yet I didn't want to leave my life or my family. I knew that came both from Grampie and Becky and that I had loved them both.

The truth. I feel like I'm scouring away the barnacles, sea worms, and sludge that have grown onto my hull over the years, and now I'm trying to find it. It's hard work stoning them away. The barnacles cut through even thick leather gloves, and my hands bleed, but what is bleeding now seems deeper. Can you love two women truly and well? I don't think so.

What is it about people that they have to cause trouble? Marge called me a few days later and said, "Thought you might want to see your old friend Becky Granger. She's Mrs. Evans now, but she's coming back to look at Captain Bunker's house. Said she'd been there before. With you. Seems she's never forgotten it. You or the house must have made quite an impression."

You're not beating me at this game, I thought. You just want to put me in a corner and create trouble, but I'm not going there. "Hey, that's good news. I think I remember her. It sure would be nice to get the house sold to someone who would fix it up and take care of it. Certainly would be a worry off my mind," I told her.

"Good. Come over to the house tomorrow afternoon around three and we'll be there. I'm sure she'd like to see you. I think she's worried that you and your family would mind if she bought it. Can't think why, though. Would be a lot better than watching it fall apart."

"That's for sure, Marge. Good luck to you."

I wanted to strangle her slowly with a bait pocket, but I hung up the phone and turned. Abby was sitting at the kitchen table and she asked who had called.

"Marge, that real estate woman. She's got someone interested in Grampie and Grammie's house."

"That's quick. It's only been on the market a couple of weeks. Let's hope they buy it."

"That would be some relief," I replied.

"Marge has done awfully well, even though I wonder sometimes what's going to happen to the island with all these houses going to summer people. No way those buyers will live here in the winter, so we'll just have one more empty house and one less family shopping at the market and using the ferry, one less family with kids in the school. Scares me sometimes. Feels like we're dying."

We both startled at the word and tried not to look as if we had, but soon we started laughing at the same time.

"That's not what I meant, and you know it, Ben Bunker. I'm a feisty old broad, and you'd better remember that."

"I know. And you're not dying, not any more than anyone else who's alive, and besides I'm not going to allow that to happen. Love you." I put my arm around her and asked if she wanted some tea, and when it was ready I poured us each a cup, and we went out onto the deck and sat in the rocking chairs. That's where we go when we're tired at the end of the day. Most often we just sit rocking and listening to the rustle of the stones jostling on the beach. The water slips between and around them in a continuous song. The nighthawks zip around catching insects, silent scimitars slashing the air. Sometimes there are shooting stars, and the rising moon shines over the undulating water, the beams catching the tops of waves in an endless light show. We go to bed already half asleep, lulled by the rhythms of the sea.

That night, however, I couldn't sleep. I raised myself up from the bed as quietly as I could and padded softly out to the back room, got a blanket off the couch, and went back to the deck. I felt numb. I stared out at the ocean, wishing I was back on the sea in a boat and had too much to do to think about Becky Granger being back on my island. My island. That's the way I thought about it when I invited her over so many years ago, but I know that's wrong. Anyone can come here, and they do.

Used to be we got the summer families that didn't want the partying and social frenzy of Northeast or Bar Harbor, then even Southwest. Used to be that we had academics, writers, painters, quiet intellectual people who came to read and write and paint and once in a while have a very sedate get-together at their houses. Then more people moved here for the summer, some of them the grown kids of families that had come for generations. Slowly at first, as the prices on the mainland got exorbitant, even more people came here for the summer and bought houses. The prices even for simple little cottages with no view got so high that local people couldn't afford to buy them. That's the problem really, our own can't stay, and the jobs aren't here to support a family.

My mind slipped back, back to Becky when we were young. I could see her hair blowing behind her as we walked along the harbor in Northeast. I needed to let the memories range through me, and then force myself to put them in a capsule and throw them away. I sat there picking them up by their scrawny rat tails and putting them into a mental box. I could hear them scurrying around inside, whining that they wanted to be let out, but I told them no. This is my life now, and you are going to stay in that box and not get in my way, or in the way of Abby or my children. The sun was just starting to color the horizon when I put the last one away, took a deep breath, and mentally threw the box into the ocean. Our minds can play tricks on us, but I was determined to trick my own mind. Determined to forget I had cared about Becky Granger, and to let her be who she was—Mrs. Evans.

The next afternoon, I walked toward Grampie and Grammie's, but stopped as I turned the corner where you can first see the house. It's a beautiful house, a Cape, added to by people in our family over generations, stretching along the shore. It knifed me to look at it now and see the shutters tossed on the ground by the wind, the gingerbread-work peeling and a few pieces missing. There were weeds in the flowerbeds Grammie was so proud of, and tall grass in the cracks of the walkway Grampie's father built from granite slag he hauled from a quarry on the mainland.

I saw Marge and Becky in one of the island's golf carts as they drove into the driveway and got out to see the house. My heart shuddered. I recognized Becky immediately, though her hair was short and flecked with gray. I had hoped she'd be a frumpy bag of a woman dressed in one of those brown tweed suits older summer ladies seem to like, but she was not. She was tall and graceful as she stood near the house, and the afternoon sun shone on her, reminding me of the sun that lighted her up when she stood in the door of the library, and everyone in my family stared at her. She was someone from another world then, and now too, I reminded myself. She was wearing an old denim jacket and a pair of corduroy pants with a turquoise scarf around her neck. She looked like the figurehead on the bow of a great ship. I've said that before, but it's still true, and the pictures I'd locked so carefully away came flooding back.

I was glad Marge had called me to tell me they were coming. I would have hated to learn from Jason that she'd been back to the house, hated to come upon Becky accidentally. At least now I'm prepared. At least now I can pretend that I'm happy to see her and she means nothing more than an old acquaintance from another life. I walked up behind her, and she turned and stared at me. The sun was so bright she blinked, but she knew me.

"Ben," she said. Her voice was deep in her throat and her eyes were soft, and I thought then that she had loved me.

I put out my hand and said, "I knew it was you last time." She took my hand, and I felt the same currents of electricity I felt the first time

I touched her. It seemed an hour that we held our hands together, but I'm sure it was seconds. Still too long. "Why didn't you come to see us," I asked her, to tell her I was we, to protect myself and her, and Abby.

She swallowed any surprise she may have felt. I was sure then that she had thought about me and prepared as best she could for seeing me, which was inevitable. Maybe she was hoping I'd be a grumpy old man fiddling around with his lobster pots, smoking Muriel cigars, and leaving a trail of white plastic stubs behind him. The thought made me laugh, which helped, and I said to her, "We heard you were here. You look good. It's good to see you. I want you to come meet my wife, Abby. She'll be glad to meet you." I took off my cap and twirled the hair over my ear. It's an old habit, and one I've never been able to break. It's something I do when I'm tense, and when I watched Becky watching me, I knew she knew I was acting out a part I'd assigned to myself, a role I couldn't quite believe.

"I'd like to do that, Ben," she replied evenly, and I thought, no, I've gotten it wrong, she's not here because of me.

"Ben, I've loved this house since I first saw it. Would you mind if I bought it? Would you mind if I lived here?"

"Becky, why would we mind?" I said as lightly as I could. I wanted to scream. Woman—don't do this to me! Don't come here where I have to see you day after day. "We can't have it ourselves, and we would be honored to have you as a neighbor," I added. I knew I sounded formal and distant, and that's exactly where I needed to be. Distant.

"Good," Marge interjected.

She's just in this for the sale, I thought. I said goodbye to them and turned to walk back to my house, confusion and guilt that I had even thought about Becky circling through my head, fear that Abby would know something had happened to me or in me as soon as she looked at my face. When I walked through the kitchen door, she asked me where I'd been, and fortunately I'd thought to buy some of her favorite cheese in the market and a couple of shedders at the dock. "Just shopping, dear," I replied, and busied myself putting them in the refrigerator. We cooked them for supper and then played backgammon, and she didn't ask me anything more.

A couple of weeks later Bernie told me that Marge had the house under contract and that the buyer was a Mrs. Evans, who'd stayed in

Northeast when she was a girl. She said, "I think she's someone you knew, Ben. Is that right?"

For a nanosecond I thought about lying. I thought about it and in a blink I knew it wouldn't work. Too many people would remember once the story came out, and I'd only give it life if I denied it.

"Yep. That was a while ago. One of Jason's tricks. He dared me to ask a summer girl over to the island and offered me some real money. Couldn't turn that down. I met her when I was with Grampie delivering the float to their dock."

"You don't say. Guess she must have liked it a lot out here."

"Guess so," I said. "Hard not to. I heard she's getting the old house for peanuts, but they're still fancy, honey-roasted peanuts, not the kind we eat. We wish we could buy the house back for ourselves, but it's still too rich for us."

"What's she like?"

"Can't say, not knowin'." That was one of Grampie's favorite sayings, and it could cover a lot. "I hardly knew her then. She was nice enough though. Not stuck up. I haven't seen her for—what is it, thirty-five or so years?"

Please leave it at that, I thought, though I knew it would soon be the gossip all over the island. Best just to let it be and wear itself out.

"Well, it will be good for the house to have someone care about it again. Marge says it's going to close fast because she's paying cash. Imagine that. I can't. Can't imagine having the money to pay cash for a house. Anyhow. No contingencies, so a fast closing, and then she's actually going to live there. Can't see a summer person doing that. They always want to change everything in the house before they set their feet in it, let alone live there. That speaks well for her."

"Yep," I mumbled and walked out of the Post Office. I was in a dream walk, floating over the island, seeing it as if I was just watching from space, a tiny slip of green on the blue of the ocean, whitened along the shore by the waves, my home, not hers. Why, why is this happening? I asked. I took a walk around Maypole Point before heading home. I knew I had to come up with something to tell Abby, something she could believe and believe in, something that wouldn't worry her. I thought of tangled lies, lies piled up on each other like debris on the beach after a storm, rotten ropes of lies, and finally I told myself, just tell her the truth, or at least most of it.

When I got home, I went into the kitchen. Abby was sitting by the woodstove. She'd started feeling cold again, so I kept the stove fired up, even though it got so warm in there I wanted to strip down to underpants or put on some fancy Bermuda shorts, 'cept I don't have any. Shorts aren't something we wear because we're always working, and you need pants to protect you. Nothing to protect me now, I thought.

"Hi, dear. How's your day been?" I asked her.

"Seems I should ask you about yours first," Abby replied, a funny smile on her face.

"What do you mean by that?"

"Seems your old girlfriend's coming back to town."

I could feel a blush rising up my chest. "It's a bit warm in here for me, dear, I just got to take this sweater off." Good, I could blame the woodstove.

"She's the girl I asked over on a dare with Jason. I made fifty bucks on that when fifty bucks was a lot of money. She's Mrs. Evans now. Seems she liked it here so much that she's come back."

"Polly told me you were sweet on her. That right?"

"Yes. Yes, I was, but that was a long time ago. Is she making you jealous? I'd like that. Just make you a little jealous so you think you have to make apple crisp for me with thick cream." I walked up behind her and put my arms around her, tickling her a little and nuzzling her throat. She stood up and I kissed her, and I meant it. I drew her against me and rubbed her back as far down as I could reach. I could feel her body tighten and then soften, working itself against me to fill every crack. I thought we might make love, but she started coughing. I'd held her too tight.

"I'm sorry, dear. I've made you cough, and I wasn't thinking. I hope I haven't hurt you." I eased her into the chair, and she sat with her head hung down and coughed again. I got her a glass of water and sat next to her.

"I'll make you apple crisp any time you want it. I think about how I look, my hair so thin. I look ten years older than you. How could I not be jealous, though you've given me no reason. Sometimes I feel so angry that my body has let us down. I can't even love you the way I want to. I'm so sorry, Ben," and she started to cry.

"I love you the way you are," I told her. "Mrs. Evans is someone from a long time ago, someone I hardly knew then and don't even know at all now." Abby sat quietly for a minute and then looked up at me.

"When she moves here, you should ask her over. When you see her, please do that. I want to meet her. I want know her for myself."

It seemed odd. Why would she want to meet someone she knows I'd cared about, even if it was so long ago? Did she believe me that Becky was just a summer fling, and a short one? Was she testing me? Did she just want to know the enemy? I had no idea.

Mackerel

CHAPTER NINE

The next few weeks I got into a pattern, working a few traps when I could, going on short trips to sea, and working on reports home. Again, Polly and Bernie got the women to cover for me and keep Abby comfortable when I had to be away at night. Chris slept at the house every other night or so, and Stan and the other men looked after the house when anything needed fixing. Ray came up from Portland when he could. Summer's an easier time in some ways, which helps, and again Jason kept the grass mowed. No one had time to plant the garden or keep it weeded, and that bothered Abby deeply. It was her garden, a place where she poured away any troubles that were brewing in her. The choking weeds took on more meaning than they should have.

Bernie told me when the house closed and said Mrs. Evans was moving in right away and bringing just a few things over on the ferry. Later she told me Mrs. Evans had hired Jane and Susan to clean, and that she was cleaning with them. Bernie was amazed. Summer ladies didn't usually clean; they hired people to clean. "Maybe she doesn't have much money so she has to do her own work," Bernie said, and she seemed worried that Becky—Mrs. Evans, I mean—wouldn't be able to fix up the house.

I ran into Stan down at the dock one morning early, and he told me that Mrs. Evans insisted he call her Becky and hoped he wouldn't mind if she called him Stan. He said she'd hired the barge to bring over a lot of personal items and furniture, and that she was scrubbing away at the dirt and dust right along with Jane and Susan. "That woman is some worker," he added.

"Seems you like her, Stan. Is she able to fix up the house?"

"I like her fine. Fine woman, no uppitiness in her. Doesn't seem to think she can own us by buying us. And the house likes her. She's going slowly, thinking things through, changing as little as she has to. First thing she wanted us to do was rip up that horrible lime-green shag carpet in the library. I can patch those little holes from where they nailed it down, and the floors will look beautiful again. Nothing a little polish won't fix. Carpet protected them. Have you seen her in the house?"

"No, not yet."

"You should stop by, seeing as you're almost neighbors."

"Good idea. I've been busy tending to Abby, but she wants to meet her. Says she wants to have her come over for tea."

"I think they'll like each other, Ben. Both smart women, handsome too, and educated. Seems they have a lot in common."

He was smiling, but I wasn't sure if it was because he was trying to get under my skin, or if I was being too sensitive. Maybe, I thought, he just likes her, and I know he likes Abby. Maybe he thinks they would enjoy knowing each other. Maybe it's that simple.

"Good idea, Stan. We'll do that. I hope she can get the house tucked in before the winter. Seems there's a lot to do to bring it back."

"It looks some shabby, Ben, but it's got good bones. She's got me making a full plan for renovating. Says we're going to bring it back to life. Seems the library is her favorite room. We hauled out all the old furniture those kids stashed in the attic. Good they didn't throw everything out. Last piece in there was the old library steps.

My great-great-great-something-grandfather's library steps. The steps I climbed as a child to reach the books Grampie set for me on the shelf. The steps I rolled toward her when she came with me to my island, to my Grampie's library. To my most favorite place. She held onto the steps where I held them before I rolled them toward her, and when she placed her hand over the top of the steps, I knew she was feeling the warmth of my hand. We were connected by those steps. Hers now, not mine. I wanted those steps when we had to sell the house, I thought, and I want them now. They should have been mine; they should be mine again.

"I wonder if she'd sell them to us?" I asked Stan. "I guess they're pretty battered up, but they mean something special to me because Grampie let me use them to reach the books he put on my shelf."

"I don't know, Ben. Seems she thinks they're something special too. When Pete set those old steps out on the lawn, I thought the woman was going to cry. She went over, put her hand on the railing, and patted it like it was her dog."

"Nuts," I replied, trying to pass it off lightly. "Maybe you'll make a set for me copied after those."

"Sure 'nuff. Just let me know."

A couple of weeks later I was standing in the line at the market about to pay for eggs and milk. I saw her come in, or maybe I just sensed it, but I didn't look at her and went up to the register. She had more guts than I did, and she walked up behind me. I turned and she said, "Good morning. It's nice to see you," and put out her hand. I took it in my own and instantly I could see us approaching the *Sea Princess* when I taught her to row. Having her so close to me again pushed me back to the smell of the sea and sun on her bare skin, to the feel of her hands beneath my own on the oars. We crashed then, and with a jolt I realized we might again.

Now I looked at her and I felt a cloud overshadow me. I saw the other scenes as well. Our fumbled lovemaking, the cold chill of that ride back to Northeast, my disgust at myself—leaving her because I couldn't think what else to do and running back to the safety of the dock, the ferry, my world not hers. Now I dragged my head back into the reality that she was standing in front of me.

"Who would have thought you'd end up here?"

"Not me."

Then what are you doing here? I wanted to ask, but I took a deep breath and said, "How're you making out at the old house? It was some mess all right."

"I'm OK. Actually I'm doing very well. I love it there, and everyone's helping and making me feel welcome."

That gave me a line to pull myself back. "We haven't. I'm sorry about that. I've been away, and Abby's not feeling well. She said if I ever saw you I should ask you to tea, to be neighborly." I paused and then asked her, "Do you want to do that?" I hoped she would say she didn't.

"Of course," she replied. "Is there anything I can bring?"

I told her no, just to come around four o'clock the next afternoon, and that we lived a little farther down North Woods Road from her, past the meadow. She must know that, I thought. But we were playing a game, acting as if this was all a coincidence and we had never meant much of anything to each other. I almost believed that was what she thought, but then I saw her hand trembling. She was holding a bottle of Heinz catsup by her side. If she was even aware of it, she may have thought her hand was out of my sight, but Ruthie had a display of mirrors on a rack next to the counter that reflected up at me. I watched Becky's hand in those mirrors multiplied into fifty hands, all quivering just so slightly.

All right, I thought. I can go along with you. "Good enough. See you then. Abby will be very pleased," I said quietly and walked out of the market.

Abby was pleased when I told her I'd run into Becky and she would come to tea the next day. "I'd like to make some cookies, dear. I just need a little more shortening and some raisins. Can you get them tomorrow?" I could have, but I didn't. The next day Abby didn't feel well, and it was a struggle for her to get the kitchen as clean as she wanted. I had to do it for her, so I just to ran to the store and asked Ruthie if she had any special cookies. She found some oatmeal cookies I thought were fine, but Abby was disappointed in herself. She's always taken pride in her baking, and she would have liked to make some coconut lemon squares or triple-chocolate brownies. My God, those are good; I can sink into them and not worry about anything.

After I got things ready, I tried to work on a report for Jim, but my mind skittered between memories of Becky and the life I'd built with Abby. I'd been a traitor to both of them, and that guilt was seeping its bitterness and anger into me. By the time I knew Becky might be walking over to see us, I was a cat pacing up and down, nervous energy making my mouth taste bitter and metallic. I heard the door knocker on the front door rap twice. We haven't used that door since— well, maybe never. The back door is what we use in Maine. Seems more friendly, I guess, and there's a mud room off it to store gear and buffer the cold air. I tramped through the house to open the front door, and it stuck. I shoved it open, and there she was, holding a basket and looking like a visiting church woman or someone selling door-to-door. I almost laughed, but I managed to spit out, "Now that you're a year-round summer person, you'll have to learn that we never use the front door."

She was embarrassed, and blushed. It made me feel easier that she cared enough about us to blush, and when she said, "I have a lot to learn," I agreed and ushered her in. I followed her down the hall to the kitchen and wondered what she thought of our small house, how it looked from her eyes. She noticed the books, and I told her they were Abby's. I couldn't acknowledge that many of them were mine. I wanted to tell her. It was tearing around in my gut, but I knew if I admitted anything,

I would want to tell her everything, and that could not be. I was a man divided, splayed out on a rock to be endlessly tormented. That was a grim realization, but it's how I felt. I was torn apart by loving two women and not wanting to hurt either of them again. Torn by the damage I knew I had already done to both of them.

When Becky went into the kitchen, she walked over to where Abby was sitting and gave her the basket of presents—lavender hand cream, and soap—fancy-looking woman stuff. She needn't have done that, but it was kind, and she'd brought Abby a bouquet with cut lavender. Turns out that's their favorite plant; something else they share. There was some of it flowering in the garden even untended. It's a tough old plant with a lot of beauty and usefulness, just like my wife.

I made tea and then sat watching these two women I loved getting to know each other. I was proud of each of them. Abby was welcoming, friendly. Becky responded with kindness and appreciation of that welcome, and she was thoughtful. She saw Abby was getting tired before I or Abby had to say anything. She said she'd be leaving, but she wanted to come back, perhaps when I was fishing or on a research boat, perhaps to read to Abby or just to talk. I was going to say, no, that's not necessary because I was worried about them getting together and comparing notes, but Abby said, "I'd like that very much." That sealed it.

Becky walked to the kitchen door, and I went outside with her. "I'm so glad I met her, Ben," she said. She was smiling. "She's a wonderful person. It makes me happy to see you with her, really it does."

Her voice had a little quiver in it that told me how hard she was struggling to stay remote and civil. What did she want to say? I wondered. "I could tell she likes you," I said. "You don't make her feel pressured. Some people want to talk and talk. Don't know when to leave, but you see what she needs. I'd like it fine if you were with her." I meant that, but I then added, "God knows it's a free country. You can live where you want." It was cruel, and I saw the hurt shadow her eyes, but I needed to push her as far away as I could. She was trying hard to tell me she wouldn't cause me a problem, but she caused me a problem just by being. That she was kind, still pretty, and good to my wife, and that I'd loved her—none of that helped me dislike her, and I needed to. I needed to keep her as far away as I could.

When I went inside, Abby was asleep, but she woke up when I set the tea kettle down on the hearth too loudly.

"I'm sorry, dear," I told her. "That was clumsy of me and I'm sorry I woke you up."

"No. That's fine. If I sleep now, I'll have a hard time sleeping tonight. Best to wake up."

She sat quietly for a while, and I waited for her to tell me what she thought of Becky. I didn't want to push her, but I wanted to know. Finally she said, "I think she's a fine woman. She's smart, but she's vulnerable and that makes her kind. She doesn't seem to think she's entitled. She listens. I like her. I think she's good for us. I think she'll be a good friend."

Her eyes burned through me, seeing so deeply into me that she was seeing things I couldn't see. She was looking at me like a mother assessing a son, and it unnerved me. "Good for us!" I retorted. "Well that's quite a comment. I don't see her becoming a friend. Don't forget where's she's coming from. She can live wherever she wants."

"And she's chosen to live here. This place is nourishing her."

That was too far beyond me. I just said, "Whatever," dismissing Abby and the possibility she had seen into my soul.

During the next week I managed to push Becky out of my mind because I was getting ready for a project on the outer edges of the Gulf of Maine. I'd be both the captain and lead researcher. The boat wasn't so big, just of enough size to sleep me and a crew of four, and we'd be making a sweep of the Gulf, along with other boats, gathering debris. We would follow a course, troll the surface for six days, and record everything we netted. We expected there would be so much we couldn't store it on board, so we would photograph every piece and record the date and time we'd trawled, fill nets, put floats on them, and attach them to one of the weather buoys for a larger ship to pick up and carry back to the lab.

You go to a beach now, and if you look hard and know what you're looking for you'll see that a lot of what you think is just natural beach litter has floated in on the tide. We're all to blame. Fishermen use old Clorox bottles cut in half as bailers. We throw unwanted crap, from fish parts to matches and gum, overboard. Storm drains overflow, carrying paper cups and other litter. The wind sucks debris off the shore and into the water. Ever think about how much dog piss and poop gets into the water along with the other crap? Bottles, shoes, cigarette butts—billions and billions of those, whose old tobacco leaches toxins and cellulose into the streams, lakes, and ocean. There are abandoned traps and buoys ripped out by storms and tossed on the beaches that tourists think are trophies, globs of oozing black tar, sludge, plastic bags, and a lot of other stuff you don't even want to think about. It's all there—the debris of a careless nation of consumers. Used to be archeologists dug up middens—old garbage dumps. Now they just have to go to the beach to see what we throw out. Pisses me off.

Plastic bags float even when they're full of water, and animals think they're jellyfish. But worst I think are the plastic beads, millions and millions of ground-up pieces of plastic that look like sand. I bet if you scooped up a handful of sand and put it under a microscope, you'd find half of it is plastic. The invisible debris, the carbon dioxide, that's making the water itself dangerous for the creatures that live in it. We're just recording, but I hope someone can take this data and do something to make people change their habits. I'm sick of seeing plastic eddying around in the harbors and out on the ocean. They say there are islands of plastic in the middle of the oceans just swirling around gathering more garbage. Gets me discouraged.

Abby was feeling better, but still weak. She could still get out of bed, and she could walk short distances and sit on the porch. The crisp fall weather agreed with her, and she liked watching the ducks coveying in the cove, the squabbling geese gathering to migrate, and kettles of hawks soaring overhead. She liked to think about the monarchs gathering for their winters so far away. The hummingbirds particularly interested her, and she read about them and then amazed me with what she'd found.

"Did you know, dear, that the hummingbird on that feeder has to increase his body weight almost forty percent to make the trip to Central America? I wonder where he lives. And he'll travel alone."

Travel alone—the phrase caught in my heart and scared the hell out of me. Is that what I'll be doing?

"Must be lonely, that," she continued, "but he'll fly low, just above the treetops or water so he can see the flowers that still have nectar, or my feeder." She loved the feeders, loved watching the birds, and getting to know some so well they were almost tame and would sit near her on the porch. Chickadees ate from her outstretched palm, and there was even a crow with a twisted wing feather that would hop up on the railing and take little pieces of food from her hand.

A week is a long time when someone is feeling sick. I wanted to be sure people knew I was going to be away and would stop by to talk or just get little things Abby might want. Chris could help, but not all the time because her kids needed her. Finally I wrote Becky a short note telling her I was going away and Abby would like to have her come for tea. I gave it to Bernie to put in her mailbox, and went to sea.

Does that seem a cop-out? Sometimes it does to me. Sometimes I have to be by myself or in the company of men. Men don't talk much, and that's a blessing and a curse. I picked the late night watch, when everyone is sleeping, the snores ruffling up through the floorboards. The guys snored like basses and tenors grunting a chant. Made me laugh to listen to them. The ship can almost run itself, but you have to have someone awake all the time to watch out that the net doesn't get too heavy. During the day, we'd troll for a few hours, then haul in and see what we got, but at night we'd just troll and stop if the pressure gauge showed the net was full.

The moon gleams over the quiet sea, an almost gentle and welcoming sea. I stand at the wheel staring out over the dark water, light waves breaking in endless ribbons of sapphire blue and white. The thrum of the engine and the swish of the hull going through water cradle me. I've listened to this lullaby, reading the sea through the sounds, for so many years that I'm oblivious, and the peril lies in not hearing any changes. But this boat is new for me, which helps me keep focused. In a few days, like after moving into a new house when the unfamiliar sounds become familiar and sink from conscious thought, I won't hear the engines or the waves and wind at all until something goes wrong. If the engine hitches, or the wave depth increases, or the wind picks up, my mind will register. But for now, on calm water in an unfamiliar boat, I'm at once lulled and alert, more free than I would like to range over my life, a soaring bird looking down on what I've done.

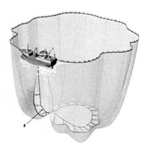

Purse-Seine

CHAPTER TEN

As I've said, there were times when I was a child that I saw what I thought would be my life. Working on the ferry. Coming home. Providing for my family. That's what it's turned out to be, but better. I felt resigned to my life when I was a kid and then scared I should be doing something better, something more important, though I didn't know what. Meeting Becky and going to college changed that. Changed me.

I think of Jason. What chance does a kid like that have? Dad was a hitter. Worst when he was drinking, and Jason's mother was tiny like a sparrow, and apprehensive. Her face was always puffy, and when I first knew her I thought she was much older than Jason's father. But she wasn't. She'd just been worn down, beaten down, and Jason hated his dad for that and for the beatings he got whenever something bad happened to his father. The drinking meant that something bad, or that Jason's dad thought was bad, was always happening.

Jason lost both his parents into a bottle, and then that was the only place he wanted to be himself. He said once he was glad he didn't have a brother, and particularly glad he didn't have a sister. It was quite an admission, and at first I didn't understand. "Would have had to try harder to stop it," he explained, but he wouldn't talk about what it was any more than that. Whenever I tried to get him talking, he'd cut me off and seal a wall around himself. He didn't want to come to our house, so we'd just play outside in the harbor or woods. When we got older, we'd hang out on boats and sneak into people's barns or garages.

There were many times, most even, Jason came to school with no lunch, and I sneaked him half a sandwich and half an apple. Mumma wondered why I was I always hungry when I got home, and I convinced her she needed to send me off with a bigger lunch. After a while, she just filled my lunch box with food for two. The teachers knew a little about what Jason was dealing with, but some of them seemed to resent that they had to deal with him.

One year we had a man come up from Connecticut, a young teacher who I guess the school department thought would be good, or more likely they were just desperate. Before we added the apartment in the attic over the school building, it was hard to get teachers out here. They couldn't afford to live on the island with prices gone so high, particularly in the summer. Now that there's the apartment, the teachers get reasonable housing with their pay, and a good place to raise their own families. That helps us get people who want to be here. We all built that apartment together once someone had the idea.

I don't know what that teacher was expecting. A little island school with eight kids. I think he had a picture postcard in his mind and didn't want anyone or anything to spoil that. But, no picture is perfect, even if it looks it. At first he just ignored Jason. Never answered his questions, just had him do foolish work like coloring while the rest of us were learning to read and write. That pushed Jason further inside himself, and he'd sit in his corner and find ways to make trouble. He'd stick his foot out just a little and trip someone who wasn't looking, or pretend to trip himself and spill water, or the free milk we got, on someone's workbook. He started bringing bugs to let loose in the school, and then snakes. He snuck a rotten mackerel in the woodstove one morning, and we had to clear out the school because it smelled so bad as it burned.

We all knew who'd done it, but we wouldn't tell. The teacher was so angry his face got blotchy red and he screamed "Fuck you!" at us. That's what we needed to get rid of him. We all knew that was a bad word. I asked Grampie why the teacher said bad words in school, and let him force the story out of me. He was disgusted and, as he was on the School Committee, he was able to tell the superintendent the teacher had to go.

As Jason got older, he got meaner. One summer his mother took him to live in their car on the mainland because they had to get away from his dad, and they had no other place to live. They'd move every few nights so the cops wouldn't catch up with them, and they used public bathrooms. Jason was ashamed, but pretended he didn't care. He wore the same clothes, and frankly he smelled, but he couldn't do anything about it. I'd give him clothes I didn't need—or want—like the upchuck-yellow sweater with the whale on it that Great-Aunt Muriel made for me one Christmas, and the puce scarf she made the next year. Lucky she lived in a nursing home on the mainland, and I didn't see her often. I bought him a shirt when Mumma and I went to Willey's. I told her why, and she chipped in too. Then I got worried Jason would think he had to give me something, so I pretended I'd won it in a drawing and it was the wrong size.

One year when Dad and I went to Portland to the boat show, I sent Jason and the other kids in school each a card telling them I was thinking of them. Each card had a different picture of the city so they could share. Mumma gave me the idea. The next morning after we got home, I looked out my bedroom window and I saw Jason standing under the apple tree waiting for me. I pulled on my pants and shirt and went out the kitchen door and then around the house to meet him. He walked slowly toward me, but as he got closer, he hung his head. When he was right next to me, I knew he was swallowing tears, and then he said, "No one ever sent me a card before. No one ever gave me a present except you. Ever." He thrust out his hand and added, "Made this for you." He opened his hand and I almost gagged at the dirt caked on his palm. In the middle of his hand was a little bird he'd whittled and set on a piece of driftwood. Then he started crying, and turned abruptly before I could say anything.

"Thank you," I called after him. "That's some fine present." There was good in him, if only more people could have reached out to it.

Tell me what chance a kid like that has to do well in school, or anything? No wonder the anger boils over on his wife and children. But he's ours. Just like with a dog that's been beaten and might bite you any time, we're wary, but we try to protect him from himself.

As I watched the ocean, I wondered, who is going to protect me from myself? How am I going to get through the waters ahead of me? I've got shoals on both sides, rocks and shoals. There's no map or beacon, and it's a cloudy night with no moon. That's some grim diagnosis, I thought, and that brought me back to Abby. A diagnosis is a chart of sorts. It tells you where you're headed, but not how long the journey, not how many storms along the way. One thing you know, it's not going to be an easy sail. How hard it was last time. I don't know that I have the guts to go through this again. Night after night of standing watch, waiting, shifting in bed, open-eyed, waiting for her to moan or twist up with the pain. Then, later, sleeping in a single bed in the room next to ours, not wanting to worry or wake her, or bump her by mistake in the night.

Sometimes I thought the strain of it would make me crazy. Trips to the doctor, waiting to hear what the latest test would tell us, too often not understanding or perhaps not wanting to understand what the doctor was saying. They can cover anything in a fog bank so you can't find your way and don't know what they expect. She's very sick. She could live. She could die. Probably they don't know themselves, but they think they should.

What's it going to be now? Couldn't be good that she's had cancer before. At least now we can say that—she's got cancer. Used to be people died peacefully in their sleep of unknown causes. Guess we all knew that was a crapper full of lies. Now at least you can die of what killed you. And the doctors keep saying that they think she's got uterine cancer, but they won't know until the tests, and another surgery. She's scheduled for that soon after I get back from this trip.

There are times I have to admit that I want her to die, quickly, painlessly, and be gone. I know. I know that is a dreadful thing to say, to even think. But here on the helm, staring at the sea, I can stare down my own demons. This is the place I am most confident, most at home and most able to see clearly. If Becky weren't back here, would I be thinking like that? Would I see a future way ahead that called like those damn Sirens luring Greek sailors to their death? Spider silk of song floating over the sea to pull them in and crack open their ships. Sometimes it's easier to think about what is right ahead, but not now. Now I know, or think I know, and I'm scared.

When I got home, I could see Abby had lost more weight, even in just a week. The sags under her eyes looked heavier and darker, and she wanted to see the doctor. We went over on the ferry, Uncle Clem making sure he had a blanket and soft cushion on an inside seat for her. When I helped her into the boat, I caught her hand and arm, and suddenly saw Becky's hand and arm. I remembered the jolt of current that spun through me when our arms and hands locked long ago. Now there was just pale flesh, and my wife, a hank of hair and a piece of bone, shackled to me. A wave of anger washed around me, and the bitterness soured my stomach. Why again? I cannot stand to go through this all again! Why doesn't she just die and leave me? I imagined a swirl of people around me commiserating. "So sorry Ben, is there anything I can do to help?" "You call us Ben, if there's anything you need." "Terrible, just terrible." "You were both so brave."

Sure, I thought, send me on a long trip, maybe to the Caribbean, or some sunny place. Let me get off this God-forsaken island. Let me run away with some gorgeous island girl and shack up on a beach eating coconuts and drinking piña coladas. Life isn't fair.

But Grampie's voice is in my head too. "Ben, life isn't fair, but you got to be fair to life. Give it what you got, work hard, love well, hope for the best, enjoy your time here. It's not long. And have a good cold beer once in a while." Grampie could always tell when I was down in my socks. He knew just by looking at me if I was gnawing on something, or feeling sorry for myself, or just had a bad day and needed someone to talk to. I need you now, Grampie. Life seems awful lonely right now.

By the time we got home and settled in the kitchen, I'd shaken loose of those thoughts. I asked Abby how she was doing, and even though she looked as pale as the belly of a cod, she was cheerful. "It's good to have you home, dear, but everyone's been tending to me. Your friend Becky came over for tea and we had such a good talk that she came over again a couple of days later."

What did you talk about? I wondered, but managed to say, "That's nice. What did you think of her?"

"She's had so many experiences beyond anything I can imagine, traveling all over the world, knowing interesting people, getting her doctorate in English. Imagine doing that when you're middle-aged. Takes some guts. She's like someone from another world dropped out of space into our kitchen."

"Good enough."

"Jane says she's working hard on the old house and it's healing. Stan's making a room like a forest for her grandchildren with cut-out animals he's painting. Says it's something he wanted to do all his life, but no one would let him. He convinced her right off, so he's happy as a clam at high tide. Helen likes her so much she gave her two coon kittens for company."

"Really? She could sell those for good money."

"Yes, but Helen thought Becky might be lonely, and she wanted to give her some company. I think she needed that."

"How so?"

"I think there are holes in her heart. There's a loneliness in her. I'm not sure she's ever had a really good friend, someone she can share her heart with. That makes her more likable. She told me about her first husband. He was a piece of work. Spoiled rich brat, if you ask me. Seems she married him to get away from her parents, and from college, and from something or someone else. I don't know, and I don't know why she put up with him for so long." Her face darkened, and she started tapping her foot, always a sign she's agitated. "And he was abusive."

My God, I thought, abusive. I'll tear the bastard apart if he hurt her. I sucked that thought deep inside and said as calmly as I could, "Well, sounds as if you hit the quick of it pretty fast."

"Yes. I liked her. She seemed eager to talk, but then maybe I just asked her the right questions."

"Always the teacher."

"That's the trick of teaching, isn't it? Asking the right questions and getting people to talk. Whoever they are." She paused, and then added, "Becky married a second time, but it wasn't any better. She married an older man, but it seems he was just looking for someone to decorate his life, and she wanted financial and social security. She laughed when she said it, like it was the first time she'd admitted that to herself. I wasn't sure what she meant by that, but she explained that in the society she came from, a single woman wasn't welcome at a party, so she would have had to stay home. But she didn't love those men she married. Sad to be married to a man you don't love. It's hard enough to be married even when you do!" She laughed and squeezed my hand.

"I love you too, dear," I said, and I meant it.

"She's a good person, dear. I'm glad she's here." But then she smiled at me in that way that let me know there was something she wasn't saying.

I managed to avoid seeing Becky, except in church where we sat in pews that were as far away as possible from each other. We'd nod if we happened to pass on the way out, but she wasn't in church the Sunday her daughter and grandchildren were visiting. Monday afternoon Abby asked me to go to the library Tuesday morning to pick up some books she'd asked Polly to get through interlibrary loan. When I opened the heavy old door with the leaded windows, I heard that voice. That voice plays melodies in my head, those chords that reverberate within me. I've craved that voice, and been scared of it, and now the last thing I wanted was to hear her voice. I would have backed out the door, but I'd taken a step too far and Polly saw me. She was sitting at her desk, putting plastic covers on new books, and I walked to the desk, keeping my eyes on her and not looking around.

"I've come for Abby's books," I said as quietly as I could, hoping I could pick them up and leave. Becky and a young woman I assumed was her daughter were looking at the display Polly'd put out of entries for the Dr. Seuss illustration contest. They were pointing and laughing at the photograph of Gus with his mountain-high belly heaving and his two-year old hopping gleefully on it. *Hop on Pop*. Good one. I thought they were so absorbed that they wouldn't hear me, but Becky turned around to face me.

"Ben," Polly said, "this is Becky's daughter, Katherine, come to visit for a bit." Polly stood up, put her arm under my elbow and steered me toward them.

"Hello, Ben," Becky said calmly. "I'd like you to meet my daughter, Katherine. She's visiting for a couple of weeks with my grandchildren."

I walked over and shook Katherine's hand. She was a blond, blue-eyed version of Becky, and when I looked at her I could see her mother as she must have been when she was a young mother. The thought that she'd had someone else's children, loved him, loved them, not me, swung out and hit me in the gut. I held out my hand and said, "It's so nice to meet you. You have your mother's eyes." But it wasn't. It was a stabbing reminder of what wasn't, of what I'd missed, and how much I'd loved her mother. I turned to face Becky. Her face was suddenly tight and blotchy, her eyes red with unwept tears. God help us, I thought. She loves me too.

I saw Polly looking at us, and could feel her questions and confusion.

"We better get going," Becky said. "We've left the children painting a chickadee and butterfly with Stan, but I don't want to impose on him."

"Oh he loves children. Adopts them as his own grandchildren if anyone lets him," Polly replied. "He'll be happy you're both out of the house."

Becky turned, and they left, but I watched Katherine walking close to her mother, asking her something, and I knew it was about me.

I started to go out too, but Polly said, "Ben? You all right? What's going on?"

"Nothing, Polly," I replied, but my heart was pumping so loudly I was afraid she could hear it. "Nothing at all."

"Ben, I've known you since we were in school together. I know Becky's the girl that won you the bet and got your daddy mad. I hadn't seen it before, but you still care for her. I know you do."

"That was a long time ago, Polly."

"Yes, and you've got a different life now. You'd better tunk that down inside yourself, Ben Bunker, like a bung in a board."

I was silent for what seemed like hours, and then I said, "I did care about her once, Polly, but we couldn't even be friends then. Not where she was coming from, and where I was. But that was a long time ago, and I don't care about her now. I love Abby, you know I do. I just saw her daughter and it took me back somewhere I thought I'd left. And I have."

I turned and walked out of the library. Tunk. A sharp blow to pound what is seen on the outside into the inside so it remains hidden; a bung in a board, carefully sanded and painted, three coats not two, so no one ever sees the nail concealed beneath it. She's right. That is what I must do.

Over the next few weeks, I went lobstering in the early mornings, leaving breakfast for Abby on the stove. Chris came over right after she'd steered the kids toward the school. They could walk most of the way with their friends, and it's a short walk anyhow. Chris would help Abby get up and give her breakfast, then get her settled and go home. Abby was all right by herself for most of the morning, but Bernie would come over from the Post Office to give her lunch and the day's gossip. Then Abby would have a nap, and about 1:00 Becky would come over. I'd hear about their visit from Abby, and that's how I learned more about Becky.

Abby told me she thought Becky had come back to Maine to pick up the pieces of her life. That after her father died, and after she was here that second summer, her life fell apart. She couldn't concentrate in school. She did badly that year, didn't go to the college she was supposed to go to, married Jordan P. Dyerman III, Jordie for short, but she didn't love him, and she had her children when she was young. She stayed with Jordie because of their children, and because she hoped it would somehow work out, but it didn't. He was very rich, so her mother encouraged her to stay married, but he was deeply wounded and he drank. At first he hid the liquor bottles and bought wine in cartons so she couldn't see the level go down. Eventually he seemed not to care and just drank. Bottles of Jameson Irish whiskey followed by chasers of crème de menthe. Foul combination. And he did drugs.

I don't think Abby told me how awful it was, but she knew. She said she admired Becky for leaving, though she left him a few times and he got her back with lies and money. Finally she did leave for good, taking the children to live with her mother and stepfather, and then in their own apartment. She went back to school and then she met Richard, her second husband. He sounds like an uptight prick, but at least he didn't hit her. Makes me want to pick Jordie up by his ears and bash him against the bait shack wall.

Abby said she thought Richard did more damage to her, though. He didn't seem as sick as Jordie, so she questioned her own worth. Richard had all the right credentials: money, class, a good job, no kids. They lived in a fancy house in Brookline, and one day Becky came home and found him in their bed with someone else. He told Becky he'd never loved her and wanted a divorce. You might have thought that would crush her, and my guess is that it did for a while. That must be what drove her up here. Maybe it seemed a refuge. I can't deny her that.

"I wonder what it does to a girl to lose her father when she's so young," Abby said one day. "Seems she'd never really grow into a sense of herself as a woman. Seems it might make her feel like she couldn't hold a man unless he was so wounded that he needed her more than she needed him. Surprising really that she's as whole as she is."

All I could think of to say was, "Yeah."

"She seems so complete until you scratch just a little and the sadness oozes out. Makes me think of her sometimes as one of my students. Odd isn't that? She who is so worldly, so at ease with people I would find intimidating, she's the one who's insecure."

"I hadn't thought of her like that," I added, realizing Abby was knowing her more deeply than I ever did. I sensed that vulnerability when we were kids. It was part of what made her approachable. Then I remembered that she said once she loved me more than she loved herself. I know now that's not a good way to love, but what happened after seems backwards. I went to college because she taught me by example that was important. She didn't finish college until she was much older. I married someone who loved me and whom I love. She did not. It's all backwards.

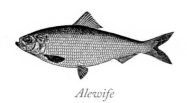

Alewife

CHAPTER ELEVEN

Abby's next appointment with the doctor was coming up, and she was apprehensive. She'd been feeling dog tired, and the pain was getting more severe in her gut. She was worried the cancer had spread and was scared about the inevitable tests. We sat tight together on the ferry, and drove the truck our family keeps at the dock in Northeast to Bar Harbor. The doctor there said he thought we should get a consultation in Bangor, and we knew from past experience that wasn't a good sign. We stayed the night in Bar Harbor because the doctor got us an appointment the next day. That was a bad sign too.

Eastern Maine Medical Center is a formidable institution, but the people are so kind that the size shrinks to who is taking care of you. I'd come to know it too well when Abby was sick the first time. When we went into the examination room, I knew Abby was frightened. I could see the pulse beating in her neck and I tried to calm her down, but I was too frightened myself. It's hard even to remember what the doctor said. The words were like clouds passing overhead, scudding along as you try to grab them and pull them down to you. He talked about the tests and the different kinds of cancer that can be associated with uterine, and he lost us in all that. Finally he just came out and told us what was happening.

"We think the cancer's gone into the ovaries."

I didn't hear much after that. Didn't have to. For so long we'd been told it was good that she had uterine, not ovarian, cancer. Now all the things we'd learned about why didn't matter; they were working against us. Ovarian was a death sentence because when the cancer metastasizes, the ovaries send the cancer cells throughout the body.

"There's a lot we can do with the new treatments. It used to be that this was one of the most difficult cancers to treat, but there are new approaches that are producing excellent results. You're a fighter. We know that." I could hear the doctor's voice, but it was disconnected, far off in a place I didn't want to be. I looked at Abby, and she was very pale, breathing shallowly, and holding her hands tight so the knuckles shown white through her almost translucent skin.

"Why did it take so long to diagnose?" she asked calmly.

"It's hard to diagnose. Sometimes the only signs are abdominal pain and bloating. In your case, we thought it was uterine, and there is some involvement of your uterus, but the reason you've felt so tired is that your body is fighting both.

I tried not to choke on the words as I said, "You are a fighter, dear. We'll fight this together. Look how long we've had since the last time. Seven years. We get another seven and we qualify as old people. Not bad for a pair of backsiders."

She knew I was trying to make her laugh, and she smiled slightly. She took my hand and said, "We'll make the best of it. We always have."

One afternoon I walked up the path from the docks after fishing. I work a small line of traps, just two hundred or so now, but enough to keep my license and pay for the boat. Most people think the lobster go into the trap after the bait and get stuck. I experimented a bit and I think they go in and out of the traps, and what you haul up is just the unlucky lobsters that happen to be in the trap. Heck, I bet some lobsters have figured out our schedules and are sitting by watching the others get hauled. I can't fish a regular schedule if I'm on a research trip, so sometimes Chris's husband works my traps for me—we split the profit—but other times I just leave traps in the water and haul them to bait when I get back. I've never hauled a load of dead lobsters in a trap I hadn't tended for a while—just empty traps. When the bait runs out, so do the lobsters.

I opened the screen door, reminded again that I had to patch it and fix the latch, backed into the door to the kitchen, and pushed it open because I was carrying my gear and six lobsters. "Hi, hon'," I said. "Long day, but a good one."

"Susan couldn't come today because one of her kids got sick, so Becky stayed with me," Abby said, and her voice sounded sunny.

I almost didn't turn around. We'd managed to avoid each other, even in church. She sat in back and usually she left while I stayed, pretending to listen to the organ music, but really just giving her time. Sometimes I saw her in the market, but we would sense each other and turn away. I've been fishing a lot anyhow. The bills. Of course, I knew she was with Abby most afternoons for an hour or so, but I'd managed not to think of her in our house. My house, my kitchen. There she was, sitting in the kitchen near the stove next to Abby, holding a skein of aquamarine wool while Abby slowly wound it into a ball.

"Thank you for staying late," I muttered.

"Of course," she said, as if it was ordinary.

"Stay for supper," Abby suggested, and Becky agreed. She took me by surprise, but there was nothing I could do to stop it.

I went to get cleaned up, and by the time I built up enough courage to go back down to the kitchen they had the lobsters and corn cooked and had warmed up some haddock chowder Chris brought over the night before. We sat around the red and white oilskin on the table because Abby said, "It's not like having company because you're here all the time, so you're more like family. You get the old tablecloth, not a fancy one."

Becky laughed, that deep musical laugh that echoed through my heart, and replied, "I'd be insulted with anything else." After a while, I relaxed. We talked about fishing, about the kids who are eager to leave school and get their lobstering licenses. Abby's worried that they won't learn other skills that might help them if the lobster fail. Becky wondered how lobster could fail, and I told her that the groundfish were failing because so many things were working against them. The lobster seem so plentiful, and it's easy for a kid to get sucked into the life when everything is pushing him, and now even a her, into it. Kids can get a loan easily to buy a boat and make $100,000 their first year. No other way around here to make that money, at least legally.

When I looked outside, I realized darkness had folded around us. Becky looked surprised and got up quickly, saying she had to leave. Abby said, "The moon gives a lot of light, but Ben should walk you home. I don't want you wandering about in the woods."

Then she asked me if that was all right and again I could only say, "Yeah."

I held the door open for Becky and followed her out. I was thinking about all the ways this was wrong and couldn't be happening. All the reasons Abby should be angry and jealous, wondering if Becky felt that too, or what if anything she felt. I had no idea what she felt then because she had kept so much to herself, or perhaps it was just me who had kept to myself. She had twined herself into Abby's life, becoming a dear and trusted friend I didn't know. She'd also wound herself into the life of the village, and people liked and respected her because she was just herself.

As we walked, we talked about Abby and how good it was to hear her laugh, and what a good day she'd had, but as we got near Becky's house, the house she had named Captain's House, which, of course, it was, I felt my heart squeezing into my throat. It was hard to breathe. I was very close to her, close enough to smell her and remember walking behind her through the woods at her father's land, watching her touching the places she loved. I took her arm and pulled her around until she was facing me. She looked at me, and I saw again the girl I had loved so deeply and for so long. I wanted to kiss her, could taste her, but instead I grabbed her arm and said, "I love her very much. She's been a good wife, a very good wife to me and a wonderful mother to my children."

"I know that," she replied. "It makes me happy to see you together, really it does."

I wished she had said anything else. Screamed at me. Thrown her arms around me, anything but that fierce, cold control. She seemed not to care or ever to have cared, and that dug a hole in the anger inside me. I took a deep breath and almost yelled at her. "Look at me. Did you ever think even once about me or what happened to me?" I watched her face whiten in the moonlight as blood drained from it and sadness tightened her eyes.

"Dad figured out what was wrong, but Mumma never knew. Dad didn't want to scare her. He was scared you would tell, that you would be pregnant and what the hell would have happened then? Or someone would find out, and we would be in awful trouble. Summer people don't forgive, he told me, and I could have gone to jail."

"Jail?"

"For rape, for Christ's sake," I yelled back at her. "For rape, and a summer girl at that."

"Oh God, I'm so sorry," she said, her hands flying up to cover her face.

"Dammit, did you ever in your stinking rich life think about me again! Of course not. I was just some goddamn backside kid. I don't know why you're here. It doesn't make sense. Sometimes I've hated you, really hated you." I could feel the veins on my neck bulging, and saw her looking at the mark where she bit me. "What do you want from me?" I yelled at her.

I turned to leave and I could hear her sobbing and saying, "I'm so sorry. I'm so sorry." There, it's out, I thought, but I could just have well have enfolded her and drawn her close to my chest before I tipped her head and kissed her, a dizzying kiss like the ones that changed my life forty years before.

I didn't see her until the next Sunday when the Stanley child got baptized. That day church was so crowded I had to sit in back where she always sat, and after the service we walked out at the same time. I steered her away from the others and said, "I need to tell you something. I'll walk you home.

"I'm sorry for what I said the other day," I started.

"No!" she replied immediately, "it's all my fault, b—"

"Be quiet. Please be quiet and let me talk. My father knew I'd fooled around with mainland girls, but it was different with you. A summer girl. You don't mess with summer people. He was furious. He grounded me, told me I couldn't play football that fall or basketball that winter. That's part of why I started reading—a gift really. Shut up in the attic room night after night, but then nothing happened. For months he thought the police would knock on the door some night and haul me off, or your mother would call, or your new stepfather, but nothing happened. I don't think he ever completely forgave me, but after a while he never mentioned it. And then I married Abby. He loves Abby."

"Ben, I'm so sorry. I was so ashamed, so totally ashamed of myself. I still am." She was looking at the ground, and I wanted to raise up her face and make her look at me. We'd reached a place on the path where there were no other houses, no one to see us. I stepped in front of her and she looked at me, a trace of fear in her eyes, and sadness.

"You marked me," I said. "When that little baby was baptized, I heard Reverend Stephens say, 'You are marked as Christ's own forever,' and I thought of you again. Again I thought of you." I pulled back the collar of my shirt to show her the mark, the mark that has reminded me almost every day of my life that I had loved her. It's faint now, a gentle tracery of dots with no discernible pattern, but she saw it. She started to stammer more apologies, but I kissed my fingers and put them over her mouth. I turned and again I walked away from her.

She made an excuse the next week about a deadline and didn't come to see Abby. Abby had a rough week, and missing her friend just added to the pain, and my guilt. I'd made Becky uncomfortable enough she wouldn't come to the house.

We moved a hospital bed into the living room, and I brought a bed from Chris's old room and set it up near Abby. I had to stoke the woodstove more often, but I could tend her easier there, and so could Chris and the others who came to help. Before I left in the morning, I'd carry her into the kitchen to sit in her chair while she still could.

The balance of our lives had shifted. I took coffee to her in the morning with the paper, instead of her having it ready for me. She'd ask me for things—never a hurry—just, "When you have time, dear, could you get me some oatmeal?" The chemo upset her stomach, and the anti-nausea medication never worked. I got so tuned in to what she was thinking and feeling that I knew sometimes what she wanted before she asked. I learned to look at the house that confined and sheltered her and ask how it would best protect her, make her comfortable. Too hot, too cold? Too much breeze, too little? Were people staying too long—there were always people who wanted to visit with her and talk or mostly to be listened to. She was a captive in her own home, and it was my job to protect her.

What did I feel most deeply? Guilt that I couldn't protect her. That was my job, a man's job, to protect the woman he loves and their children. To keep away the pain and fear, the awful cold fear that extinguishes the light. I couldn't fight the cancer, and I failed at keeping her alive. I failed at protecting my children from losing their mother. God knows I wish it had been me who got the cancer, but it wasn't. I couldn't even do that for her.

The first time she got sick, it was so soon after the kids left—grown up to start their jobs and families. We didn't have a lot of time to adjust back to being a couple, not just parents who conversed about and through their children. Children take over so much of your life and love that it's hard to see yourself as anything but a father—not a lover or friend. But we did that when she was sick. There is nothing I wouldn't have done for her, and I know she would have done the same for me. I wish I had gone first.

She couldn't reciprocate when she was sick, and it troubled her. She tried, though, by nagging me to eat and sleep. I tried, but too often I lay awake, attentive to her every move after being jerked awake by a slight whimper, or the move of her turning in bed. I began to long to be in a bed in the guest room so I could sleep through the night. Now I would tear out my eyes to have moments of that time back so I could lie awake and listen to her breathing, or move my arm near her back and feel the warmth.

I felt proud of her and awed. I couldn't have borne the pain and the fear as well as she did. I need to be alone most of the time, and so did she. But she couldn't even do that when she got sicker. She needed someone to help her do everything—sip tea, nibble a rice cake, nothing on it, that and oatmeal the only things she wanted to eat, a walk to the bathroom—but then that became too hard. Take her hand, hold her, look away—it all became a way to share and trust. Then even that got too hard. Diapers—three in the morning—changing her, she's too weak to stand or too sick from the medicine to do much but moan as quietly as she could, clenching and unclenching her fists.

Of course, people helped, but then I felt dependent on them. When Abby got sick the first time, Mumma came over every day to help. She cleaned and shopped and worked as she could in the garden. But she tired easily, and the work made her arthritis flare in her knees and hands, so making beds and scrubbing pots became too painful. Then she'd just sit with Abby while she slept, and knit. Abby said the clicking of those needles, like a tiny train, was a source of comfort. She knew Mumma was always there watching out for her, even though they didn't talk much, or perhaps, Abby just didn't talk about what they said.

This time Abby got sick, I thought it would kill Mumma and Dad too. Sometimes Abby's parents would come over from Brant's Island to see us, but it was a hard trip for them. They spent a lot of time sitting with Abby, but also with Mumma and Dad at their house.

One afternoon I was sitting with Mumma next to Abby as she lay asleep in the bed in our kitchen. "It's not right, Ben," Mumma said. "It's not right if the children die before their parents. I should be the one dying."

There was part of my mind that agreed. Mumma was in her seventies. That was pretty good for a person who'd worked all her life, had a heart condition, and some seen some scares along the way. "That's not how it works," I replied, but I wondered, how does it work? Are there any rules? Do the good die young? Does that mean the rest of us who live longer are any less good? I guess that was a trite thing to say—to think—but sometimes I felt it was true.

The next morning I sat in the chair near Abby's bed while she tried to eat some breakfast. I had to put oatmeal on a spoon and guide her hand to her mouth, so it was a slow process and she was tired. She lay back trying to swallow and turned her head toward me. "Dearest, we need to talk about something," she said, her voice thin and high.

I wanted to beg her not to, as if saying the truth, the now inevitable truth, would only make it real. I wanted to get up and walk outside, anything to get outside into the air, perhaps to go on the boat, pretending to take care of the traps, but just taking care of myself. But she wouldn't let me be and she continued.

"I'm dying. You know that and I know that, and we're hiding from it if we don't talk about it. Please, I need to talk about it."

"Oh Abby, I don't think I can't stand it. How can I stand it? I can't let it happen!"

"You can't stop it now, Ben. It's gone too far. I know it. I feel death creeping its way through me, and besides, I see it in my own face."

I looked at her, not wanting to understand what she meant. Then I saw the light through the window burnishing her face, making it golden, beautiful, almost translucent, but doomed.

"You remember when my Aunt Emma was dying, we noticed her skin was yellowish, and the doctor said the cancer had gone to her liver. I think that's what's happening to me now."

"Oh, my dearest," I said, and I could hold the tears back no longer. I was crying from such a deep place of sadness and fear for her and for me that the sobs contracted my body. I wanted to scream and beat the walls, but I pushed the pain down, put out my hand to her, and we sat for a long time not speaking.

"I am scared," she said. "I admit that, but the pain isn't going to be so bad this time. I know that. They'll give me all the pain medication I want, and everyone will help. But what hurts me is leaving you." Her words rushed out faster. "I don't want to leave you. I love you and I don't want to leave. Please know that. Please don't be angry with me. I know sometimes people who are left are angry, and I don't want you to be angry."

"How could I ever be angry, Abby?"

"Please, just know I don't want to leave you."

"I'm not angry, just very sad."

"On the cold January nights when you get home and there's no one there with a hot rum cider in her hands, you'll be angry. I know you." She smiled, and I tried to as well.

"There is something I want for you that you may say is none of my business, but it is."

I couldn't think what she might mean, so I waited. She was very tired now, and cold. I wrapped another blanket around her and put a log in the woodstove.

"Sit near me please," she said, and I sat as gently as I could on the bed next to her and she laid her hand on mine. "I know you loved Becky."

I opened my mouth to protest, but she moved her head just slightly back and forth to say no.

"She and I have only talked a little about you. That won't salve your male vanity, but we had lots of other things and people to talk about. But I told her I knew, and I told her that sometime, after I've gone, I want you to love each other again."

"No! I don't want to think like that. Not now, not ever."

She winced as she turned to look at me directly. "Life is too cold and lonely, and love is too rare to let it go without fighting for it to live. It would make me happy to think of you loving each other. If I can't do it myself, that is." She raised her head, a smile lighted her eyes, and then she winked. She never winked, but now she did, or did her eye just flutter involuntarily? I don't know.

"It was a long time ago, but I know you loved each other. A deep love. And I understand it. I've grown to love her too. I love that she is my friend."

I stared at my feet. I couldn't face her.

"You and I have always tried to find the best in whatever floated in on the tide. We have to find that now."

I could only nod.

"I don't know where Becky's been the last week, and I've missed her, but I think something happened between you two when you walked her home. Am I right about that?"

"Yes," I admitted. "I told her how I was angry with her for how it was between us when we were kids."

"What do you mean?"

"She was playing with me, using me because she was sad about her father dying. But she was from a different world, and it wasn't a world I could be in. I was just convenient."

"You don't know her very well. There's more to it than that."

"This is a damned odd conversation, if you ask me," I said, trying to laugh, and then the laugh caught me in the throat. "How can I think about being with anyone else, Abby? Not now, not ever. I can't go through this again. I can't lose you. I can't think about this; it's too hard."

"It is, but it's what I want. Right now I'm too tired to talk more. Please just sit near me," and she drifted asleep.

She had given me a gift so steeped in love and kindness it drove me a little crazy. I knew it was freely given, given because she cared about me and how I was going to spend my time when she was gone, and that she was taking care of me in the only way she could. It was an extraordinary act of generosity, and it made me love her even more, but to know she cared about me that deeply made me shrink into myself and away from Becky.

How could I think about loving another woman? I didn't want that pain ever again. You might have thought being given the release to love her after Abby died would have catapulted me into that future, but it didn't. It shut down any feelings I might have had for Becky, as if I'd been cauterized or castrated. That was not what Abby had wanted, but it's where I went. Down, down into blackness, closed in, separating into two selves, the self that could care for Abby, go through the day, and hide in the motions, the rituals, the expectations. But there was also the self that was dying. Crying like a child in the loneliness, curled up in my single bed, clutching for her at night, and then waking fully, staring at the ceiling, listening to the sounds of night—rustling of mice, and the waiting owls. Shrinking into bitterness and anger even before she'd gone.

Capelin or Sardine

CHAPTER TWELVE

When Amy, the visiting nurse, came to see Abby that week, I knew she was worried. I could overhear some of her side of the conversation from the living room, and her tone was different. They weren't joking around; there was no laughter, and Amy's voice was deeper than usual. I heard only her calm, serious voice, but only a few words and nothing from Abby. I knew Amy would be checking for any changes in Abby's functions, to see if she could eat anything solid, or was relying now entirely on Ensure or Hormel's Magic Frozen Cup, the only food she seemed to enjoy. Was she getting enough fluid, what was her skin tone, and most important to me, was she in pain? Abby always tried to hide her pain from me.

But I heard nothing from Abby. Her voice seemed to have disappeared, to have slid down her throat, and the effort of speaking, forcing air through her throat and voice box, the effort even to breathe was becoming too much. Perhaps most telling, though something I realized only later, Amy was only trying to make Abby more comfortable. She wasn't doing any tests, she wasn't asking Abby to do anything, and finally I heard Amy ask if there was someone with her all the time. Abby must have nodded yes, because Amy said, "Good."

Then I heard the creak of the springs in the old chair Amy always sat in, and I knew it was time for me to go into the kitchen—that together the three of us would plan Abby's treatment for the next week. This time, though, Amy walked out of the kitchen and met me in the hall.

"Ben, she needs more care now than you can give her here. It's time to take her to the hospital and start hospice care." The lines of her face were like gutters, and she was clenching and unclenching her fists in the pockets of her white starched apron, which told me this was for real.

I stared at the photographs lining the hall—pictures of Chris and Ray when they were young, of Abby holding Chris when Chris was a baby, of Rufus our dangle-eared, half-Bassett, half-retriever we'd put to sleep when he was ancient. I wished now I could put Abby to sleep, to spare her the pain and ugliness of dying.

"I don't think I can bear to do that."

"I know, Ben. I'm going to do it for you. It's the only way to spare her more pain and keep her safe now."

"I can take care of her. I know a lot more about it now than I did, and I can tend her."

"No, Ben. I'm calling Seacoast Mission to send the boat to come pick her up, and the ambulance. She needs to be in Maine Medical now. Things will happen that you won't know how to cope with, and it's kinder to her to let us take care of her."

"Please, no."

"Ben," she said insistently, "Your wife needs more care than I can give her here. Every day—every hour. I can't do that for her. You need to do this for her."

I let Abby be taken to the boat, and then to the hospital. It was a place we knew too well. The antiseptic sprays couldn't mask the smell of shit, sickness, and death, a pallid sweet smell of old air and fear. Hushed voices, nurses in sneakers, doctors walking fast and urgently, bells, dials, pulsating screens, bedpans, and catheters. Worst for Abby was knowing there were children there in pain. Somehow, she sensed they were near and asked about them while she still could. The nondescript paintings on the walls and the cheerful floral or geometric patterns on the nurses' uniforms couldn't disguise the work they needed to do—pushing, poking, prodding, taking samples, invading places once private. Giving yourself up to the system. I would never be good at that, but Abby could do it because she could imagine herself as the other person. I knew that was what she wanted to do—what she'd been able to do before—make their work easier, make them feel easier by joking with them, accept their care with no complaints, do what they asked of her. But now she was helpless, and so was I.

When they first wheeled Abby onto the ward, several of the nurses recognized her, and Stacy was head nurse now, which made us feel better. I hated that Abby had to share a room with an ancient woman who wanted the television on high, but there was nothing I could do to change that. I got a room in a B&B nearby, but stayed with Abby at the hospital most of the day and night. Sometimes I walked up and down the corridors just to get out of that room, but mostly I just sat next to her bed, feeling myself drifting through a black space. Tuned now to the padding of nameless feet, the coughing and occasional moaning through doors in the long corridor, in days defined by the rotation of nurses, doctors appearing and quickly disappearing, cheerful Pink Candy Stripers with trays of food Abby couldn't eat, orderlies turning Abby so she wouldn't get sores, and the constant drip through the shiny plastic tube of morphine that would save her from pain and kill her in the process.

Chris came up from the island and stayed overnight when she could to see Abby in the evening and then in the morning, and Ray took time off from work and drove up from Portland. He was shocked to see how much his mother's condition had deteriorated, and I know he regretted that he hadn't made more of an effort earlier to come see us. "It came on hard and fast this time," I told him. "She understands. So do I." We had our first honest conversation in many years. I told him I was sorry that I'd hurt his mother long ago, and that I'd hurt him.

"That's really all you have to say, Dad? 'Sorry.' Mom said the same thing to me a couple of months ago, and that helps. I guess it helps me understand to know because I've come so close to doing the same thing."

"The same thing?"

"Yes, to Joyce."

"The bed isn't always lined with rose petals," I replied. "There are a hell of a lot of thorns."

"We're going through a bad time. Sometimes I feel the pressure in my shoulders so hard it hurts. I just want to go get drunk, horse around with the guys, or go sit next to the river and smoke a cigar. Joyce hates that."

I looked at him and saw myself years before, bitching about the chores, the sounds of children whining and asking for things I couldn't afford to give them, the relentless lists of things Abby needed me to do after I got back from fishing or being on the ships. Ordinary stuff, but it grinds you down. Of course, I always had a legitimate reason to go to sea, to just leave when things got too rough at home. I looked at Ray and saw the shadows behind his eyes, the guilt and pain.

"Bad, huh? How can I help?"

"You've got enough to deal with now, Dad; I'm the one who has to help you."

"Helps me that you understand more now. Can you stick with her? It's better, I think, if you can. Better for the child. She needs you both." I was thinking of the damage losing her father and being a stepchild had done to Becky, but I couldn't tell him that. All I could say was, "Let me know how I can help, and besides, I like cigars too, and you know your mother hates them. Next time you're here, I'll get some good ones from the smoke shop on Main Street."

"Thank you, Dad. I'd like that."

And we did. A few days later when he came up again, because we knew Abby was going down fast, Ray and I went to the smoke shop, sat in velvet chairs overlooking Main Street, and smoked two Churchill cigars. He told me that one of the kids at school had told him years ago that his mother was messing around with the music teacher, but that he refused to believe it. He told me he threw all his anger up against me, and that he wanted me to stop him, to tell him it was his mother's fault, but that I never did.

"I respect you for that now, Dad, but then I wanted you to stand up for yourself, so I was mad at both of you. Now I get it that you were trying to protect us."

"Ayuh."

He grinned, and then knocking ash off into the large crystal—or at least glass—ashtray, he said, "Mom told me the first time she was sick that you were a wonderful man, and that she'd not fully appreciated that or you until she got sick. She told me she'd hurt you, but not how or why. She asked me to forgive her. Goddamn, there's nothing to forgive. I understand that now."

Tears were skim-coating his eyes, and he took a long drag on the cigar.

"Thank you," I said. "That means the world to me, and I know it does to your mother." I didn't add what I was thinking, that she's wrapping everything up. Wrapping up everyone she loves with love.

I could feel the tears coming up to grab me, and I took a deep breath, just as Ray did. Then almost simultaneously we looked up at each other, smiled and said, "What about them Red Sox?" We burst into laughter and walked out of the smoke shop back to the hospital with our arms around each other. I felt like one slab of granite just got lifted off my back, but there is still the other. Ray may have forgiven me, but his mother is still dying.

The next day Polly phoned to tell me she and Bernie and Becky were taking the early boat over and driving up, but I decided to leave just before they arrived. I couldn't face them or other people who came to visit, expecting to see Abby as she had been, not as she was, struggling to suffocate their own fears when they saw her, trying to smile. The pretense of it made me feel toxic. I resented their relief when they left, and wished I could as well, while I also hoped I would remember every last moment I spent with my wife.

Stacy told me Polly and her friends were surprised and disappointed I wasn't there, but I was too wrought up to stay. I felt the anger writhing up through me, and it scared me. I was edgy from too little sleep, and the sick taste of fear and sadness puckered my mouth. Worst was the feeling someone was tightening a vise around my chest, the wooden claws squeezing until sometimes I couldn't breathe. My shoulders ached, and the only relief I could find was in more walking. Pacing, really, up and down the corridors, and sometimes outside and into the little garden in the back of the hospital. There were other people there walking off their fear, or trying to, but we never talked. We barely nodded, just passed each other, wound up in our own grief.

Stacy said Abby was able to smile and talk just a little with her friends. She told me they sat around her and talked about things they'd enjoyed doing, like parties to knit for the church fair or make heads for lobster bait. In the old days the women wove the bait pockets, and the men set them out on the beach and slathered them with tar. Now we just order them through a catalogue, but sometimes the women make the pockets to enjoy each other's company and keep up the tradition.

They told stories about school and special things Abby had done with the children. Stacy said it was good to listen to them and learn about Abby when she was healthy. "They talked with her, though she couldn't answer much. But I could tell she was a great teacher. That's the way learning should be," she said, "doing things instead of just sitting on your butt and listening." Stacy particularly liked the story about when the kids would boil down maple sap in the spring and make syrup. It took a lot of fathers to chop wood for the stove, but when the syrup was done we had a pancake breakfast at school for all the dads and kids to celebrate spring. Abby used to say it gave her a way to teach botany, chemistry, history, math, and writing each year, and the kids never got tired of it. Never tired either of having their dads at school for breakfast. Stacy knew Abby was listening because the monitors she was hooked into registered a change when someone spoke to her, and sometimes she tapped a finger, or fluttered her eyelids, but she was too tired to talk.

Then Stacy told me that the woman she hadn't met when we were there before had been so overcome by seeing Abby that she had to leave the room.

"She got queasy seeing the tubes going into Abby's hand. Kept rubbing her own hand like she was feeling it herself. I watched her looking at Abby and I knew she was going to have to duck out for a bit. Good Abby was sleeping then, and she didn't really know who was there and who wasn't."

"So what happened?" I asked.

"The woman left and stood out in the hall. I stayed with Abby in case I could help her or her other friends, but a couple of the other nurses told me the woman stood with her back to the wall trying to hold in tears. Where'd you know her from?"

It was a question I couldn't answer, but fortunately Stacy continued.

"She must really care about Abby."

"Yes, I think she does."

"But, she seems like a summer person. Did she come up from wherever she lives? Did Abby work for her?"

"No!" I almost shouted at Stacy, but managed to stop myself by pretending to cough. Don't do that in front of a nurse.

Stacy laughed at me, raised her eyebrows and said, "More to it, huh?"

"Or less," I replied. "I think you mean Becky Granger. She's a summer person. Well, now a year-round summer person because she moved to Islesford. In fact she bought my Grampie's old house and is fixing it up. She's fitting in."

"Seems she cares a lot about Abby."

"They have some things in common," I added lamely.

"Your wife's a good woman, Ben. I know you're going to miss her. It's not easy to lose someone you love. Be gentle with yourself."

I could only look at her; the confusion I felt bound me in knots tied with in hawsers.

Stacy said, "I remember when Abby was hospitalized before, the whole time she was more worried about a student of hers whose father had run off, and the mother was drinking and maybe worse. The poor kid was an only child and would have stayed in her room at home all day. Abby used to pick her up on her way to school and take her home just to give her some time at school with her friends. Abby was worried that with her being in the hospital, the girl wouldn't go to school at all."

"I remember. She got Polly to pick her up."

"Yes, Abby's a good woman." She looked at me and added, "But you know that. Look at what she's had to put up with," and she laughed, then looked at her watch. "Time for meds and then I'm off, but I'll be back first thing in the morning."

I began thinking about the things Abby does—the smell of my favorite coffee sifting up through the kitchen floor to the bathroom where I'd be getting ready to leave. She doesn't have to get up when I do. I told her that. It's wicked early, and she doesn't have to be at school for hours, but she always gets up to see me off. Said she uses the time after I leave to get ready for her day. She makes great popovers, and the rich buttery smell mixes with the aroma of coffee—I almost didn't have to eat to enjoy them. Could I just capture that smell and store it in bottles on our pantry shelves the way Abby canned and bottled preserves and tomato sauce? Cooking for her myself has been a struggle, but it's going to get worse, isn't it? Cooking for myself. Just myself. By myself, to eat alone. What's the point? What's the point of any of it?

She's right, I thought. I do feel angry, but not at her. At life? God? I've prayed that God would take me instead. The anger is etching its way into me like acid and hollowing me out. I want to turn my back on people and their fucking kindness, all of them. Except perhaps my grandchildren. I can be with them without feeling the anger. But not with adults. I don't want their pity, their self-conscious and self-righteous pity. Damn them. They can go back to their lives as they know them. I can't. Instead, I walk back into the room, and Abby is lying in the bed, tubes with God knows what going in and out, machines flickering, and humming. I sit by her bed and stare at the floor.

"Home," she says softly. "Take me home."

Thank God Stacy heard her. I turned to Stacy and begged her with my eyes.

"We can't release her unless a hospice nurse goes with her, but let me get to work on that."

A few hours later Stacy came back into the room smiling. "OK, we're all set. In the morning, you'll go down to Northeast by ambulance, and then the *Sunbeam* will take you back to the island. You'll like the hospice nurse, Jenny. She'll go over with you now, and she or her partner will check on Abby every day, and Amy will stay. They'll take good care of you."

The next morning Abby was pretty well drugged up, so she wasn't restless in the ambulance, but when we transferred her to the deck of the *Sunbeam*, she smiled. She was hooked up, of course, to the morphine drip, but Jenny carried that and then sat right next to her and monitored her breathing and pulse. The weather cooperated, and Abby lay on the stretcher, lulled by the wash of the waves and breathing more deeply than I had seen her doing for a long time. I talked to her about the special places we'd been to—the picnics we took with our kids on the lawns of summer places after the owners had gone back to Philadelphia, or Texas, or wherever they were from.

I joked about good times, like once when chipmunks joined us and we threw bits of our peanut butter sandwiches to them, and one came right up to her hand. I wanted to talk *with* her, but she couldn't respond, so I fell silent. Then I remembered that Stacy had told me to talk as if she could hear us, because most of the time she could. Stacy said hearing is the last sense to go before someone dies, and that Abby would be aware that people she loved were around her as long as we talked to her. Talking about her when we were in her room was the worst thing we could do, so I just stood next to where she was lying and talked about the good times.

As we neared Islesford, I saw people gathered on the float and the ramp. They were standing together all the way up to the parking area, and I realized just about everyone on the island had come to welcome her home. That set me back a bit. It's harder for me to bear kindness than when someone's angry or nasty with me. When the guys set the stretcher on the float, a few people clapped, and Abby roused a bit, but Jenny quickly shushed them and they fell quiet. I felt a sweep of sadness coming toward me, shrouding us like a thick fog.

It took her two weeks to let go, and during that time everyone she loved sat by her bedside for at least a little bit, took her hand, talked to her. Chris was there every day and brought our grandchildren, and Ray brought Joyce, who was pregnant, and their daughter to the island for long weekends. Polly and Stan brought their guitars and sang to Abby. Another morning the church choir members same into her room and asked which hymns we wanted to hear. Abby was moving her mouth, and I saw her fingers moving on the sheet and knew she was joining as best she could.

Sometimes it was hard to believe she could hear us. She lay so quietly under the sheet that I checked again and again for the gentle rising and falling that indicated she was still alive. We took turns. Chris would stay with her after she dropped the kids off at school. I'd take a walk then to the store or the harbor, but I couldn't stay away long. I felt as if I were tied to her, and that when I left I was still there. One morning, very close to the end, just before it, she opened her eyes, turned to me and said clearly, "Remember what I told you. You will remember?"

"What, dear?" I asked, shocked to be talking with her, though I had read in the hospice pamphlet that people who are dying will do that. They will come out of the fog of death for a few moments to tell people they love something that is important to them before they slip away again.

"You and Becky. Take care of her for me."

"I don't..."

"I know. But she needs you, and you need her. I told her the same thing when she was here yesterday."

And then she was gone, back into the cloud of medication, but not in pain. She died the next morning, and our children and I watched her spirit ebbing away. Amy had given her medicine to spare Abby and us the death rattle, but we knew she was dying when her breath came in gasps punctuating long periods of complete silence. Ray and I stood at her bedside, and Chris sat in a chair next to her, and then for several minutes Abby didn't move at all, and neither did we. Finally Amy said, "She's gone now," and it was over.

I didn't want to see anyone. I just wanted to take a bottle of bourbon down to the harbor and drink until I fell asleep. That's what I would have done when Jason and I were teenagers, but we would have drunk a can of beer or a bottle of bad wine.

We had a service for her in the church, and then we all walked together down to the graveyard. I could have sunk down into that grave next to her with no regrets. Strange to look at the plot where you know you're going to end up. Seems almost a waste of energy to fight it—why not just hurry the process of dying when living is hard? I looked over to where Becky was standing with Polly and Bernie. They had their arms around each other and they were crying. Sometimes I envy the women who can cry out their pain. With me, it just sticks in my craw like a fish bone, digging pain in deeper.

When everyone had left, after we'd sung "'Tis a Gift to be Simple," Abby's favorite hymn, and everyone had hugged me, and Chris and Ray had gone home, I walked down to the beach at the end of Bar Point and sat on the wall looking at the tide washing against the rock. The sound of pebbles and water swishing against each other is a lullaby for me, always has been. I don't think, I just let the rhythm of the breaking waves roll against me. I could hear harbor porpoise chirping to each other as they cruised past where I was sitting, and the muffled quacking of ducks settling in coveys near the shore. It all has its rhythm, its time and place, and its season. But Bar Island points to the Thrumcap, and beyond that is Baker Island, and that brought me back to when I sneaked up on Becky as she danced on the flat rocks. *Rock, Rock, Around the Clock.* I could hear her voice now as I heard it then, and it turned my sadness back to anger.

I walked back down to the harbor to my boat, grabbed one of the blue wool blankets I store under the seats with the cushions, and made myself a bed. I didn't sleep that night, but I watched the stars and listened to the water, held in place by powers too far beyond me to comprehend, but comforting. The next morning, I called Jim and told him I needed to be out on the water. I said I had some short trips to make that I'd planned before, but that I needed a big one and I needed to get away from Islesford, from too many people who loved Abby.

I didn't tell him about Becky, but most of all I needed to get away from her. We'd run into each other, of course, but I couldn't bear to look at her. My grief and anger all settled on her. It didn't make sense, but I resented her more deeply than I had ever been angry about anyone. I couldn't bear to think of her being alive and Abby dead. Truth is, right then I wanted her dead.

She came up to me in the market one morning and told me she'd been planning to have a party before Abby got so sick—a party to celebrate the house and that she was almost finished with the work on it. She asked me how I would feel about going ahead. What the hell am I supposed to say about that? Sure, have your party. Get all your fancy friends together. Show off what you've done to the house; show off the things we couldn't do, but you could. Stan says it does look some nice. Just don't make me go and look at my old house. The house I loved that we couldn't keep. Anger is corrosive, and I was being eaten away by it. I felt like its prisoner, as if I too had a cancer spreading inside me. But I kept remembering Abby, my dear Abby, telling me I would be angry, and that I needed to feel it to understand it and to grow past it.

I told Becky to go ahead. That Abby would have loved the party. She would have too. Particularly the dancing. I was going to be away, and that was a relief. I saw Becky looking at me, her eyes wide, then narrowing suddenly. I guess I didn't look so great. These past few months plastered a few years over me, and it's hard to get up the energy to shave or do much of anything. I probably looked as scraggly as I was feeling.

Depression can lead you by the nose if you let it. There've been times I felt as if the only way I had the energy to do anything was to let myself be led. Go through the motions. Hide in my own wallow. The routine of being on a ship was the only way to escape. I was used to being without Abby on board, used to the chatter and grumbling of men, used to the rocking of waves, the creaking of a ship, and to being attentive to it all. Used to having a job to do. Losing myself in the job at hand, using my hands to stop using my brain.

This next little run was to check out the pogies. Funny word—it means a lot of things that seem unconnected. A welfare check, like— Sam went to pick up his pogy. Or it means a special kind of mitten the women used to knit that had a hole in the side for an oar handle so a man could row and keep his hands warm. That's a useful piece of gear. But the main thing the word means is the fish. They're a small fish about twelve inches long that's so oily you can stick a wick in one and light it up like a candle. There used to be millions, but there hardly seem enough now to fill a whale.

We're assessing the pogy fishery, which is a lot more important than it sounds. People used to think the pogies ate mud, but now we know they siphon their food from the water. It's comical to watch them because they raise their snouts out of the water and cruise along letting plankton and microscopic plants like diatoms filter through their gills. Pogies clean the ocean by filtering enormous amounts of water, or did when there were millions of them. With just one fish filtering around four gallons a minute, they kept the algae blooms under control. Pogies feed the fish that feed people, whales, sharks, pollock, cod, hake, swordfish and especially the bluefish. You name it—it eats the pogies, or did. The birds too—gulls, cormorant.

The bluefish kill a lot more pogies than they eat by herding them toward the shore. If the pogies try to escape by swimming close to shore, they can get stranded by the ebbing tide, or suffocated when they use up all the oxygen in the water. Then they'd die by the thousands, maybe even millions. Terrible waste and the carcasses stink.

Without the pogy, or menhaden as they call them south of here, the fisheries wither. Now factory ships out of Virginia trap schools of menhaden in purse seines, then vacuum them into refrigerated holds, and on shore they're "reduced"—no awareness of the irony in the word—they are reduced to oil, pet food, and fertilizer. Millions at a time—eighty percent of the pogy caught off the east coast end up that way. Maine's got the sense not to allow that, so our pogies are caught for bait, but that fishery isn't regulated. Of course, fishermen don't want it to be regulated, and some of the guys who know the work I'm doing are some pissed, but I want to understand how we can keep this fishery going.

The population of pogies used to come and go, and we're trying to figure out now why it's going and not coming back, because they are perhaps the most fecund fish in the ocean. They start being sexually active when they're about two years old and they never stop 'til they die. No little blue pills for them, and a female can lay about 300,000 eggs a year! People have been keeping track for some years now, and we'll continue that work. It's a good distraction.

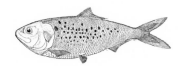

Pogy or Menhaden

CHAPTER THIRTEEN

The job was hard, and we didn't find many pogy. At least the work kept me tired so I couldn't think much, but I did have to go back home. We worked our way back to our port—Woods Hole—offloaded our gear and data, and finally headed for our own homes. I walked down to the Northeast docks to take the ferry, and my heart jumped a mile because she was standing there, right by the ramp to the dock where the ferry leaves. I watched the wind playing with her skirt, and her hair like a silk veil waving, and saw myself walking up to her so many years ago, reaching for her, and then suddenly she was in my arms and I was holding her close, and she cried. When she cried, she released the sadness I felt after her father died because I couldn't help her. Now I could do something—I could hold her and let her cry. I walked closer now, and then she turned around and I saw it was Ralph's daughter Lilah, pretty as Becky was then, well almost, and almost as excited to see me.

"Hi, Uncle Ben! You're home! Everyone's going to be some glad to see you."

She's my honorary niece, not blood kin, but Ralph and I go so way back that calling me Captain Bunker like the other kids do seemed strange.

"Hi, Lilah. How's everyone been doing?"

"Real good! So much going on. Mrs. Jones had her baby, a boy, named him Graham after his great-grandfather. Mrs. Able's having a devil of a time with her arthritis. She stopped eating tomatoes and potatoes because someone told her they're bad for arthritis. Said she grew eight kinds of potatoes last summer and now she has to give them away. And best of all, Mrs. Evans had a party. A real big party! She invited everyone on the island to celebrate finishing the work on her house. She had food for everyone, and there was even music. We danced and danced..."

I let her go on because it was easier than trying to stop her. She told me about the boys she danced with and the boys she wanted to dance with, and then we were at Islesford. I hadn't told anyone I was on my way back, so I had a lot of people to greet on my way to the house. I ran into Ralph at the dock and he asked if I wanted him to come so I didn't walk into a lonely cold house. I told him no, that was exactly what I wanted: just to be alone, let the house welcome me, hear Abby's voice in the kitchen, and smell what she was cooking. I could fool myself for a while, but when it was time to go to bed, the room seemed so empty and cold that I went back to the kitchen and lay down on the couch the way I did when she was sick.

I managed not to run into Becky for weeks. As I've told you, that's not easy on a small island, but if you know someone's habits—when they go to the market, when they go for a walk or to the mail—you can avoid them most times. It was awkward, though, because so many people seemed to know or sense that we had cared about each other once, and that Abby thought we could again. Hell, I guess being the only single man and woman our age on Little Cranberry would give even the numbest person a hint. So at the Post Office Bernie would say, trying to make it sound as if she'd just been struck by the coincidence, "Becky was just in getting her mail. I told her there was going to be a bean supper at the church on Saturday night. I don't suppose you're going too?"

I got used to it and played with them for the delight of making them stammer and shut up. "That's great," I'd say. "Maybe she'll go. Hope she has a good time. Personally, I never did like beans." Polly would tell me when they were having an event at the library and suggest I come, but I'd tell her that reading was Abby's thing, not mine, and I didn't want to go anywhere near the library. I hurt her feelings with that one, and I was sorry. Then she told me that Becky had started volunteering, reading to the kids, and that she was so good at it that they wanted her there every day. Finally, Polly let on that Becky did go there every day and she even started a program after school for the kids. It got so popular most of the kids stayed for it. That's something Abby would have liked. No wonder they were friends.

That fall and winter I brooded and kept to myself, turning away from people when I saw them coming toward me, going out early to fish, and coming home late, after dark some evenings. Ralph, Durlin, and Jason tried to get me to go out, to play cards in the evenings or have a beer, and Chris and Will, Mumma and Dad, and cousins often invited me to supper. I went sometimes, but not often. Mostly I just sat at home and played the scenes of my life over and over again in my head. And I drank too much. Foolish that, and my head hurt in the morning. I know I worried people, and finally Ralph came over in the late evening as spring was flirting with us. I'd tossed back too many beers, and a glass of whiskey as well.

Ralph knocked, but didn't wait for me to open the door. Instead, he walked into the kitchen, plunked down a thermos of hot chocolate, a batch of his wife's shortbread cookies, and sat across the table from me. I looked at him and I knew what he was going to say. He didn't have to say a thing.

"I know," I said.

"Enough. It's time to quit feeling sorry for yourself and get off your sorry ass."

"I know." And I did. I knew he was right, and we're good enough friends that I also knew he wasn't looking down at me, just caring about me.

"I know," I repeated, "but it's hard."

"Damn right it's hard. But Abby'd be some pissed. Some pissed and disappointed to see you here looking like a dragged-out piece of crap and drinking yourself to oblivion. She'd be right angry to see her house looking raggedy and dirty. It's time to get on with your own life."

He told me we were going for a walk, and the cold air soon cleared my head. We walked to the harbor, then along the beach and finally back past Becky's house and through the woods to my house. Mine and Abby's.

"Ben, I don't care if you live by yourself for the rest of your foolish life, or you do what the women say you should and go courting Becky Evans. I don't give a damn about that, but I'm not going to sit back and let you feel sorry for yourself, drown your sadness in booze, and shame your kids and the memory of your wife. She loved you. Don't do this to her or yourself."

"Ralphie," I pleaded, thrown back to when we were children, when there were too many times he drew me back from the crap Jason wanted me to get into. "Ralphie, I don't know how. The loneliness and the anger bore their way into me, and I feel like I'm poisoned."

"Of course you are, you damn fool. You're poisoned with drink, and some guilt, and a lot of sadness. The stress of it poisons you. The only way to get rid of it is to stop drinking, take a lot of long walks, and find other people to be with. You stick yourself here alone, and of course the world seems lonely. But you don't have to be alone. There's lots of people who want to spend time with you and, you know, you are a total fucked up idiot. There's a beautiful woman just down the road who'd love to go for a walk with you."

"That's about all I'm good for right now."

"It's enough. Just take a walk. See where it leads. Beats getting drunk by yourself, and you won't get anyone 'cept Jason joining you in that shit."

The next morning after I got up, I walked over to the kitchen cupboard where I kept the booze, and I poured it out. It's never meant so much to me that I couldn't pour it out, except when I was hurting and hiding in it. I knew that's what I was doing and it wouldn't work. So I poured it all out, and went for a walk. I walked around the entire island, and in early winter that's not easy. The ground is frozen and there are places where the ice catches your boots. It coats the stones in the streams, and even the edge of the sea, beautiful and shining, but daring you to step on it and slide on your ass—always there waiting for you to miss your step. The cold pierces your chest, and you can feel the icicles each time you breathe. Of course, I wear three layers and wrap a scarf around my mouth and throat, but the cold finds its way through.

I like to walk on the beach, looking out at the ocean, thinking about what the fish and birds are doing, but when the ice skims the rocks, it's easy to twist or break an ankle. I'm a stubborn cuss to be out here, I thought. Damn dumb. Stubborn as a pig on ice. Then I laughed at myself, remembering so many years ago, when Becky jumped off the high table rock on Baker Island. I told her Grammie would call her stubborn as a pig on ice. Laughed to think of her laughing, and for that moment I missed her. It was just a moment, but a good one, and the start of wanting to see her.

At first I was the stubborn pig. I wouldn't go near the library, or any of the places where I knew I might see her. No matter, the rumors persisted as well as the sly grins and silly smiles, the innuendos that there was something between us or could be. It irritated me, and one day when I was about to walk past the library, instead I walked in. I walked over to where she was working with some children's books and stood next to her. She smelled like lavender and she was wearing a blue and white apron over her sweater and pants. I thought, how settled she looks. How easily she's fitted herself into a world that was so different from the world she came from, and I wondered if she wasn't more at home on my island now than I was.

She looked up at me and smiled in welcome. That gave me courage, but I was still tight in my gut. All I could spit out was, "I don't like the way things are between us. Would you go for a walk with me?"

She seemed calm, but then I noticed her fingers twitching against the books she was holding. This is hard for her too, I thought, and that eased me a bit.

"I can't now," she said, and I felt the wall go up between us again, but then she explained, "because the children will be here in a minute. But after? Yes, I'd like to."

"I'll come back." I turned abruptly to walk away from her before I could change my mind.

I walked down to the docks and then around the harbor, killing time and trying to unknot my nerves. I felt like a pimply teenager before his first date. Like there was a clump of elvers in my stomach swirling around. Glass eels in the stomach! That's a damn ugly thought, and it made me laugh at myself. "Just a walk," I kept saying to myself. "Just a walk."

When I opened the door of the library, Becky was standing behind the main desk putting books into a leather satchel. I'll offer to carry them just like a school kid, I thought, but I hope she doesn't pile any more in there. I watched her walking toward me, grabbing her coat off the hook, and wondered what would happen. Would this be a moment that changed everything, or just another moment. Or both.

"Thank you for coming back," she said, and her voice covered me like a velvet cape. Of course, I've never had a velvet cape and don't want one, but she has a voice I could listen to for a long time.

"It's a little dark for a walk, but the moon is coming up full. Let's just walk around the shore path for a bit. Are you going to be warm enough?" I asked her.

"Yes, and the exercise and fresh air will be good."

"Give me those books. You read too much!"

She laughed, and I did too.

"We were friends once," I started.

"I know what you mean," she interrupted. "I feel as if I know you and don't know you all at the same time. Like I should know you better, but I know you as a child, and now you're a man. Like I lived with you in my head for many years, and now we're friends again, and Abby..."

The words poured out like alewives over a dam. I felt them rush past me and thought, this is a mistake. This is too damn complicated.

"I didn't ask for a psychological evaluation," I told her. "Just a walk." We walked silently along the harbor listening to the birds settling in for the night. I saw a light on in the bait shack and figured someone would be watching us.

"There's lots of talk about us now, so I figure we'll just go for a walk and let everyone see there's nothing going on."

She took a deep breath, exhaled, then asked, "Did someone dare you this time?"

Now that was a low blow and it irritated me. I blew back at her, "No, just me. I'm a very ordinary man, you know. Sometimes I think you're just slumming by living here." I watched her wince. "Like we're so ordinary we make you feel like *Queen for a Day*. Like we're your serfs in the village around your castle."

She was silent for several minutes, at least that's what it felt like, and I had time to see I'd hurt her.

"Ouch, that's harsh," she countered.

It wasn't kind of me, and I was almost sorry, but I watched her as she thought about what I'd said, seeing the truth in it. Then she shook her head a little and looked straight at me as if she had absorbed the truth of what I'd said but cast out what didn't fit. I sensed she was shaking off my accusation and that she had come home.

I didn't realize until much later how important it was that she was coming home, making a new home for herself. That eased up the burden of having her there and I began to understand that her vulnerability, so seductive when we were kids, was a sucking void. There was no way I could fill the emptiness inside her, the black pit from losing her father and sister and having such a cold mother, unless she had already filled it. I began to sense she was doing that, and it freed me to love her as a woman, not just the memory of a girl.

"Can you ever forgive me?" she asked.

"For what?"

"Ben, you know. For the way I acted when we were kids. For the trouble I made for you. I've felt so sorry, so sad I ruined everything. So ashamed of myself."

"God, woman, you're clueless sometimes. I was angry. Angry at myself that I didn't know how to make love to you. Angry at you because I knew you weren't after me—even then I knew that. You were such a hurting puppy. Becky, I loved you then. Love and forgiveness. Abby taught me that. Of course, I forgive you and I hope you forgive me."

She watched me as I was watching her, seeing her not just as a beautiful seductive child, not just as a prize, or a mysterious stranger from another world, but as a friend, and a woman I could love.

She turned to me and said, "I don't know who you were to me, or even who I was then, or who we might be to each other, but I'd like to be friends. You're a good man, Ben. A good person, and you make me feel as if I am too."

That was enough. Best really. To be friends. I'd learned that from Abby. More than anything, we need friends. People who care about us. People we can count on.

We walked past the dock and Hadlock Cove and headed down along Maypole Point Road. The moon was shining on the waves lapping the shore, and the sounds, sights, and smells we both loved were a gentle companion. Finally I said, "I need to thank you for something."

"What?" she said, as if it was impossible there was something she could have done for which I was grateful.

"When we were young. You made me think about my life in a different way, as if I could do some of the things you took for granted."

"I never thought about that. I never thought you thought about me like that."

I told her she was foolish, and that I had thought about her too many times. Cramped up in my room at home, or my room in the back of Aunt Cissy and Uncle Albert's house. Staring at the ceiling. Though I didn't tell her then that I threw away hours thinking about her and what she looked like with the moonlight on her skin. I just told her how I learned to want something more than being a sternman because of her. I told her I sat up in the attic so long by myself, finally I just bored myself. Eventually, I had to pick up a book, and then the more I read, the more I wanted to read, and I did well in school. I told her about getting into college and working with Jim Acheson at UMO. Telling her all this seemed to give her some peace—as if what had happened between us hadn't all been a mistake.

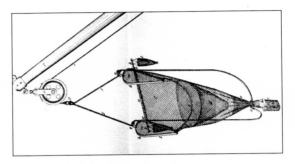

Design of an early beam trawl—from Wikipedia

CHAPTER FOURTEEN

I walked her back to her house, and I was going to ask myself in, but I thought no, let this be whatever it is going to be; let it just be. We got into the habit of walking every afternoon. Whenever I was home, and not on a ship, I'd pick her up after her program at the library ended, and we'd walk. As we walked, we filled in the gaps—she told me her mother had married again, a wealthy man Becky didn't like much at first. She talked about going back to her boarding school after her father died, and how she shriveled into a cold angry lump of misery, alienating her friends, not doing her schoolwork, and not getting into a college she wanted to be at. She told me about marrying Jordie.

Made me angry to hear about the way he treated her and their kids, boozing and drugging himself to oblivion. Night after night. Only reason she stayed was for the kids, but finally she had the courage to leave. She told me how much she missed her kids now that she lived in Islesford, but how she had hidden from her own life behind theirs for so many years that she knew she had to be on her own to find herself. That was what she was doing.

We talked about Abby. She already knew a lot of it, how we'd met, how we'd lost each other over the years with all the work, and me being away so much. How we'd hurt each other by messing around with people who didn't mean anything to us, but then come back together when she got sick.

"You were her best friend, Ben. You got her through the cancer—the pain. The god-awful treatments. She loved you very much."

I started to cry once when I was with Becky because I missed Abby. I missed her confidence in herself, her wise-ass remarks, and her patient wisdom. I missed sitting next to her in the evening going over the day, or listening to her gentle breathing at night like the waves against the shore when she was sleeping next to me. I started tearing up as Becky and I walked out to Bar Point. I could have used a hug then, but we seemed to have an unspoken agreement not to touch.

I told Becky things I've never said to anyone about Vietnam. Those were the toughest times to talk about, but she walked alongside me just absorbing what I was saying, hearing my pain and fear, and that drew some of it out of me.

I was sitting at home one evening eating franks and warmed-over beans when Ralph dropped by. He's rarely without a purpose, so I waited to see what was on his mind. Finally he told me.

"Seems you and Becky are becoming very good friends. See you walking all the time. Must be colder than a witch's tit out there this time of year. Late afternoon and all. I'm surprised you don't go in somewhere for some warmth."

"Ayuh," I replied.

"Don't you ayuh me, buddy. I'm not one of them god-damned tourists."

"Getting as nosy as one."

"Well, you are the talk of the island."

"Don't take much to earn that sobriquet."

"What the hell's a sobriquet? Sounds like something to do with grilling. You're just trying to change the subject by showing off your fancy learning."

"Ayuh."

We could play this game for hours, but then Ralph looked at me sharply and said, "Stop. Stop avoiding what I'm talking about. You know I want to know what's going on with you and Becky, and it's time you figured that out yourself."

I was quiet for what seemed a long time, and finally I answered him. "I don't know Ralph. I just don't know. It seems too easy to take up with her. I worry I would do it just because she's a fancy rich person from away, or people would think that. They'd think I was just her pretty boy. That's ugly. That's not what I want."

"Her neither, I don't suppose," Ralph replied.

"No, her neither. But I don't know how to get past that."

"Have you talked to her about it?"

"No, we've talked about everything else in the world. From how to catch lobster to world peace. Even took her out on the boat a few times. Bet I could make her into a good sternman. But we haven't talked about us."

"Seems it might be time to start."

"Too soon, Ralph. I loved Abby, and I haven't said goodbye to her yet."

"Fair enough." He paused, then added, "Becky loved her too, and she loved both of you. Never understood what that woman saw in you, but some men are born dumb lucky." Ralph smiled. He always knew how to gentle the tension, and he was right. I needed to figure out where I was, and where Becky was, and if we could ever really be together.

"Seems if you can't ask her, you might want to go where you can figure best."

"And where's that?" I asked him.

"You know the answer to that one too," Ralph replied.

"Go to sea."

"Yup—see your way on the sea. Corny, but it works for you, always has."

"You're probably right, Ralph. I'll ask Jim and the others to see if something big's available. Thank you."

The next day I called Jim, and he told me there was a ship out of Woods Hole that was about to head out for back-to-back trips over at least four months. They'd trawl for plankton, then study the declining fisheries and their effects on marine mammals and apex predators, but the first mate had just taken sick. A colleague of Jim's had called to ask him if he knew anyone who could fill in at the last minute. They had wanted another researcher on board, but didn't have the budget to pay someone, and that I could do both jobs would be a great help to the captain. I said I'd go.

I packed. I told Christine and took Abby's plants over to her to care for, including the gardenia Abby had raised for years. The damn thing wouldn't die. I asked Chris if her husband would drain the pipes after I'd left, and she said he would.

"What are you going to say to Becky?" she asked me.

I started to tell her I didn't have to say anything to Becky, but I knew she'd see through that. "I don't know, Chris. Maybe just the truth. I need to be alone on the sea with your mother. I don't know what will happen when I come back, I just don't."

"Don't over-think this, Dad."

"Don't tell anyone yet. You're right, I need to talk with Becky."

It was a nasty blustery day in January, and I wondered what the hell I was doing going out on a ship for three to four months, maybe longer. Memories of gloves freezing to the handrails, slipping on the steps to the deck below, salt spray freezing to oilskins—it made me think I was nuts, but I felt driven to leave. I dialed her number, but I felt as if I had already left. My voice was tight in my throat, and I was about to put down the phone when she picked up.

"I want to come talk with you. Would that be all right?"

"Here, or do you want to meet at school like we usually do?"

"No. There."

"Of course. I'll make some tea."

I went to the front door, the way Becky had done when she first came to our house. It was more formal, and I needed formality to get through what I needed to say to her. She opened the door, and I think she was about to tease me for being at the front door, but she looked at me and knew immediately something was wrong. I guess I looked grubby—two days of stubble on my chin, the start of a beard. I never grow a beard unless I'm going to sea.

"Come in," she said. Even that wasn't a simple sentence, because we were breaking our unspoken agreement that I would never come in. It wasn't simple for me to go into that house. Grampie and Grammie's house, our family's house, now hers.

"Come into the library. I've some tea there, and scones; we can sit and talk." It was my favorite part of the house, and I dreaded seeing it, but I followed her down the hall. I had to stop in front of an old photograph of the house, and another of my great-grandfather working a pair of oxen. She told me Uncle Curly had copies made for her.

When I walked into the library, I almost cried. Memories flooded over me. Sitting in Grampie's lap while he read to me. Going to my shelf to find the new books he'd gotten from the library for me. As I got older, I could stand on the library steps and move them around the room on the brass rail, so I got to have a higher shelf. I went over to pat the old steps, losing myself in the moment. Then looking at Becky and smiling, I pushed the steps toward her as I had so many years before, and she caught them and held the place where I had held them. Perhaps my heart knew then how it would end, but not my head, and I pushed the idea away, just as I had the steps.

I turned to look at the old books on the shelves. Books I didn't recognize and then, with a jolt, books I did. Books that had belonged to Grampie and Grammie, and generations of Bunkers before them. "Aristotle," I whispered, drawing the book from the shelf and holding it in my hands. "Becky, it's the same one my grandfather had. How did you get this?"

"I went to the Chicken Barn on the outskirts of Ellsworth and looked through the old books there. I bought quite a few." She moved her hand over the books, "This one and this." She pulled *The Poems of Edgar Allen Poe* from the shelf, opened it to the first page, and handed it to me.

I knew instantly it had belonged to my great-great-grandfather. I read the inscription: *To my Annabel, from her Captain, for our kingdom by the sea.* "My God, they were some romantic, those old guys, though I wouldn't have chosen that poem," I said, trying make a joke of it. That she had cared enough to find the books, to bring them home. That got to me. I could feel my neck burning, the scar where she had marked me flaming hot. I walked quickly over to the table where she had set the tea tray, and sat on the couch. She sat across from me on a wing chair and poured the tea. I was frozen—running over all the things to say and saying nothing.

"Becky, I have to go away," I blurted. "I'm going to be away for four months, more or less. I'm going to take the place of a guy who got sick, perhaps just until he gets back again. There's a series of research projects—I'll be second in command—sort of a combination researcher and first mate."

"Ben, that's perfect," she said calmly.

Damn her uptight WASP control. She could show some emotion that I was leaving. Then I thought, that's not fair. I'm not letting on how I feel about this—I don't even know.

"Well, you could be just a little sad. You could think you'd miss me just a little," and I smiled at her. I guess that made it easier for us both.

"Ben, I will miss you terribly. I'm glad we're friends again, but it's hard when people seem to think we're…" then she paused and looked at the tea leaves swimming around in her cup.

She was right. Everyone thought we were having an affair, and I told her she was right, and then she said it.

"Well, sometimes I've wished we had been—whatever they're thinking." She had a lot more courage and honesty than I did. I wanted to jump across that table, take her in my arms, and kiss her until we sank back onto the couch and made love for hours. In the flight of a swallow, the flash of a dragonfly's wing, I saw it all, but I couldn't say it. Instead, I was silent, and then I said, "Not yet, Becky. Not yet." I hurt her then by not admitting that I loved her, but I was twisting inside, torn by loving them both.

"She loved us both," I added, in part to soften what I had said, for both of us. "The greatest gift is to be able to let the people you love be happy, even if it's not with you." As I said it, I understood it better, and I felt a layer of the cloud around me lifting.

"She was a very good friend to me, Ben, and I loved her for that." Then she leaned back and looked out the window. I wondered if she was thinking about me on the ship, a place she couldn't imagine or understand. How hard this must be for her.

I said that when I'd walked her home from our house after we'd all had lobsters, I'd almost told her I married Abby because she reminded me of her. Becky looked as if I'd slapped her, but then she told me she was glad I hadn't because it would have gotten in her way of knowing Abby.

We talked about Jason's dare that I couldn't get a summer girl to come to the island with me. We were easier with each other by then, joking a little, and I said something that surprised me, "I think a man can love two women. Hey it works for Mormons and Muslims. Why not Mainers?" She laughed at that one, and told me she'd boasted about me to friends, though she'd taken me out of Maine and Mount Desert High School and plunked me into a suburb of Philadelphia and a fancy boarding school. Don't think I would have liked that much.

I told her I was scared she'd be bored living on the island for the rest of her life, and she said, "No. I'm not bored here. I'm not angry with myself or anyone else anymore. I like being where I am, and there's lots of things I enjoy doing here. And lots of people I love to be with. I'm never going to get tired of feeling cared about. That's what I feel here, and it frees me to do many other things." I think I knew then that I loved her and wanted her, but also that I had to go away and make peace with myself and Abby.

I stood up and told her I was going and that she wouldn't see me for months, that I wouldn't call or write her, that she wouldn't know what was happening to me. I suppose if I'm rock honest with myself, I was testing her and also myself. "I need to be by myself for a while."

"I know," she said, and she seemed to understand.

I opened my arms, hoping she would rush in and hold me so tight that I wouldn't leave, that she would tip her head back and I would kiss her, but she didn't. She buried her head against my shoulder. I could smell the mist of lavender she wore, and feel the softness of her sweater in my arms, but also the sinew and muscle beneath it.

"God be with you," she said.

"Goodbye. Thank you for waiting," I replied. "If you miss me, go look on the back side of the fifth tree from the house behind the kids' bunk room, facing away from the path. You'll find something that's been there a while. Then I turned and walked through the door she opened. When I heard the door shut behind me, I wanted to turn around again, pound on the door, beg her to let me back in and kiss her, a long, deep, and exploring kiss. A kiss to make up for a lot of lost time. Going off to sea in the winter was damned dumb when I'd just found her again, but all I could do was whisper, "I love you, Becky Granger," and walk away.

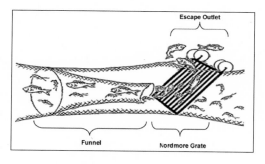

Design of an otter trawl

CHAPTER FIFTEEN

I'd be heading out on *Research Vessel Delaware II*, run by NOAA's Northeast Fisheries Science Center out of Woods Hole, to study aspects of the groundfishery, particularly the condition of phytoplankton, and then marine mammals and predators. The fisheries have deteriorated so severely that we were desperate to understand the complex factors strangling them and fishing communities. If there are no fish, there can be no fishermen. On August 2, 1995, the Secretary of Commerce declared the northeast fishery a disaster. Fishing communities had been begging him to do that because fishermen were going broke and needed federal money to survive. There weren't many fish to catch, and not enough money coming in to feed their families and pay the enormous loans they had on boats and gear.

Ralph and so many others struggled for years. Being in a disaster area isn't what anyone wants, but at least federal loans and other funding would provide some financial relief, technical assistance, and training for new work. Not that fishermen want to change the way they make a living—the way they live—they just want to fish. It was discouraging for everyone, particularly after all the regulations the New England Fishery Management Council (NEFMC) had imposed to deal with the issue of overfishing. Our Council was one of eight set up in 1976 by the Feds as part of Magnuson-Stevens. It put fifteen different fish stocks under federal regulation, then set limits on the catch. You can imagine how well that went over with fishermen.

Ralph and his father were still fishing the Gulf of Maine up until a few years ago, or trying. They had changed gear a few times to meet new regulations about mesh size. Regulators were worried about the loss of by-catch—creatures caught by mistake—and were trying to reduce it, particularly young and smaller fish. Then in 1994 regulators limited the days a fisherman could work. Fishermen also had to get access permits, and the areas closed to fishing were expanded. Hardest was that new guys couldn't get permits, so they couldn't fish. That was discouraging for whole families. The death knell, it seemed, for a way of life.

Many guys with small boats were cut to just forty days at sea, which isn't enough to sustain a family. A lot of guys left fishing entirely and moved off-island, trying to figure out new ways to make money, or sold their trawlers, including Ralph. Cut him to the quick to do that, and I thought we were going to lose him to depression. His wife had to clean for summer people and take in laundry just to keep food on the table. She brought him around eventually, after a few very tough years. She showed some of his paintings of the sea and boats to summer people she worked for and sold them without him knowing. Finally, she got him commissions to paint pictures of their boats, and that got him going again. Now he's got a third-hand boat and fishes for lobster too. It's best he got out of the groundfishery because it's headed nowhere but down further.

The loss of the fisheries—and the loss of jobs in old Maine industries like forestry products, paper, and shoes—increased the pain for out-of-work fishermen. There just wasn't much work to do except slam meat on a grill or clean up after tourists in the summer. I don't understand why we rely on the tourists so much. I think we've created a monster because they buy up the houses, even the little houses local families have lived in for generations, and they drive up the price, which makes it difficult for young people to find decent places to live. Summer people? Problem is, of course, they're only here in the summer, and mostly along the coast. Locals can soon become second-class citizens, in large part because we make our money here and we can't make as much of it as people from away.

The Council set up the Northeast Multispecies Fishery Management Plan (FMP...fishermen have their own words for that acronym), but the regulations were complicated and changed so often everyone was confused. NEFMC sent out long technical updates fishermen were supposed to understand, and we were supposed to attend training sessions that are a lot like school. Not many guys liked school. We have to follow the regulations no matter how complicated, expensive, and confusing, but it isn't easy. The government tried everything it could think of—restricting gear, trips, days-at-sea, and sections of the ocean open to fishing—but nothing seemed to be working. Then money was appropriated to buy groundfishing vessels, just to get them off the water.

That's when Ralph decided to sell his boat. It almost broke his heart because it had been his father's boat and was named after his mother: *The Mary-Anne.* His father died a few years back, and then his mother, and he was glad they didn't live to see him sell the boat. He couldn't bear to watch it being towed away, so he asked me to turn in the papers after he signed them. He was lucky he had a good wife and another skill to fall back on, lucky too that a few years later he could buy an old lobster boat and fix it up. There's a rumor now the government may expand the pilot program to buy back even more boats because the groundfishing's not good enough to sustain the ones that are left. It's hard to know what fishermen will do then if they aren't resilient like Ralph, or have other skills.

The Delaware was 155 feet with a 14' 9" draft. She could cruise at over 10 knots and range over 6,000 nautical miles before she had to come back to port. We could stay out for twenty-four days, then come back to Woods Hole for a few days of R&R for the crew and servicing of the ship. I'd served on other research vessels before, and on bigger ships, but this was going to be an extended tour of back-to-back voyages. Most of the time the Delaware worked in the Gulf of Maine on the Bank, and along the continental slope from southern New England to Cape Hatteras in North Carolina.

There were eighteen crew, including the master or captain, me as chief mate, three officers with NOAA, three engineers, and ten other crew. *The Delaware* had special equipment, including five winches—each suited to a particular job—a boom crane, and a movable gantry that gave her the ability to lift up to 7,000 pounds. She could handle almost 20,000 feet of cable and pull 20,000 pounds. That meant we could haul a lot of net, and a lot of creatures within those nets. Of course, we also had echo sounders and a Doppler current profiler, because her mission was to research the living marine resources for the National Marine Fisheries— that meant fish, and everything else that lives in the ocean. There was also a lot of research equipment, a lab of almost 700 square feet, and a big refrigerator we expected to fill.

Our first job was to assess the relationship of phytoplankton and zooplankton to the groundfishery in hopes we could add to our understanding of the physical and biological processes affecting the health of the fish and the fishery. NOAA's Northeast Center conducts year-round assessments to see patterns and changes. Then it tries to predict what's likely to happen so people in management of the fisheries can set policy.

I've been hated and feared by some fishermen for working with the scientists who provide data for the regulators. Some guys tell me I've gone to the other side, the side of the enemy. They see the regulators as capricious guys in ivory towers manipulating our livelihoods by deciding at the last minute to close a fishery, just after the fishermen have invested time and money getting ready to fish. I'm not going to forget getting back to the dock in Northeast after a trip and finding my truck plastered with bumper-stickers that damn fishing supply company in Portsmouth printed up: "National Marine Service: Destroying Fishermen and Their Communities." It's ugly sometimes, and hard for me to convince people at home that we have to understand what's happening so we can help the fish come back. Some guys just avoid me now, and that hurts. Sometimes I think it would be a damn sight simpler if I could just see one side.

We'd be sailing in winter weather when the storms are harsh and the waves can batter even a solid steel hull apart. That should be enough to clear my head, I thought. The first mission was to collect water samples and samples of phytoplankton—the food base for the oceans. We'd measure the availability of plankton, scooping up batches in a systematic grid and recording what we found. The plankton feed the baby fish, and we hoped to get a sense of what there was for the young fish to eat. Phytoplankton are so dense they color the water, and NASA launched a satellite to monitor the blooms and track their movements. The SeaWIFS (that's short for Sea-viewing Wide Field-of-View Sensor) would guide us to changes in areas in the Gulf and along the Bank.

This first trip, we'd only be gone for ten days, then come back to refit for a hydroacoustic study measuring the density of both phytoplankton and fish. You can pick up the echoes of schools of jellyfish, marine mammals, pretty much anything in the sea, and charting their activity helps us understand how many organisms, small and large, there are and where they live. Later we'd do a study of marine mammals, and finally a series of apex predator surveys along the East Coast all the way down to Florida and back. Think sharks. It's not my favorite work, catching and bisecting sharks, but it's important to understand how they're faring and what they're eating. Dismaying that so many slither helplessly to die in agony on the ocean floor, their fins sliced away to make soup.

The first week we were out in the Gulf, there was a massive storm. Worse on land than on the sea because it coated the Northeast with ice, and I thought, I've left Becky alone in that house, and she probably doesn't have power. I worried about her getting cold, wondered if she had a generator, and hoped that Stan would help her. We had power, of course, on the ship, and the wind wasn't so bad. Easy enough for us; much harder to be on land. I learned later that there were places where three inches of ice coated tree limbs and they crashed down, roofs sagged under the weight of the ice or gave up, and livestock and people died. If I'd known how bad it was, I wonder if I would have gone back. But I didn't.

I brought my favorite photo albums with me, ones in which Abby had carefully chronicled our lives together. After my watch, chow, and a drink, I'd go to my cabin and look at them. Pictures of Abby and me when we were just going out, the black and white photographs grainy, with the edges looking like they'd been cut with pinking shears. Photographs all stuck in the books with those nasty little corner tabs that kept falling off. I loved staring at them, conjuring up conversations and feelings when I had touched her cheek or run my hands through her hair, smelling the lavender scent she loved. Abby, standing on the deck of the *State of Maine*, the training ship we had at Maine Maritime, on the day they welcomed family and we went for a short sail out of Castine Harbor.

Hard to imagine the American fleet sailing up through the narrows there and being beaten back by the British, but that's what happened in 1779. Was it the only defeat on American soil or waters after we became a country—not including Pearl Harbor, of course? Need to check that. Abby would know. She could talk so easily with people—probably because she liked them—no matter who they were or where they came from.

Like Jason. She took him under her wing when most people would hardly speak to him. Some people just shunned him, but Abby asked him to help her do things at school that she didn't really need done.

Halloween pictures; I laughed till cried, though I guess that isn't saying much. The tears were close to the surface. Still, Halloween is a big celebration here. We're about to put fall to bed and welcome winter, so we make an effort for the kids. They all get dressed up in costumes the women make—no store-bought ones for us—and then everyone lines up along the road between the school and the library. There are little girls dressed like flowers, and boys in boxes made to look like Rubik's Cubes. One year a mother made gray corduroy masks with whiskers and suits with tails for friends who wanted to be the three blind mice. Those were so fancy they got passed along for years to other children. Later we'd end up at the library and enjoy a chowder cook off. Clam, fish, corn and seafood chowder, that's my favorite because it includes shrimp. Made me hungry to think of it. I could smell the steam rising from the huge kettles, and the garlic bread toasting.

I could see the kids, our kids. Babies sucking on my finger to stop their crying in church, or toddling their first steps. Ray when he fell into his first birthday cake, grinning as he stuffed his chubby face with vanilla icing. Chris when she played in the mud puddle she found while Abby was hanging out the laundry. Always worry when they're too quiet. Chris had painted herself brown and was chewing on her muddy fingers. Or blueberry picking—the photos reminded me that the kids ate more than they put in their little buckets, and their faces were stained blue. Abby told them their ancestors the Celts did the same thing and showed them a picture book to make her point. Chris asked if the Celts used blueberries, and that stopped Abby for a minute, until she looked it up and found they used *woad*, were much taller than their Roman opponents, matted their hair up, and wore great helmets to make themselves look taller. She was always learning, and I learned a lot from that woman, all of it interesting, and some of it even useful.

During the weeks aboard, I got in the habit of looking at a few photographs when I was off duty, trying to sleep, and trying to remember when they were taken and what was said. I relived my life with my wife and children, and I ached for them and the days we were together. It got so I couldn't even imagine Becky, or wanting to be with her. I just sank into my old life and recreated it, picture by picture.

I wrote Becky many letters I didn't mail ending our relationship, though there really wasn't anything to end. Still, I thought I owed her that. I told her that I was sorry to hurt her, but that I couldn't see getting married again. The guilt of all those years of thinking about her when I was married to Abby had choked the love out of me. I tried, but I couldn't find it again.

I thought about the house, my house, and I was angry at her for being so damn rich that she could buy it and do whatever she wanted with it.

That she'd done some good things—ripped out that rancid green rug in the library, repaired the library steps, named it Captain's House—none of that mattered to me. It got so bad I hated her because she had done all the right things, things I'd wanted to do. She hadn't even done them herself, just hired Stan and the women to do the work. Then I remembered again Abby saying Stan called her "some fine worker," and that Jane and Susan were amazed she scrubbed floors, bathrooms, anything, right along with them, and that sometimes she sang as she worked.

I was turning into a bitter old man—resenting the crew who were happy with their wives, or even unhappy, just had a wife to go home to. Resenting the men who had someone and forgetting I had kids and grandkids. The captain was a little older than I was, but we weren't friends. He was a distant man and may have thought he needed to be that way with the men. Some captains seem to have no problem being friendly, though not friends. This man, Captain Ned Tate, didn't have a natural ease with his crew, but he was a good captain, and they trusted him. He was just what you would call a little crusty, so I was surprised when he singled me out to talk to.

We weren't often alone, because we took different shifts. But he pulled me aside one morning when I was heading to my cabin to bunk down and he was just starting his day. He asked me what was eating away at me. I was taken aback that he had noticed anything, and started to protest that I was fine.

"Ben, I know you just lost your wife. How could you be fine? I've cut you some slack, but you're awful grouchy with the men sometimes. How long were you married?"

"Twenty-eight years."

"It's a long time. Long time of living and working together. Even if every day wasn't perfect, the accumulation of days, having some company, someone to complain to, to…. Well. Don't kid yourself. There's a lot of missing to get through."

I called him "sir" then, or "Captain," never by his first name. I realized later I was just trying to push him away. Trouble was that he wouldn't stay pushed. He sought me out, asked me to eat with him, to go over the logs and data with him when we didn't really need to, and he kept trying to get me to talk about Abby. I give him credit. He cared enough to work on me, but he irritated me.

One time I was talking with Jamie, the bosun's mate, about storing some fish in the hold, and Jamie turned the conversation to the captain. "He's a good man, Captain Tate. Been on the sea most of his life, so he knows what he's doing. Not such an outgoing man, though, and worse since his wife died."

"I didn't know."

"That's why I told you, so you understand that even if he don't know you, he knows what you're going through."

The next time I saw Captain Tate, I said, "I understand you've been where I am. I know I haven't been easy to talk with. Thank you for trying."

"Jim knew we had that in common, losing someone we loved, but I didn't have the courage to talk with you about it directly. It's still..." and he stopped. But I knew what he wanted to say. It still hurts so much sometimes he can't breathe.

"I know," I answered.

Ned Tate wasn't easy or outgoing, and he didn't have much of a sense of humor, but he was a good and kind man, though tough if someone slacked off. He was about sixty-five, near retirement. He was shorter and rounder than I am, but he had a lot of solid muscle on him, a deeply lined face, and a mustache that made me laugh, though not in front of him, because it was so exaggerated.

But he got us through, every day, and even what lay ahead that we couldn't foresee. He had his routines, and I think they kept him sane. He spent time every day going over the ship, section by section, so that at the end of each week he'd examined the entire ship. He'd look so carefully at every square inch that once I saw him take out a little magnifying glass and a flashlight from his pocket to look at a patch of rust on the bilge. "Hard to keep paint on the bilge," he explained, "and when the salt exposes something like that patch over there, the rust can take over faster than you'd imagine." He got to know all the men that way, too, because he went everywhere and he listened to them.

We got in the habit of meeting for supper. Sometimes we played cards or talked about the Patriots. He was a huge fan, and that helped us work through our reticence. One night we had a particularly good dinner; afterwards he praised Cookie for the grilled haddock with baked potato, and the cook said, "Just wanted to make something special for you for tonight."

"Appreciate the thought. Thank you."

After Cookie left, Ned sat back in his chair and looked at me through his glasses, over that foolish mustache, and I sensed he was almost daring me to ask what Cookie was talking about.

Instead, I sat quietly and stared back at him. "It's my anniversary," he explained finally.

"You and your wife?"

"Yes."

"How long were you married?"

"Thirty-seven years. Married right out of high school."

"And when did she die?"

"Eight years, three months, and fourteen days ago," he answered without a pause.

"And fourteen days," I murmured, astonished.

"Doctor says I need to get on with things, get on with my life, forget her," he said, and then looked embarrassed. I let him be. "I can't forget her," he continued. "Can't think of anyone else I want to be with. Seems silly to try. Don't know what I'll do when I have to retire. No point."

"Do you have children?" I asked, and he grew tense and quiet.

"No. She wanted them; I didn't. I'm a selfish bastard really, deep down just a selfish bastard. Couldn't think how to take care of a wife and kids if I was at sea all the time. Didn't want to leave the sea. She told me I cared more about the sea than her, and she may have been right. She told me I was always thinking about myself. That I was as much of a self-concerned dandy as Commander Whitehead on the can of Schweppes with the stupid mustache." He put his hand to his face. "Like this one. After she died, I grew this as a reminder."

He started dealing canasta, and after we played a hand in silence he looked up and said, "Don't let it happen to you, Ben. The loneliness kills you. I may not look dead, but I'm walking dead."

Watching that poor man day after day made me think about what Ralph had told me. "Don't do this to yourself, your kids, or Abby." And it made me think that I was being a fool not to let myself love a good woman, a woman Abby had told me I could love again because she knew me so well. She knew I'd sink into a trough without her, or someone else to love.

I spent a lot of time in my bunk staring at the ceiling, or out on deck. I took up smoking there for a while, but I hated it and I quit. Finally I wrote Becky a letter. A letter that I'd written and rewritten so often there were times I thought I'd already sent it.

"My Dearest Becky, You are in my thoughts now all the time. I know now that I want to come home to love you and live with you, to grow old with you, to see our children and our grandchildren and, if we are so lucky, our great-grandchildren growing up. I want to sit with you looking at the ocean and hold your hand. With all my love, Ben." I did have to add, "P.S. It sure will beat counting cod." I hoped Becky would understand. I put the letter in the pouch where we collect mail to post when we get into port.

The rest of the time we pretty much were counting cod, phytoplankton, or anything else we could find to count, but there wasn't much. It was discouraging to realize how far down the catch had fallen.

In late spring, just as the air gentled and the sun warmed the deck so you could stand watch without shivering, we were working our way up from Cape Hatteras toward home. On the last leg of the trip, as we passed Cape May, we began to get weather data that suggested a front was building to the south. We weren't worried, though, because we could see sunny skies, light seas, and winds, and the prediction of a slight increase in wind and wave height wasn't alarming. That was Wednesday and Thursday, but by Friday morning we knew wave height to the south and east had increased to fourteen feet.

What NOAA reports as "Significant Wave Height" (SWH) is the average of the highest third of the waves. "Average" is the key word. All averages reduce a range to one number, but waves vary widely, and individual waves can be twice the height of the SWH. Rogue waves even higher.

Captain Tate pushed Gus our navigator to use the Dial-A-Buoy system that NOAA had just created. Gus was wary, but I thought it was going to prove useful. Of course, anyone can use it, and that means that mariners' families will know what their men are facing. Sometimes I think the women endure more anxiety than the men because if we're in the middle of a gale or storm, we don't have time to worry. People on shore do.

So as we sailed the coast off New Jersey, Gus kept calling on the ship-to-shore to get the report from the buoy known as "Hotel" because it replaced *Ship Hotel*, a manned ship formerly stationed 200 nautical miles east of Cape May. A canned woman's voice he called Hotel Girl reported conditions, including SWH and frequency, air and water temps, wind velocity, and visibility. Useful stuff and up-to-date. There used to be other ships stationed along the coast, and men who collected and transmitted data, but now there are automated buoys. It's safer, though I guess a lot of guys had to find new work. I think Gus was getting to like the woman who gives the reports. I told him that he was listening to a Siren's call, but he didn't understand that so I dropped it. Stupid joke anyhow.

By Friday morning the skies were clouding up, and a light rain started falling about 1100 hours; winds were gusting to 30 knots, but the waves were still light. We were so close to home, Captain Tate and I thought we would make it easily given weather reports and the buoy data. Of course we have NAVTEX, the Navigational Telex that radios the weather conditions to us, and we thought the ship was big enough to get through the weather. This time of year, between the harsh nor'easters of winter and the hurricanes of summer, weather eases up. So when it first seemed we'd run into deteriorating weather, we decided not to make a run for the coast. If you can't get to harbor, you're better just out on the sea, but thinking back, we might have tried running to shore or at least behind one of the outer islands.

We were working our way toward Cape Cod, our samples in the hold, but not much else. We were down on fuel, food, and water, and the ship didn't belly into the waves as she did when she was full. We were riding high, which is not what you want when the wind picks up the water and the waves throw gnarled fingers in front of you.

Some people think a gale is worse than a storm, but it's not. A storm is stronger in force than a gale, just up to the level of a hurricane. We were at what we knew later was the beginning of the worst El Niño season in the Pacific, which ushered in the most destructive hurricanes ever recorded along the Atlantic coast. I've got a strong stomach, and I've been in rough weather, but this was bad, and it scared me, probably because I had so much to lose.

By early afternoon the Nantucket buoy was reporting winds gusting to 46 knots, the rain had picked up, and the SWH was fourteen. The sea wasn't too rough, but by 1700 the buoy reported winds gusting to

55, and by eight we faced a storm, not just a gale—winds to 68 knots, SWH at twenty, with heavy rain and even thunder and lightning. And rogue waves. They're the ones that empty your gut and can break a hull, unpredictable high waves building above the ship, crashing down on it with incredible force and weight. Rogue waves are the terror.

Up on the bridge, I looked out at the ship's bow fighting through the water and saw a wall of water tower above me as we fell into the trough of a giant wave. Ernie, the young helmsman, looked at me in panic and said, "Sir, I don't know if I can hold it steady."

"Take the speed down," I replied. "Keep her facing the waves and ride it like a bucking bronco. We don't have much ballast, and that will make her shimmy around, so head right into the wave." I could hear my voice trying to keep steady, trying to stare down the next wave as the ship fell over the edge of the last one, trying to keep Ernie strong. "Joe," I said to the mate who had just come into the wheelhouse, "you might want to wake the captain. He can sleep through anything, even a freak storm, but he'd want to be here."

"Right, sir," Joe said, and he spun around and ran for the stairs to the deck below.

You have to keep your ship facing the wave, slicing through it, but if you lose the engine, you'll be at the mercy of the sea. The sea is a merciless mistress, pitching the ship up and down, heeling it over until you are sure it can't right itself, rocking it sickeningly back and forth until at last the water wins, crashes over the sides, and sinks you. The waves were twenty or so feet, but then there were the great waves, that rush at you like angry bull elephants, determined to pound you down under the water.

When the ship is on top of a large wave, the stern can be out of the water, and the prop too. That makes the engine overspin and wear out. That's what scared me most. Losing the engine and depending on the electric back-up system to turn the prop. I didn't think it could do what we needed in those conditions.

Captain Tate came into the wheelhouse wearing his pajamas and a sea jacket. "What's our sea room?" he asked me.

"No problem, sir. We're far off the coast. No reports of ships nearby."

"Steerageway?"

"Good enough. I slowed us down a bit so the engines wouldn't heat up, and we've got enough headway, but I'm worried about overspin."

"Good enough. Joe, go get Donovan up here at the wheel. Son," he added, turning to Ernie, "you're doing just fine, but you're going to get tired, and Donovan's gotten this old girl through other storms. He'll get her through this one too."

I watched him staring at the enormous walls of water cresting over our heads as we fell into the troughs of the waves. I tried to gauge his fear, but I couldn't. Consummate pro, Captain Tate.

Perhaps worst for me in a storm is the creaking. The ship is in pain, and it sounds like the ice cracking in winter, or a witch screaming. The torrent of water crashing against the hull still doesn't cover the creaking of metal against metal and the screeching of the wind. Sometimes it seems the ship would rather break apart than endure the wrenching and crushing.

Donovan ran into the wheelhouse, pulling his hands over his scraggly red-gray hair to mat it down, and put his arm on Ernie's shoulder. "Good job, good job. I've got her now," he said as he eased his hands onto the wheel. He planted his feet in a wide stance and stared down each wave, keeping us sharp through the water, finding the path that minimized buffeting against the hull. I knew he was a good helmsman, but I hadn't realized how good. He and the ship were one being; he was the brains and she the body. Donovan worked to steer her on a slight angle against the water and wind, instead of straight into the waves, to try to keep the prop in the water.

The barometer was still sinking—over 30.00 in the morning, but then sliding down to 29.56 by 2000 hours, and its lowest of 29.21 around 2300. We watch that because the barometer tells us which way the weather is going—better or worse. By 2300 the winds were down to 47 knots, still gusting to 60, but the waves were higher.

The tension was palpable—you could taste it and smell it. I felt as if I was standing above the ship, above myself. Out of my own body—not even thinking about my body, just the ship. If you stop to worry, you sink yourself. But you want to be with good men—and women. I've seen women in a wheelhouse who were tougher and more calm than the men. You need to go to a place of cold and total focus. Your senses are heightened, adrenaline coursing through you; no matter how long you've been on watch, you stay alert.

Together, Donovan and the ship fought the winds and waves so they couldn't roll her over. Together, they brought us home. It was a long night, but by around 0200 hours we could tell the wind was down, and the Nantucket Shoals buoy reported we were right, winds WSW at 47, gusts to 60, and the storm was moving, up to Georges Bank and Islesford, I imagined. I wondered how Becky and my family would fare. When the sky finally lightened, the winds were down in the 30s and the wave height about 15 feet.

When the winds had abated and I was sure we were safe, I asked Gus to call the buoy off Islesford, then the one on the Georges Bank. I wondered what people on Islesford might be experiencing, what Becky might be going through without me there to help. The Islesford buoy reported that there would be heavy rain, but the winds were lighter than where we were, and the waves about twelve feet. I hoped no one had taught Becky how to dial the buoys and she hadn't heard how bad the storm was at sea. But then, she didn't know where I was, so which buoy would she call? Georges Bank probably, and the report coming from that buoy showed there had been heavy rain, winds gusting to 60 knots and seas up to 19 SWH. I hoped that hadn't scared her, and I wanted to be home with her.

Captain Tate ended his long night with a two-hour inspection of the ship. There was some damage to the deck, but nothing that couldn't be fixed. Most important, he assured the men that they had all done their work well, and that was why their ship survived. He asked Cookie about the condition of the galley, and when Cookie assured him that everything had been made fast before the storm, Captain Tate asked if he could make a special breakfast of pancakes and sausage, which we usually only had on Sundays. We had reason to celebrate.

factory ship

CHAPTER SIXTEEN

The engineers worked on the engine, oiling and cleaning it, and finally got it purring again, but we were a wounded cat and clawed our way slowly home while the crew cleaned up the ship. We'd been numbed by the storm, and now we stretched in the sun and gloried in being alive. I knew we had come close to death, and that made me cherish my chance to live, to see Becky again. To love her. To live with her. To watch our children and grandchildren growing up. God works in mysterious ways.

There's a lot you have to go through when you disembark from a long trip, and it's best not to go home until you get that all sorted out, and that's what I had to do. After we docked at Woods Hole, it took a solid week to finish reports and supervise offloading the samples we'd collected and our gear. I didn't call Becky; I wanted to see her. I took the bus back up to Mount Desert, then hitched a ride down to the dock in Northeast and stood in line to get a ticket for the ferry, wondering how my life was going to change yet again. I wondered what Becky might be doing, wondered if she had gotten my letter, and if she was thinking of me.

I turned toward the ferry, looked out toward my island, and then saw Ralphie on the dock waiting in line. He was surrounded by large canvas bags, so I knew he'd been doing the monthly shopping in Bar Harbor. I called out to him, and when he saw me, he threw open his arms, his eyes and smile lighting up as he loped over to me. Real men hug. Ralph put his arms around me and held me for a long time. "Missed you," he said. "Got worried when that storm hit, but then we didn't hear anything, so we hoped it meant you were OK."

"We got her back, but not at full power. Didn't dare. Man, am I tired."

"You look like hell, if you ask me."

"Didn't."

"So what are you going to do?"

"Go home and have a long hot shower and cup of real coffee. We were down to instant by the end, and I make the best."

"I meant about your life. About Becky."

"Can't say, not knowin'," I replied, smiling coyly.

"Total bullshit. You must have had time to think about her, to figure out what you want."

"Did."

"OK. This should be worth waiting for." Ralph grinned, and I think he knew then what I hoped to do, but he agreed not to pry any harder. Instead, he caught me up on news of the island and the mainland. It was a short trip, and I didn't want to ask him about Becky, but I felt the tension growing inside me—did she get my letter? Did she love me too? What did she want from me, with me?

As we walked off the float up to the Islesford dock, I hoped I wouldn't see anyone else before I could see Becky, so I decided not to go home, but to call her from the bait shack. My fingers were trembling when I dialed her number, just as my legs had trembled from being on land. It takes a while for me to get used to walking on something that doesn't move.

The phone rang several times. Damn, she's not home, I thought, and then she picked up and said, "Hello."

Talk about music. Stupid songs rang through my head. Bells chimed—*The Bells are Ringing for Me*—I could hear her breathing, waiting, and I blurted out, "Will you marry me?" Then it was my turn to wait. Total silence.

Finally she answered, "Yes, Ben, more than anything in my entire life, I want to marry you,"

"Well now, that's a relief. You were taking so long I thought you were going to say no."

"Once I figured out who was doing the asking, I wasn't going to give you a chance to change your mind."

"I love you Becky. I loved you then and I love you now. I've loved you ever since we were kids." I could hear her crying softly, and imagined her face shining up at me. "Now woman don't get gormy on me. Hush up and look out your window for me."

She asked me where I was, so I told her and said I was going home to get cleaned up.

"No, you come right here." I guess I was a bit forward—horny actually—but I said that was what I had in mind. Thank God she laughed.

I heard her throw down the phone and I guessed she was running to meet me. Now I've done it, I thought. And then replied to myself, Yes, you have, and you've done it well, and you're a goddamn lucky bastard. I hitched up my seabag and started walking fast toward her house. I imagined her running along the path through the field where purple lupine would stand sentinel in the sun, then down to the dock. She must have run hard, and I was slow because I was carrying my sea bag, but suddenly there she was, just at the edge of the main road and Chapel Lane. I swept her up in my arms and swung her around. I could see us on a carousel, whirling and whirling around in a space we carved just for ourselves, and then I put her down and she hugged me, and I tipped her face back to kiss. And kiss we did. A deep kiss of love and exploration, of past and future, pushing to make ourselves one person.

I heard other people clapping and cheering and stood back from her, my legs shaking and laughter pouring out of me uncontrolled. Joy. Explosive, wonderful joy bubbled over me like uncorked champagne, and if I'd had a bottle, I would have poured it over us. Polly, Bernie, Stan, Susan, Jane and Hubert, Ruthie, Helen, Uncle Clem, and then Jason, and Chris with Mumma, Dad, and my grandchildren all cheering and making a circle around us. I grabbed Becky's hand, raised our arms together and announced, "We're getting married!"

My God, the cheering! It sounded as if we were in Gillette Stadium and the Patriots had just won. The men thumped me on the back so hard I thought I'd have bruises, and Becky started to cry again. Damn that woman gets weepy easily. Polly gave her a handkerchief and said, "Give it a good blow." Dogs were barking, children doing cartwheels, and we made a hell of a noise.

Chris went over to Becky, and I heard her say she missed her mother, but if Abby couldn't be with me, she was glad that Becky would be. That caught me in the throat and I thought I would cry too. Then one of the women said, "Let's have a party to celebrate," and I thought, shit. That is not how I want to celebrate. Polly understood, and added, "We'll make it a short one," and we all laughed.

And then it was time for Becky and me to be alone with each other, and suddenly we both felt shy. I could sense her drawing back, so I picked up my seabag and slung my arm around her shoulder. I needed to touch her, to feel she and this moment were real, and to dissipate the awkwardness slipping between us. I tickled her neck and she laughed, and that gave me the courage to ask, "Your place or mine?" Her answer surprised me and helped me know we were right together.

"Well, really they are both your places, so I think you should come to the Captain's House."

"I'm wicked dirty," I warned her.

She told me I smelled like fish, grease, and dirty laundry, but that she loved it and me. We stood for a moment on the big doorstone in front of the house, and I dropped my bag, picked her up and carried her over the threshold.

"Oh Ben," she said, laughing and crying at the same time. "No one ever did that before."

I told her it was good there was at least one thing she'd never done, and she told me she had never really loved any man, except her father.

"Well, my deah," I told her in my deepest Maine accent, "now's your chance."

Strange how dreams, when faced with reality, can dissolve into fear. I knew we were avoiding each other as I led her down the hall to the master bedroom. I'd been there so many times to see Grampie and Grammie when each of them got older and then sick.

I visited Grammie to read to her, or just hold her hand, and I was glad to be with her when she died. She just ebbed away, talking with us, and then closing her eyes and drifting away. It's the way to go, surrounded by people you love. I hope I can be so lucky, but I hope it doesn't happen for years. And Grampie. The feisty old bird, telling jokes and playing canasta with us the night before he died. Never letting on how sick he was, then just going to sleep and not waking up. The shock was for us, not him, and that's really the best.

I laughed at myself, thinking these mournful thoughts when for so long I'd been thinking about making love to this woman again, and this time doing it well. Peeled her out of her clothes so many times that now I had the chance, I was tongue- and hand-tied. I just wanted to walk along a beach with her, and yet here we were walking to her bedroom. She was actually stomping, not walking, and that made me know she was scared too. Well, one of us has to not be scared, and that's my job, I thought. I teased her about the fancy bathroom, the Mexican tile, and then I saw the deep soaking tub and imagined us leaning against each other, or sitting opposite each other in the tub and enjoying just looking and feeling our bodies close in the water. She said she'd get me a towel, but I told her I wanted her to stay and we'd just talk like old married people.

I started unbuttoning my shirt, figuring maybe that would be more like old married people than unbuttoning hers, and I turned on the water, but she left, so I stripped and sank down into the hot clean water. I imagined the dirt floating off me and turning the water dark, not a welcoming bath for a lady. She came back so quickly that I couldn't wash and get rid of the water as I'd hoped, and then she flipped some button and jets of warm water played over my entire body and I sank back again the tub. "It's making my di—" Well, I thought, maybe not get so graphic so quickly. She picked up a bar of soap and the wash cloth and started to scrub me. Feeling her hands on my body, even through the cloth, relaxed and excited me simultaneously, and I thought, I'm just going to enjoy every moment of this.

"Get yourself in here," I said hopefully.

She looked at the clock and said, with some relief, "No. We've got to get to dinner, and there's not enough time."

"Spoken like a wife," I chided her.

We walked to the party at the church hall swinging our arms, but just before we got there, I stopped, pulled her toward me and kissed her the way I had wanted to do for so many years. I told her with that kiss that I had loved her for most of my life, and would love her for whatever was left to us. It was a kiss I will always remember—deep, passionate, sending sparks up and down my spine, and a flow of glowing warmth that made me know she loved me too. I was oblivious to everything but her, but when we moved apart, I looked at the stars showering heaven, heard the owls hooting, and the sharp calls of nighthawks, smelled the dew on the lupine and the firs, and held her hand. What more is there to ask for from life?

As we opened the door to the church, a shower of confetti and paper rose petals cascaded around us, and we saw all our friends and relatives cheering and smiling. The hall was decorated with flowers, candles, and pink and lilac crepe paper streamers left over from Auntie Harriet's 90th birthday. An amazing array of food graced the table, and we wondered how they had assembled it so quickly, particularly the cake, but they explained everyone had brought something. Bernie had thawed and iced a cake, then written on it: "Welcome Home Ben, and Congratulations Ben and Becky!" Hard to fit that all in, but she's got neat handwriting. After dinner, Polly asked the men and women to make separate circles, so the men pulled me into their circle as the women pulled Becky into theirs.

"All right, Ben," Ralph announced cheerfully, "We know you've done this marriage thing before, but we think you're going to need some help. We've got a few things to get you through it. You go first, Hubert."

Hubert drew in his breath, put his nose in the air and said, "When Hubby Jr. married that summer girl, we used this book. Lovely book. Just divine. So helpful if you want to keep up with the Hoity Toiters…" He pulled a slightly tattered volume of Emily Post's *Wedding Etiquette* out from behind his back. "I figure you may need it so's you bow and scrape at the right time. Truth is I want to get rid of this foolish book and, actually, I don't think you're goin' to need it."

Ralph told Stan he was next. When Stan moved forward a step, he extended his hands and offered a new set of ear plugs, "This is for you, but really for your wife. Had an extra pair. You snored even when you were a kid."

Clem gave me a pint of rum. "Know you loved having Abby make a rum toddy for you, so you'll teach this new wife how. Bet she'll pick up on it real quick."

Dad took a step toward me and said, "Better late than never, if you know what I mean," and he handed me a frame with my acceptance letter to UMO. It took me a few seconds to realize it was set on a background of the hideous wallpaper from my room at Cissie and Albert's house.

"They decided to upgrade, and I know you always loved it."

I started to protest, but then just laughed and hugged him.

Then Jason stepped forward into the circle, and everyone held his breath. What would Jason do or give, we wondered. He was sober, at least, and he'd shaved.

Jason looked up at me, his wiry lined face tight, and he took a deep breath. "Ben," he said. "You've always been my friend. Somehow. Don't know how when I think about some of the things I've done. But you have. Don't have much to give you except a promise." Someone in the circle sighed when he heard that, but Jason continued. "I know. My promises may not mean much. But Ben, I promise you I'm going sober. I haven't had a drink in three days, and I'm going clean. You believed in me, and I'm going to do that too."

I was almost in tears, and so were some of the other guys. We drew the circle tight around Jason and put our arms around him.

"You can do it, Jason," someone said, and others joined in.

Then Ralph said, "And, my God, if you don't I'm going to beat up your scraggly ass, so you best not break this promise. We care about you too much to lose you."

So everyone chipped in something, and everyone laughed, teased and made me know I'm theirs and they are mine. No matter what happens, I'm loved here, and here I want to stay. I teared up a bit knowing how much I loved them, and when I turned to Becky, she was muffled up in a large handkerchief, so I know she was feeling the same way. All we could do was laugh, and then hug each other.

"All right, off you go. We're cleaning up," Polly told us. "We'll see you in the morning," and she shooed us out the door.

Calm down, I told myself as Becky and I walked home. Home, amazing that. My home and hers. Let's just pretend this is an ordinary day, a day like any other, and we've been living together for months. Horse crap. I haven't made love to a woman in how many years. Since Abby took sick the last time. I hope it's like riding a bicycle.

Becky asked me if I wanted some champagne, but I've never understood the charm of that. Bubbles up the nose and a headache in the morning. "No," I told her. "Let's just go out on the porch for a minute. I want to sit there like Grammie and Grampie."

We sat in the faded green wicker rocking chairs. She still had the old ones, and I settled in like I had so many times. I just rocked and listened to the tide coming in, the rush of water through the pebbles on the beach. You could almost rock in time with the waves. Sometimes we hear the osprey that live in the woods behind the house, up in the large pines where they have protection from the wind and a high perch from which to observe us all. What are they thinking of me right now? I wondered. He's damn lucky, I bet.

"Let's go back and soak in that tub of yours," I suggested, thinking that would be a way to ease into making love. "If you'd told me about that, I'd have been back months ago."

We'd drunk some cider at the party, which helped, but we were awkward and skittish with each other. Becky reached into a drawer, held out a little packet, and dumped it into the bath, which immediately grew mountains of bubbles. "You think you can hide in that?" I teased. She dialed the light down and told me she was glad she'd had a dimmer installed.

She told me she wished she was young, and not an old woman with cellulite and wrinkles. I told her I wished I wasn't an old man with my own wrinkles and thinning hair. I also told her she was beautiful, and she was. I walked over to her, put my arms around her, and when she started to speak, I put my finger over her mouth and caressed it. She began slowly to kiss my finger, running her tongue over it, while I gently opened the buttons of her blouse and put my hand over her breast. I could feel her beginning to sway against me, so I slipped off her blouse and bra and cupped both her breasts with my hands, then I stood back and looked at her.

There she was again, the figurehead on the bow of a ship. "My God, you're beautiful," I said, astounded by seeing her, even more beautiful than I had imagined, grown to a woman, a woman who loved me. "You're as beautiful as you were when you were sixteen, even more so." I knelt in front of her and slowly peeled off her pants and underpants, until she was standing in front of me totally naked, her waist curving into the broadening of her thighs. Thighs that would hold me against her, folding into a sweet mound where I longed to put my head. I kissed her there, and was going to explore more deeply when I felt a rush of water over my feet and knees and she jumped. The water was gushing over the top of the bathtub, carrying clouds of bubbles with it. She picked up a handful and threw them at me, while I got undressed, and then it was her turn to look at me. I guess I had a big erection, and she teased me that I was young at heart, or at least somewhere, and threw a wreath of bubbles over me, which made us both laugh.

We got into the tub and lay back in the water, exploring, telling each other about the accumulated scrapes, scars, bruises, our own histories written onto our bodies. She told me she'd walked into the woods in back of the house to look for what I'd said she would find—the heart I'd carved there with our initials when we were kids. "I found it," she said. "And when I missed you most, I'd go there and trace the carving. Then I added my own for you to find."

We let the soapy water run out, then rinsed and dried each other, and she slipped on a blue silk nightdress and led me, still naked, to bed. She lay next to me, turned so her breasts stood out from her body. I was fixated by those breasts, the most beautiful I had even seen, let alone touched. I put my hand over one of them and thought about kissing her and feeling that beautiful mound between my hands, and making love.

It was a lovely dream, and in the morning when I woke up I realized I had faded into sleep before I'd made it a reality. My God! What a waste! Time to make up for that. She was still asleep, so I walked quietly to the kitchen, used the guest bath to clean up, and then made breakfast. There wasn't any coffee machine, but there certainly was a lot of tea. I found some vegetarian sausage that looked scrummy, but better than none at all, free-range eggs and fancy bread, and real maple syrup, so I made French toast with sausage. I was pretty proud of myself, and I walked back into the room carrying a tray and sat down. "This is the first course; I'm the second."

Her hair curled away from her face in squiggles, and with no make-up on she looked like a young girl. Then she smiled, and I thought, My God, I'm a lucky man! She said she had to go to the bathroom to get cleaned up, and when she came back she bent over to kiss me, and I told her how I felt. We ate breakfast, and when I told her I couldn't find any coffee but that Abby had taught me how to make a pot of tea, that opened the way to talking about Abby. This time, though, we talked about the bad times, the times Abby had an affair with the music teacher and then I did the same to her just to get even.

"We always have to talk," I said to Becky. "I don't want to live with a woman who's got secrets and things she can't say—or is scared to say—because she thinks I'll be mad."

"It's hard, Ben. I haven't had much practice at that," she replied.

That shoved a spline into me, showed me how long she had been alone, most of her life I guessed. I took her plate and mug, set them gently on the floor, turned to her, grinned like a foolish person, said, "Ready or not," blew a rhubarb on her neck, then nuzzled and tickled her. I wanted her to laugh; I wanted her to be totally at ease with me and with herself, so that I could show her how deeply I loved her. I wanted her to trust me with her body, her soul, and her heart.

I explored her body, gently probing for the places that would lift her out of herself, to where her body would take over her mind and even her heart, where she would feel only her own body and mine. I ran my hands slowly over her mouth and then around her back to her breasts, circled them slowly with my fingers, feeling her soften beneath my hands. Then she curled up next to me and I slipped my hands down to her waist and pulled her against me. I stroked her the way I would a beloved cat, until she was purring softly in my ear, answering in touch. Her thighs parted and we were moving together, gently, then in fierce rhythm, fierce love, love I had felt for so long, but delayed, constricted, forced away, held back. Making love to her burst all those frustrations away, swept them behind me until I was just in the present, lying with the woman I loved, in a place I loved, with time ahead of us.

She lay on top of my chest and smiled down at me.

"Well, that was worth waiting for," I said, laughing.

I was glad it wasn't longer, but the lost years engulfed me. Forty years? Could it have been that long? But, I remembered, they weren't bad years, most of them. I'd married, had children, built a career, loved Abby. But forty years meant there wasn't as much ahead of us as behind, not as much time for loving this woman as I wished.

"I need to buy you a ring," I told her, and I knew then she'd been thinking about it too because she said she knew what she wanted.

"What's that?" I asked,

"One from the Rock Shop that makes me think of you and the places I love. Not diamonds; they're too cold and ugly."

Bless her for that! Saved me a few thousand dollars. More important, it showed me she wanted me, not some stud stand-in for a fancy pants summer guy. It's still hard to understand that it's me she wants, me she loves, and me she wants to love. All my life I've been told that I'm just a kid from the backside, a Mainer who isn't quite as good as the people from away, or the people from here who went away. Hard to dredge that out of my system.

Three days later we went to Bar Harbor and talked with Sandy at the Rock Shop about having a ring made. I'd called ahead because Clem's wife's brother is Sandy's boss, and asked if they would make it fast so I could take it home with us. When I gave it to Becky that night at dinner, I thought she would faint before I got it on her hand. She'd picked out a deep green tourmaline from Maine, a purple amethyst, and an aquamarine because they made her think of the forest, the lupine, the sky, and most of all, she said, of me. Now that's a hell of a compliment that your woman—my woman—wants me on her hand. She leaned over and kissed me, kept looking at the ring and at me and smiling.

We got married in July when her family and some of her friends could be with us. We decided to have the wedding on the lawn in back of our house with the guests facing the ocean. Stan built an arbor of branches, and we covered it with roses and other flowers. We made a path from the library to the arbor, and Becky asked Stephen to give her away, Katherine to be her matron of honor, and all our grandchildren to scatter petals as she walked along the path to where I would be waiting.

I asked Ray to be my best man, and Ralph, Durlin, and Jason to be my ushers. Jason was so surprised and touched that he sat down on a rock and put his face in his hands. He's been having pretty tough time, though he has been sober. I told Polly I was going to ask him, and at first she didn't understand why. "Why? Well, because he's been my friend a long time, and because without him, without the dare, I never would have gotten to know Becky. I never would have loved her."

"I understand. He is trying to stay sober. So, I'll get him cleaned up for you. A good scrub, a shave and a haircut, and maybe a suit would make a big difference. Might make him feel better about himself too."

Ray, Ralph, Durlin, and Jason met me at my old house, and we walked together over to the Captain's House. Polly had done such a good job on Jason that he was still pink around the ears. She'd given him a haircut, someone had shaved him, and he was wearing a suit. I wondered whose it was, but it fit him pretty well, though I could see the pants had just been cuffed. Ralph asked me if this was what I really wanted, to marry Becky, and I told him it was, and I knew that was true. I hadn't been a hundred percent sure when I married Abby, but that was because getting married to anyone seemed so strange. Now, after that long marriage, and being alone, and finding Becky again, growing to love her as her own person, I knew this was what I wanted.

Jason told me he didn't think marriage was a great idea, but that if I was going to marry again, marrying Becky was the best I was going to do. I guess it was a compliment, or an assurance, or whatever—he was happy for me, he wasn't drunk, he'd gotten cleaned up for my wedding, and he was there. That was quite an accomplishment. And, he thanked me. As we turned the corner of the house to walk over to the arbor, he said, "Means a lot to me that you'd want me here. Most people don't want me anywhere near. Got to try harder. Thank you."

I stood under the arch with Reverend Stephens, my son, and my three friends, and then the music started. We looked toward the library door, but there was no one there and it didn't open. For one moment I thought, my God, she's seen some sense and changed her mind, but then the door opened and she stood in the sunlight with her son and smiled at me. Stephen leaned over to her and whispered something and she laughed, gathered up the long aquamarine skirt she was wearing, and started skipping down the path holding his hand, laughing and skipping toward me, grand-kids running ahead throwing petals! I laughed too, and everyone started clapping. I reached out for her as soon as she came near me, and I wanted to kiss her but I knew I couldn't. Not yet. I don't remember the ceremony. I just remember smiling, and holding her hand, and wanting everyone else to go home. Just after Reverend Stephens pronounced us man and wife, a pair of eagles soared overhead, circling us several times, and we felt blessed.

Despite the fact that I wanted to be home alone with my wife, we had a great party. Music, dancing, everyone from the island, Becky's friend Monica with her new man, Chuck, who was a retired player for the Patriots. Now that was exciting, though we had to tear some of the men away from him. Becky's mother and stepfather gave her a pair of paintings that had been in her father's family for generations. Miniatures, thankfully, because they were of two ancestors dressed in severe black clothing who lived in the late 1700s. Becky said the man looked like Mozart's father in Amadeus, but she loved them. Becky and her mother, Anne, had talked through their problems with each other, and were laughing and gossiping like old friends. Anne came over to me later and said, "I've never seen my daughter so happy. What's your secret?"

"I love her."

"Yes, I think you do. Lucky her!"

I watched Becky as she moved between summer people, island people, her own family, and friends, and just watching her made me happy. She must be about hugged out, I thought. I watched as she introduced people who would not otherwise have known each other socially, even though this is a small island. I overheard her tell Mrs. Bartlett that she wanted her to meet Matt Small, who did the plumbing on the large shorefront cottage she and her husband had bought two years before. Seemed as if Mrs. Bartlett and Matt might both pass out at the thought of talking to each other, but Becky got them laughing, and later I saw them still talking. They'd moved past pipes and were discussing bees. Matt's a master bee keeper and he offered to help Mrs. Bartlett set up hives in her field and promised to tend them for her when she wasn't there. Matt's trying to increase the number of hives on the island and he's always looking for people to teach and new places to raise bees. He never takes any money, and I think that amazed Mrs. Bartlett, as well as how much he knows.

Finally everyone left, and Becky and I walked out onto the porch and sat in Grammie and Grampie's rockers and held hands. By then we really were old married people, so we took our time, enjoyed rocking to the sounds of waves swishing through the pebbles on the beach, and then we went to bed.

And you thought that was the end. No, it was the beginning. The beginning of understanding her and myself, of finding ourselves in each other, of tolerating and even appreciating our differences.

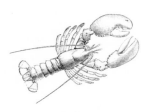

Lobster

EPILOGUE

Change is hard for anyone, and we've had our share here. Global warming, rising tides, falling number of fish, overfishing, government intervention, destruction of the estuaries and marshes for spawning and raising young fish, ocean acidification. What did I leave out—growing pollution, drugs, a terrible dependence on tourism? Well, it's forced us to think about ways to change together so the island could survive. It made us go back through our history to figure out how people before us survived before factory fishing and worked in ways that helped the fish survive as well.

We had meetings—lots of meetings. Everyone from the island— men, women, older children, and the little ones tended by all of us. We know we're a small island in a sea that has changed beyond our control and will continue to do so. We searched for ways to still afford to go fishing when the cost of licensing, owning, and maintaining a boat just goes up, and the returns, except for lobstering, have gone so far down. We decided we need to share licenses and boats, just as Mainers used to. We realized we have to be entrepreneurs because no one is going to bring business here. We can't depend on, or be subservient to, summer people or tourists, though they are welcome to add to our economy and life. And we began to think it was risky to get even more dependent on one fishery—lobsters. What would we do, we wondered, if something happened to the lobster the way it has with the fish?

We each thought about what we wanted to do and what we could do. Fishing is part of us, being on the sea is part of us, so most people wanted to fish at least part-time, but we thought about other things we can do—some new, some old. Jack, one of Stan's boys, decided he would start an eco-tourism business off the town dock. Now he trains people in survival skills and takes them on kayak trips around the islands. He also takes groups of all ages camping on the uninhabited islands. That only lasts the summer, of course, but he's trying to think of ways to extend the season. Winter camping anyone? Well, Outward Bound is interested, and someone suggested starting school vacation survival courses for summer and island kids. Guess that would help kids and parents get through vacations, which some of them seem to find a problem. Never did understand why rich people send their kids away to school just when they're turning into people you can talk with, let alone get to do some useful work.

Several people started selling crafts on Etsy. It's amazing what Gertie gets for her decoupage waste paper baskets and tissue holders. Sells them all around the world because she's very good at design and makes them to fit someone's decor. Shipping isn't a problem because we just take packages to the Post Office and Bernie handles everything from there.

Ralph and Stan started another business, in addition to painting pictures and fishing part-time. They make really strong and solid racks for people who want to save energy on drying their clothes. Shipping could have been a problem, but they solved it, and improved their product, by figuring out a way the rack can be folded into a very small package and then opened to dry a whole load of laundry. Patented that idea, they did! Ralph still paints, and he also makes intricate wooden maps of the islands and locates people's houses on them to personalize them.

We started a nonprofit housing trust and worked with summer people to establish it as a 1031 exchange. Now, the summer residents can invest in the trust, which subsidizes housing for young families, and know they have a stable and profitable investment. We're trying to buy the old barn out on North Wood Road and turn it into several suites we'll rent inexpensively to anyone who's got a business idea they want to develop. We're hoping to teach a class in entrepreneurialism to our island kids during school vacations, and to host a conference in the spring about education, the environment, and growing a business. Local people, year-round summer people, and our summer residents have a lot of experience in running successful businesses, and we'll mentor the young ones just coming up, while trying not to be controlling busybodies. Fine line that.

The kids are the ones we worry about. We're trying to show them that they can live here and make a decent living. Each of our kids in the school has an island mentor, and some of them have email buddies from away as well—people they've met here in the summer, or who have contributed to the school. We always ask one of the students to write a letter of thanks when someone makes a donation, and sometimes that leads to long correspondences and friendships. About eight years back, Jed, the son of one of the fishermen, wrote a letter to a well-known TV producer who had contributed to the school fund when he was visiting, and they stayed in touch. Now Jed's working on a movie about the island, and the guy is helping him and says they might even make a television pilot from it.

Becky's first children's book was such a success that she decided to start a small publishing house. Now she handles several Maine authors, and has written five other books herself. She's working on a young adult book and a novel. I help her with that business by tracking sales and orders, but I'm also writing a book about the changing fisheries, and I learned to needlepoint. Don't laugh. Well, do if you want, but you can buy my needlepoint pillows and stool covers on Etsy and eBay for enough money that you'll cry. Besides, it's fun to work on in the evenings. I guess we've learned that we can live here and take our time to enjoy our families and being together.

Chris took over the afterschool program so Becky could write and run the publishing company, and expanded it to include summer programs for kids who come to the island with their parents. Poor kids never get to do anything on their own. Here we can get them away from their helicopter parents—so Jack takes parents on trips separately—and we let the kids get wet and dirty. We have waterproof jumpsuits for them to wear so their parents won't freak out when their children come back covered in mud, with their Zulily and Nordstrom shorts and shirts ruined. If we're lucky, the parents have gotten dirty too and discovered it won't kill them.

We've got a lot of talent here, so we hold weekly "sessions" on Thursday evenings at someone's house, like they do in Irish villages. Anyone's welcome. We sing old songs and new ones people write, and trade stories, just as people in Ireland have been doing for centuries. Polly wrote a musical play about island life, and then everyone pitched in to help produce it. Especially Ashley. He's our resident artist, a poet, and our friend. He moved here year-round so many years ago after teaching at Dartmouth that we made him an honorary islander. We waited until summer to present the play because so many people from the island were involved that we wouldn't have had an audience.

Mr. Phillips hooted with laughter until I thought he would fall backwards in his chair when Stan did an imitation of him, and Polly played his wife. We knew they would figure it out, but they each have a good sense of humor, so we played them pretty close. Mrs. Phillips always wears a wide-brimmed straw hat. She's a large woman who wears bright flowered print dresses that make her look like an expansive garden. He's never without a blue captain's hat and wildly patterned silk ascot. Turns out he's trying to hide a lumpy Adam's apple that quivers when he talks.

When Maggie and Ralph sang a song about two aging summer people who are very generous in donating to the library and the school, but expect to be treated very well, Mrs. Phillips looked like she'd been poked in the fanny, but then her husband laughed hard and nudged her and she started laughing too. Thank God. It's a narrow line we tread, but we all get along now, better than in a lot of places.

Oh—and I forgot the kids' band. Ralphie's boy Brad and some of his friends at the high school started a rock band, The Backside Boys. They combine jazz, rock, and folk all in one pretty engaging sound. They made a CD, and *The Bangor Daily News* wrote it up as one of the best to come out of Maine in the last decade. I guess their sound holds something for everyone.

Bernie started a knitting co-op with one of the summer ladies who retired here after her husband died. Turned out she'd thought they were comfortable financially, but then she found out everything they owned was mortgaged over the eyebrows. She sold their house in New Canaan, Connecticut, and moved to the little house they have on the shore of Hadlock Point. She's always loved to knit, so she joined the knitting circle and then started designing sweaters. Some of them have island scenes, and the women started knitting them up for her. She got contracts with fancy stores in New York to sell the sweaters, and also sells knitting kits online that anyone can use to make up an Island Lives sweater. She made up the name knowing most people would think of it as "the lives of island people," but she and the women know it's really that the co-op is helping us "live" on our island. She splits the money with the women, so everyone does well.

Jane and Stan's son Tom wrote a computer program that links to satellites and can scan oceans anywhere in the world. Tom can watch the patterns of the ships and figure out if they're fishing in places they shouldn't. He even has a contract with some of the island nations in the Pacific to track fishing pirates. Some of those nations are tiny—just strings of atolls and very few people. The 200-mile limit gives them control over huge areas of the ocean, but they can't exercise that control without investing money they don't have in policing. Tom helps them surveil their ocean without having to spend much money. He's done well enough to hire my son Ray, and together they're monitoring 24/7 and training a few other people to help them.

It's not all good, of course. We've had our disappointments and troubles. Jason fell hard when his son got into trouble over drugs. The poor kid didn't have much of a role model, and Jason knew that. The guilt got him. He went up to Ellsworth, where few people know him, and he got tanked. Got into a fight at a bar and clocked a guy. Both of them went to the county jail for a time because they couldn't make bail—but when we heard, we put the money together and dragged Jason home. He's better now, and he's trying to get his son to come back to live with him. Might be good for both of them, though there are some people here who worry the kid might get into worse trouble. They worry he might bring friends who are looking for trouble, or get our own kids in trouble.

Ralph had an idea, though, that we're working on. Jason likes to carve birds. He'll find an old piece of wood no one wants, carve a little bird, paint it, and then set it on a piece of driftwood he collects at the beach. He's gotten pretty good, but we think if he takes a class or two at the Gilley Museum in Southwest, he can get good enough to sell the birds at one of the craft stores on the Islesford dock. We're putting together the money for the ferry—though we might make him an honorary hand for some trips—and to pay for the classes.

It's a good thing that years ago we renovated the shed behind Dad and Mumma's house where we stored the boats. It has a view of the ocean, and Dad decided it would be worth fixing it up to rent to summer people. At first he was thinking summer help, people coming to the island to work in the restaurant, but then he realized he could make good money if he made it a little fancier. Renters loved it—booked it way ahead and loved cooking lobsters on the beach, or sitting on the deck where we used to drag the boats from the water. We couldn't have built that if there hadn't been something there before, as it's so close to the water.

Of course, we never used to think much about the water, but summer people come for it, and we've had a parade of people through the Boat Shed in summer. Mumma cleaned after them and did the booking, and Dad the maintenance and welcoming. Mumma never was much on socializing, and as she and Dad got older, the work hung heavy on them. The renters changed too—got so they didn't take as good care of the place. They'd move all the furniture around to suit them, but never move anything back, burn a pot and never tell you, and leave the trash barrels full of stinking lobster and clam shells. As their lives got more complicated and everything got expensive, they came for just a week, not a month like they used to do, and that added to the work as well.

Dad figured the expense for hiring someone to take the trash, clean, and everything else wasn't worth the trouble, so when Chris and her husband Will wanted to move back to the island, Dad said they could have his house, and he and Mumma would live in the Boat House. Only thing Chris and Will have to do is keep the place kept-up, mow the grass, and go with Mumma to the mainland to shop. Things like that. Works fine for everyone, and Mumma likes to have cookies and milk ready for any children who want to drop by after school. I worry about them. They're frail, but being old in a community that loves you sure beats being old and lonely in a place where no one cares.

And perhaps best of all, Ray and Joyce moved into Chris and Will's old house. They'd rented it out after they moved into Dad and Mumma's house, but were happy to give it back to someone in the family. Ray told me Joyce asked him to marry her. He said yes. But, seems they don't want to rush into this, so they're going to get married next summer. Well, as Dad says, better late than…

The biggest challenge is still the fishing. The government doesn't make it easy to fish the way people used to in the 1700s, in small boats families shared, going after different creatures at different times of the year. Licensing is the worst. A fisherman has to buy a license for each kind of fish he wants to catch, and right now boats can only fish a certain number of days a year, and I bet that will keep changing. No one has time to read the treatises the government puts out. I make a point of it, but, my God, they are dry. They can put a man to sleep faster than Aleve

PM. And confusing. We get summaries, but sometimes I wonder if the person writing the summary has even read the report.

We're trying, but it's hard. We're struggling to keep fishing, and I don't know how our grandkids are going to survive. Worries me. Most of the kids think that lobstering is the way to make a fortune, and some years it is. But I wonder what will happen when the lobsters run out, or move north. We've got other fisheries—of course, the groundfishing is pretty much shot, but there's shrimp, scallops, clams, and mussels. As Grampie would have said, it's hard to say not knowing.

But we're doing well now, or well enough. There's a lot of talent and initiative here, and life—as we say in Maine—life is good and the way it's supposed to be, at least for some of the people most of the time, and most of the people some of the time. But I have to tell you one thing I've finally figured out. Best to live in the day you're actually in—not in the days past. Best to look ahead, not behind. Best to have a good friend at your side, and be at her side too. And at night, best to curl up against each other on the porch, listening to the tide coming in or the waves going out, the birds gathering in the cove, and then to walk into your house holding hands.

You can do everything you want to, just not all at the same time. Me, what am I doing? I've fished and studied the oceans, and now I'm ready to turn into one of the old guys at the docks who gather in the mornings to jaw about the weather, the tides, the tourists and summer people, or the lack of tourists and summer people. Becky and I live together, love each other, and together we've created a life that is a blessing on us both. Now is my time for my family, my island, my good woman, myself, and to try to leave this a better world than I found it.

SELECTED REFERENCES:

BOOKS:

Acheson, James M., 1988. *The Lobster Gangs of Maine*, University Press of New England, Hanover and London.

Beam, Lura, 1957. *A Maine Hamlet*, Maine Humanities Council, Augusta, Maine.

Bolster, W. Jeffrey, 2012. *The Mortal Sea: Fishing the Atlantic in the Age of Sail*, The Belknap Press of Harvard University, Cambridge, Massachusetts and London, England.

Carpenter, William, 2002. *The Wooden Nickel*, Little Brown & Company, Boston, New York, London.

Corson, Trevor, 2005. *The Secret Life of Lobsters*, Harper Perennial, New York.

Duncan, Roger F., 1992. *Coastal Maine: A Maritime History*, W.W. Norton & Company, New York.

Dwelley, Hugh L., 2000. *A History of Little Cranberry Island, Maine*, Islesford Historical Society, Islesford, Maine.

Franklin, H. Bruce, 2008. *The Most Important Fish in the Sea: Menhaden and America*, a Shearwater Book, Island Press, Washington, DC.

Goode, George Brown, 1887. *The Fisheries and Fishing Industries of the United States*, Government Printing Office, Washington, DC.

Greenlaw, Linda, 2002. *The Lobster Chronicles: Life on a Very Small Island*, Hyperion, New York.

Jewett, Sarah Orne, 1981. *The Country of the Pointed Firs and Other Stories*, WW. Norton & Company, New York, (See also *The Country Doctor.*)

Kurlansky, Mark, 1998. *Cod: A Biography of the Fish that Changed the World*, Penguin Books, New York and London.

Kurlansky, Mark. 2008. *The Last Fish Tale: The Fate of the Atlantic and Survival in Gloucester, America's Oldest Fishing Port and Most Original Town.* Riverhead Books, Penguin Group, New York.

Larzelere, Alex, 1997. *The Coast Guard at War: Vietnam, 1965-75*, Naval Institute Press, Annapolis, Maryland.

Lawrence, Barbara Kent, 1998. *Working Memory: The influence of culture on aspirations in Downeast Maine*, Dissertation, Boston University.

Lawrence, Barbara Kent, 2016. *Islands of Time*, Maine Authors Publishing, Thomaston, Maine.

Lewis, Gerald E., 1989. *How to Talk Yankee*, North Country Press, Unity, Maine.

Lunt, Dean Lawrence, 1999. *Hauling by Hand: The Life and Times of a Maine Island*, Islandport Press, Yarmouth, Maine.

Moore, Ruth, 1986. *The Weir*, Blackberry Books, Chimney Farm, Nobleboro, Maine. (See also her many other fine books and poems, including *Cold as a Dog and the Wind Northeast*.)

Oragano, Christina Lemieux, 2012. *How to Catch a Lobster in Down East Maine,* The History Press, Charleston, South Carolina.

Phippen, Sanford, (Ed.), 1993. *High Clouds Soaring, Storms Driving Low: The Letters of Ruth Moore*, Blackberry Press, Nobleboro, Maine.

Safina, Carl, 1989. *Song for the Blue Ocean: Encounters Along the World's Coasts and Beneath the Seas,* Holt, New York.

Scotti, Paul C., CW04, USCG (Retired), 2004. *Coast Guard Action in Vietnam: Stories of Those Who Served,* Hellgate Press.

Small, H.W., M.D., 2001. *History of Swan's Island Maine,* Picton Press, Rockland, Maine.

Upton, Joe, 2015. *Herring Nights: Remembering a Lost Fishery.* Tilbury House Publishers, Thomaston, Maine.

Woodard, Colin, 2005. *The Lobster Coast, Rebels, Rusticators, and theStruggle for a Forgotten Frontier,* Penguin Books, New York and London.

ARTICLES:

Acheson, James M., 1993. "Capturing the Commons: Legal and Illegal Strategies." In *The Political Economy of Customs and Culture: Informal Solutions to the Commons Problems,* Terry L. Anderson, and Randy T. Simmons Editors, Rowman & Littlefield Publishers, Inc., Lanham, Maryland.

Alden, Robin, 2011. "Building a Sustainable Seafood System for Maine," *Maine Policy Review,* Vol. 20, Number 1.

American Museum of Natural History, August 10, 2016. *The Sorry State of Georges Bank, What Does the Seafloor Say? Trawling Takes a Toll.* amnh. org.

Ames, Edward, Stephanie Watson, James Wilson, May 1999. *Rethinking Overfishing: Insights from Oral Histories with Retired Groundfishermen,* The PEW Environment Group.

Ames, Ted, 2001. *Locating Historical Fishing Grounds and Tracking the*

Movements of Cod in the Gulf of Maine with GIS.

Ames, Edward P., January, 2004. *Atlantic Cod Stock Structure in the Gulf of Maine Fisheries*, Vol 29.

Bolster, W. Jeffrey, January 1, 2015. "Where Have All the Cod Gone?" Op-ed, *The New York Times.*

Chen, C.Y., C.T. Driscoll, K.F. Lambert, R.P. Mason, L.R. Rardin, C.V. Schmitt, N.S. Serrell, and E.M. Sunderland, 2012. *Sources to Seafood: Mercury Pollution in the Marine Environment.* Toxic Metals Superfund Research Program, Dartmouth College, Hanover, New Hampshire.

Fairbrother, Allison, May/June 2012, "A Fish Story," *Washington Monthly.*

Fogarty, Michael J. and Steven A. Murawski, 1998. "Large-Scale Disturbance and the Structure of Marine Systems: Fishery Impacts on Georges Bank," *Ecological Applications*, 8 (1) Supplement, pp. S6—S22, The Ecological Society of America.

Jensen, Albert C., 1967. *A Brief History of the New England Offshore Fisheries*, US Department of the Interior, Fishery Leaflet 594, Washington, DC.

Li, Bai, Jie Cao, Jui-Han Chang, Carl Wilson, Yong Chen, School of Marine Sciences, University of Maine, Orono, 2015. "Evaluation of Effectiveness of Fixed-Station Sampling for Monitoring American Lobster Settlement," *North American Journal of Fisheries Management*, 35:942-957.

Losonci, Ildiko, Natalie Springuel, and Catherine Schmidt, (Reviewed by Karen Alexander, Ted Ames, and William Leavenworth). *Fisheries Then: Cod*, Downeast Fisheries Trail, www.downeastfisheriestrail.org, downloaded June, 24, 2016.

Natural Resources Canada, Nova Scotia Petroleum Directorate, June, 1999. *Georges Bank Review Panel Report.* http://www.cnsopb.ns.ca/pdfs/

georgesbankreport.pdf.

MacLeish, William H., September, 1981. "Oil, Fish, and Georges Bank," *The Atlantic.*

Pershing, Andrew J., John H. Annala, Steve Eayrs, Lisa A. Kerr, Jonathan Labaree, Jennifer Levin, Katherine E. Mills, Jeffrey A. Runge, Graham D. Sherwod, Jenny C. Sun, and Shelly Tallak Caporossi. June, 2013. *The Future of Cod in the Gulf of Maine*, Gulf of Maine Research Institute.

Ropeik, David, Dec. 3, 2014. "Atlantic Cod and 'The Human Tragedy of the Commons.'" *Cognoscenti*, www.wbur.org/cognoscenti/2014/12/03/overfishing-georges-bank-david-reopeik.

Scheina, Robert, *The Coast Guard At War*, Public Affairs Division, US Coast Guard, https://www.uscg.mil/history/articles/h_cgatwar.asp.

Springuel, Natalie, Bill Leavenworth, and Karen Alexander, 2015. *From Wealth to Poverty: the Rise and Fall of Cod around Mount Desert Island*, Mount Desert Island Historical Society, Mount Desert, Maine, Vol. XV.

Thompson, Colleen, June, 2010. *The Gulf of Maine in Context: State of the Gulf of Maine Report*, Gulf of Maine Council on the Marine Environment, and Fisheries and Oceans Canada.

Tredwell, Brenda, July, 2006. "Menhaden: Bait, Oil, and Water," *Fishermen's Voice.*

Tulich, Eugene N., USCG, 1986. *The United States Coast Guard in South East Asia During the Vietnam Conflict*. Public Affairs Division, US Coast Guard, https://www.uscg.mil/history/articles/h_tulichvietnam.asp.

Wahle, Richard A., Lanny Dellinger, Scott Olszewski, and Phoebe Jeikelek. "American lobster nurseries of southern New England receding in the face of climate change," *ICES Journal of Marine Science*, doi: 10.1093/icesjms/fsv093.

Wheal, Caroline, December, 1994. "No More Fish in the Sea: Lessons from New England," *Calypso Log*, www.calwater.ca.gov/Admin_Record/C-048159.pdf.

Woodard, Colin, October 26, 2015. "As Gulf of Maine warms, puffins cast as canaries in a coal mine. Mayday: Gulf of Maine in Distress," *Portland Press Herald.*

Yeh, Jennifer, 2002. "Catadromous—Diadromous and Anadromous Fish," Animal Science, The Gale Group. http://www.encyclopedia.com/doc/1G2-3400500059.html.

WEBSITES:

Catch Share Indicators, and online dashboard of interactive graphs and maps offering best available data on catch share programs: www.catchshareindicators.org

Department of Marine Resources: www.maine.gov/dmr

Dial-A-Buoy gives mariners an easy way to obtain weather reports when away from a computer or the internet: www.ndbc.noaa.gov/dial.shtml

Downeast Lobstermen's Association: www.downeastlobstermen.org

Gulf of Maine Council on the Maine Environment: www.gulfofmaine.org

Gulf of Maine Research Institute: www.gmri.org

Island Institute, working to sustain Maine's island and remote coastal communities: www.islandinstitute.org

National Oceanic and Atmospheric Agency: http://noaa.govand http://www.greateratlantic.fisheries.noaa.gov

New England Fishery Management Council: www.nefmc.org

Northeast Fisheries Science Center: www.nefsc.noaa.gov

Penobscot East Resource Center, a nonprofit organization that works to secure a diversified fishing future for the communities of Eastern Maine and beyond: www.penobscoteast.org

Penobscot Marine Museum: www.penobscotmarinemuseum.org

TIMELINE FOR THE FISHERIES
IN THE GULF OF MAINE AND THE GEORGES BANK

1100: Basque fishermen begin to exploit the rich cod fishing area off Newfoundland using small boats and hand lines. Cod salts well and can be preserved for long voyages home.

1497: Genovese navigator Giovanni Caboto, better known as John Cabot, explores the Western Atlantic, including Newfoundland, and finds Basques who have been fishing its rich waters for hundreds of years.

Early 1500s: Italian explorer Giovanni da Verrazano discovers what is now Georges Bank and names it Armeline Shoals after a papal tax collector.

1500s: Northwest Atlantic cod fished heavily by the French and Portuguese on the Grand Bank off Newfoundland.

1600s: New England colonists fish for cod in local waters using hand lines, as well as with weirs and traps adapted from those used by native people.

1605: English colonists rename Armeline Shoals Georges Bank for St. George.

1708: New England vessels are fishing on the Nova Scotia banks.

1748: First fishing for cod on the Georges Bank. The fishery quickly grows, and cod remains the most sought-after fish for 200 years because it salts well and is plentiful.

1761: Great Britain wins the French and Indian War, and British colonists begin settling on Mount Desert, initially in what is now Somesville.

1788: About 60 vessels from Gloucester, Massachusetts, fish on the Grand Banks.

1792: A federal bounty instituted of one to two and a half dollars per ton if fishermen fished for cod at least four months a year, which subsidized independent fishermen with smaller boats. Maine fishermen earn about 40% of these federal funds.

1818: The cod fishery dominates until about 1860, although mackerel are fished for bait. Fishermen still use lines, each with two baited hooks on a hand reel.

1819: Fisheries in severe economic depression.

1819: Congress passes a "bounty act," which is a form of subsidy.

1830: Mackerel, herring, white hake, menhaden, shad, and halibut fished extensively; later, haddock, whiting, flounder, and ocean perch harvested extensively.

1840: First pogy/menhaden oil extraction facility opens in Blue Hill.

1848: Mount Desert Island fishermen petition the Maine State Legislature to close the pogy/menhaden fisheries to oil-factory seiners, but industrial interests win out.

1850: Dory fishing and tub trawls with long lines of 500 to 1000 baited hooks begin to be used for cod fishing. Near disappearance of halibut around 1850 after intense overfishing.

1852: Captains required to present a log when applying for the cod bounty. These diaries show boats from Mount Desert Island fished from eastern Penobscot Bay to Grand Manan. In 1861 alone they caught nearly 27 million pounds of cod in this area, and over 9 million pounds of cod around Mount Desert—90% within 25 miles of the shore.

1857: Fishermen from Gouldsboro, Maine ask the Legislature to limit pogy/menhaden fishing because they fear the effect on cod.

1865: After the Civil War, the cod bounty ends, favoring larger boats that can afford to operate without a subsidy. Larger boats can catch in two days what had taken smaller vessels a week to catch before the Civil War.

1865: Whale fishery in decline, which puts pressure on pogy/menhaden to be processed for industrial oil.

1866: The cod bounty is repealed under pressure from states that do not have cod fisheries and from lobbyists for owners of larger boats.

1871: The United States Commission of Fish and Fisheries is established under the leadership of Spencer F. Baird. Woods Hole selected to be its central location for research. Congress directs Commissioner Baird "to determine whether a diminution of the number of food-fishes of the coast and lakes of the US has taken place."

1877: One hundred and thirty-seven Block Island fishermen protest the use of line trawls, a long line with a series of baited hooks, as fish are thought to be leaving the fishing grounds because of lacerations and other trauma imposed by this new method of fishing. However, longline trawling becomes the accepted practice and is an efficient method for catching all species of groundfish except ocean perch, flounder, small haddock, and cod, which will not take a large hook.

1877: First successful US East Coast sardine cannery started in Eastport, Maine.

1879: Pogy/menhaden and the industrial fishery it supplied collapse along the Maine coast. Only herring and alewives, many blocked by dams, are left to attract cod inshore.

1879: About 92 million pounds of fresh cod landed by the salt-bankers, which are fishing schooners out of Gloucester, Massachusetts.

1880: A record catch of 294 million pounds of cod landed.

1882: Cod are scarce, but the price is high so fishermen count the catch a success.

1886: Active herring fishery with weirs on Mount Desert Island.

1890s: There is a flourishing cod fishery on the Georges and Brown's Banks, including 174 dory schooners. Improved technology and diversification obscure the declining number of fish.

1891–92: First beam trawl tried in New England after successful use in British Isles. Thin twine is susceptible to breaking, however.

1898: The Norwegian gill net is introduced to the cod fishery in Cape Ann, but the twine is too thin and the nets break.

1905: The otter trawl, a very efficient technology for catching fish, used in the late 1800s in Britain, is introduced in New England. It is improved and becomes an even more powerful harvester of fish after steam trawlers, again used in Britain and France earlier, are introduced to New England in 1915. Species previously protected from fishing because they would not take a hook, such as halibut and other flounders, can now be caught in nets.

(Gill nets, beam trawls and otter trawls catch fish of all ages and sizes indiscriminately and greatly increase the by-catch of fish that are not the targeted species. These fish are discarded, often bruised, dying, or too young to have spawned.)

1908: Gill nets popularized by fishermen from the Great Lakes.

1914–1916: World War I interrupts fisheries, and fish landings decrease.

1919: First steam-powered otter trawler, like those widely used in Europe since the 1880s, starts to fish in Hancock County and takes 10,000 pounds of flounder. Otter trawls become more affordable and increase in numbers along the coast. Boston trawler fleet develops.

1921: Filleting machinery introduced to New England in 1921. Fish are filleted at the port of Boston, which makes it possible to sell iced and frozen fillets to retailers. Haddock becomes very popular and is heavily fished by trawlers.

1925: Clarence Birdseye invents way to fast-freeze fish and, in conjunction with Harden F. Taylor of the Bureau of Fisheries, opens markets for other species besides cod. The fish stick is invented.

1929: Diesel power introduced, which makes ships even more efficient.

1927–1934: Haddock landings decline severely. Otter trawls, skippered by increasingly skillful captains and using huge nets, can catch almost anything in the water column, even whole schools including juvenile fish that have not yet spawned and are too small for the market.

1935–1941: Haddock landings increase due to greater fishing effort and some increase in abundance.

1943–1946: World War II decreases fish landings because men are at war, and there are fleet requisitions, but profitability increases.

1946: Beginning of postwar industrial fishing, enabled by technology invented during the war including sonar, radar, LORAN, steel-hulled ships, and use of airplanes to spot schools of fish. California sardine fishery fails, which puts pressure on the pogy/menhaden fishery in New England.

1950s: Serious groundfishing in Frenchman's Bay ends as there are too few fish left to catch.

1952: Regulation bans the use of trawl nets with mesh smaller than 4 1/2 inches for cod or haddock fishing. As fish tire and are pushed deeper into the nets, however, they fill the mesh so that smaller ones can not escape.

1960s: Distant water fleets, or foreign ships, begin to fish the Georges Bank and Gulf of Maine extensively.

1965: Haddock landings at record high, but decline rapidly after that.

1970–1973: Catch quotas put in place to stop further declines in fish population.

1974: A two-tier management system starts that recognizes and allows for by-catch, and establishes practices for discarding fish caught inadvertently. Data shows many groundfish populations have declined to lowest levels ever recorded.

1976: Magnuson-Stevens Act establishes 200-mile limit, or Exclusive Economic Zone (EEZ), banning foreign ships from fishing in US waters and creating eight management zones, including the Northeast Fisheries Management Council (NEFMC).

1976: US promotes investment in modernizing and expanding the fishing fleet, which results immediately in higher catch of cod, haddock, and yellowtail flounder, exceeding recommended levels.

1976–1984: The number of domestic vessels in the Northeast groundfish trawl fleet doubles, even as each ship's capacity to harvest fish increases because of better hulls, better technology for finding fish, and more efficient and effective gear.

1986: Portland Fish Exchange established.

1985: All northeast groundfish brought under one management plan through NEFMC.

1986: Northeast Multispecies Fishery Management Plan (FMP) initiated.

1989: World catch peaks at around 86 million tons of fish and shellfish.

1990–1991: After increasing fivefold over forty years, the annual catch begins to decline. In 1991 Maine's cod catch peaks at more than 21 million pounds, five times higher than in 1974.

1992: Maine's cod population collapses. (Between 1991 and 2013, the catch falls almost 99%.)

1992: UN bans drift nets.

1993: Canada declares a moratorium on fishing northern cod and places strict quotas on other species.

1994: National Marine Fisheries Service (NMFS) finds a 40% decline of cod stock over four years and concludes the fishing fleet is about twice as large as the Georges Bank can sustain.

1994: On December 4, officials close 9600 square kilometers of fishing grounds on the Georges Bank.

1995: In April, the ban on fishing in specific areas of the Georges Bank is extended. US Secretary of Commerce declares the Northeast groundfishery a disaster, making federal disaster relief of $90 million available for retraining, technical assistance, loans, health insurance, and family assistance centers.

1995: NMFS establishes a pilot program to buy back groundfish vessels, which is expanded in 1997 and 1998.

1997: NEFSC reports that groundfish are still being fished too hard to regain healthy levels.

(Mid to late 1990s: The era of cod fishing around Mount Desert Island ends.)

1999: In January, scientists at NEFSC Woods Hole report "a continued rapid decline in cod stock."

I prepared this timeline using sources cited in the bibliography, including those by Jeffrey Bolster, Natalie Springuel, Jonathan Labarree, Kate Mills, Michael Fogarty and Stephen Murawski, Albert C. Jensen, Catch

Share Indicators, The Fishermen's Voice, Maine's Department of Marine Resources, New England Management Fishery Council, NEFSC and NOAA, the American Museum of Natural History, the Penobscot East Resource Center, and the Penobscot Marine Museum.

Any errors are my own, and I welcome comments that will make this timeline more complete and accurate.

GLOSSARY OF TERMS:

Alewife: fish of the herring family that swim up rivers from the northwestern Atlantic to spawn in freshwater.

Anadromous: meaning "upward running," describes a subset of diadromous fish that spend part of their lives in the ocean, as well as part in freshwater (see catadromous). Anadromous fish, including salmon, striped bass, sturgeon, shad, and herring, are born in freshwater but live most of their lives in the ocean, then return to lakes and streams to spawn.

Backsider: resident of the western and more rural side of Mount Desert Island, as well as outer islands.

Bait: the smellier the better, to attract fish or lobsters. (See chum and gurry.)

Bank: a large submerged plateau or shelf of land rising from the ocean floor and creating an area of shallow water in the ocean.

Beam trawl: the simplest trawl, on which the net is held open by metal beams and dragged along the bottom of the ocean. Used on smaller boats working close to shore, the beam trawl was introduced to New England in the nineteenth century, but never became popular.

Benthic: bottom-dwelling organisms.

Benthopelagic: living or feeding near the bottom of the ocean, as well as in the mid-water and on the surface.

Capelin: (also known as a sardine) a member of the smelt family that feeds on plankton, spawns in sandy beaches and shallows, and is eaten by many ocean creatures, including seabirds, whales, cod, seals, squid and mackerel.

Catadromous: diadromous fish that spend part of their lives in the ocean, as well as in freshwater. (See anadromous.) Catadromous fish, such as true eels, run downward (the meaning of catadromous) to the sea to breed and spawn.

Chum: a Maine term for bait.

Cod: once the most important fish caught by fishermen in the Western Atlantic. Human depredation has decreased their number, as well as size.

Demersal: the area of the sea just above the seabed. Demersal fish, including flounder and halibut, rest on the seafloor, while cod, haddock, hake, and cusk cruise through higher levels of the water column.

Dial-a-buoy: a system of weather buoys throughout the Western Atlantic sending data to a center that mariners can call for up-to-date weather and sea conditions.

Dory: a small boat with shallow draft, used for fishing because it could carry heavy loads and was cheap to build.

Draggers: the word is used interchangeably with trawlers, but traditionally referred to smaller boats that fished closer to shore.

Drift net: a large net for herring and similar fish, kept upright by floats at the top and weights at the bottom, and allowed to drift with the tide.

EEZ: Exclusive Economic Zone extending 200 miles over the ocean from US coasts established by the Magnuson-Stevens Act in 1976.

Elvers: young eels, also called glass eels because their bodies are almost transparent.

Estuary: the tidal mouth of a river.

Factory ship: a large fishing vessel equipped with freezers and many amenities so a crew could fish for extended periods of time without visiting a port to resupply.

Fare: another word for fishing trip.

Gale: a very strong wind. The US National Weather Service defines a gale as 34–47 knots or 39–54 miles per hour of sustained surface winds.

Gig: a hook with molten pewter or tin cast around its shank. Gigs for mackerel were shiny to attract the fish.

Gigging: lowering a hook on a hand line and repeatedly jerking it to attract fish.

Gill net: a net suspended below the surface of the water at a set depth, secured with anchors, and used at night when fish can't see them. Spawning cod will not take a hook and had been protected from fishermen until gill nets were introduced.

Georges Bank: the most westward of the great Atlantic fishing banks. It is the now-submerged portion of the North American mainland that makes up the continental shelf running from the Grand Banks of Newfoundland. Georges Bank was part of the North American mainland as recently as 12,000 years ago.

Grand Banks: relatively shallow underwater plateaus southeast of Newfoundland on the North American continental shelf. The cold Labrador Current mixes with the warm waters of the Gulf Stream, which lifts nutrients to the surface and helps create rich fishing grounds.

Groundfish: fish that live on, or near, the bottom of the body of water they inhabit. Examples are cod, flounder, halibut, and sole.

Gurry: fish guts and discarded parts used for bait.

Gulf of Maine: the area of the Western Atlantic bounded by Cape Cod and Nova Scotia.

Gyre: a circular or spiral motion or form; here, a giant circular oceanic surface current.

Haddock: a fish similar to cod, but smaller. They did not salt as well, so were not heavily fished until invention of the otter trawl and refrigeration.

Halibut: the largest of the flounder and flatfish, they could grow to 600–700 pounds. They are heavy eaters of other fish, clams, lobsters, mussels, and even seabirds.

Herring: small schooling fish commonly eaten in Europe, but not fished in the Western Atlantic until the nineteenth century when they could be canned as sardines. In the US, herring were primarily used for bait.

Hotel Buoy: buoy that replaced a ship reporting weather conditions east of Cape May, New Jersey.

High-line: the most successful fisherman or fishing boat.

Hurricane: a storm with a wind-force equal to or exceeding 64 knots or 74 miles per hour.

Long line: an apparatus of hook fishing consisting of a mainline to which shorter lines (called snoods) were attached at regular intervals. Each snood had one hook at its end.

Mackerel: an oily pelagic fish that used to swim in dense schools. During the late nineteenth century, they were the favorite food of American consumers and were heavily fished.

Magnuson-Stevens Act: the Magnuson-Stevens Fishery Conservation and Management Act is the primary law governing marine fisheries management in US federal waters. Passed in 1976, the Magnuson-Stevens Act fosters long-term biological and economic sustainability of our nation's marine fisheries out to 200 nautical miles from shore.

Maine Coastal Current: a plume of relatively fresh water that hugs the coast, fed by streams and rivers.

Menhaden: a small oily fish, once traveling in slow-moving and enormous schools, heavily fished for oil, bait, and to be made into fertilizer. (See pogy.)

NAVTEX: Navigational Telex is an international automated, medium frequency, direct-printing service for delivery of navigational and meteorological warnings and forecasts, as well as urgent maritime safety information, to ships. NAVTEX was developed to provide a low-cost, simple, and automated means of receiving this information aboard ships within approximately 370 km (200 nautical miles) of shore.

New England Fisheries Management Council: one of eight regional fisheries management councils established by the Magnuson-Stephens Act in 1976 and charged with conserving and managing new England's fisheries.

NOAA: the National Oceanic and Atmospheric Administration is an American scientific agency within the United States Department of Commerce focused on the conditions of the oceans and the atmosphere.

Northeast Fisheries Management Plan (FMP): replaced an interim plan in 1998 and specifies management for groundfish species in the waters off the coast of New England and the Mid-Atlantic. By 2017, the covered thirteen species of groundfish.

Otter trawl: a cone-shaped net consisting of a body, normally made from two or more panels and secured by one or two closures called cod ends, and with lateral wings extending forward from the opening. A bottom trawl is kept open horizontally by two otter boards. A boat can be rigged to tow a single trawl from the stern or two from outriggers.

Pelagic: inhabiting the upper layers of the ocean.

Phytoplankton: free-floating algae and other creatures able to photosynthesize that are the beginning of the food chain.

Plankton: small and microscopic organisms drifting or floating in the sea or fresh water. These include diatoms, protozoans, small crustaceans, and the eggs and larval stages of larger animals.

Pogy, (also Porgy): the Maine name for menhaden, which have been called "the most important fish in the sea" because their bodies are rich in oil needed by larger fish in order to fatten up to spawn. Pogies were heavily fished to fuel post-Civil War industrial development. After oil was extracted, the remains were ground up to be used as fertilizer. The name comes, in fact, from the Abenaki and Penobscot word *pauhagen*, meaning fertilizer. Pogies filter phytoplankton from water at a rate of 4 to 6 gallons per minute and contribute significantly to cleaning the oceans.

Purse seine: a large seine, often drawn by two boats around a school of fish and tightened along the bottom to trap it.

Rockhoppers: large rollers that allow an otter trawl to be dragged very close to the bottom but to skip over rocks and reduce damage to the net.

Salt marsh: an area of grassland along the coast that is regularly flooded by seawater, making it rich in minerals.

Scrod: baby haddock, and occasionally cod, weighing between 1 1/2 and 2 1/2 pounds, caught in otter trawls. Because they were too small to take a hook, they escaped to mature and breed until the invention of trawls that scooped fish indiscriminately. The name was invented to market them.

Sea room: clear and sufficient space for a ship to turn around.

SeaWIFS: Sea-Viewing Wide Field-of-View Sensor, a satellite-borne sensor designed to collect global ocean biological data and to provide quantitative data about marine phytoplankton.

Significant Wave Height (SWH): the mean wave height of the higher third of the waves. Because this is an average, individual waves can vary and may even double the SWH in height.

Steerageway: the rate of motion sufficient to keep a ship responding to its rudder.

Storm: any disturbed state of the atmosphere, especially one affecting the Earth's surface, and strongly implying destructive and otherwise unpleasant weather with sustained winds of 35 mph or greater, or frequent gusts to 35 mph or greater.

Striped bass (Atlantic striped bass): anadromous fish that can live for thirty years and grow over four feet. They spawn in fresh water and prey on oily fish, such as herring and pogy, as well as young lobsters.

Tickler chains: a device to stir up the bottom and flush fish into the nets pulled by a trawl.

Tidal flats: coastal wetlands formed when mud is deposited by tides or rivers. They are found in sheltered areas, such as bays, bayous, lagoons, and estuaries.

Trawl: a net towed by a vessel, as well as the action of trawling. Includes tub trawl, beam trawl, and otter trawl.

Trawlers: used interchangeably with draggers, but usually referring to larger boats that fish farther offshore.

Water column: a column of water stretching between the surface of an ocean or lake to the bottom.

Weir: a blockade made of varying materials that channel fish into a trap where they are easily caught.

Zooplankton: organisms in plankton consisting of small animals and the immature stages of larger animals.

Definitions are from nonproprietary sources, such as NOAA, Wikipedia, and the US Weather Service.

About the Author
Barbara Kent Lawrence

As a summer resident of Mount Desert Island, beginning in 1948, a "year-round summer person" from 1979 to 1995, and then living Camden from 2015 to the present, I've seen many faces of Maine. My academic background in anthropology, sociology and education, and my love of Maine and its people, made me aware of, as Bill Carpenter put it when reviewing *Islands of Time*, "the long-standing divisions of the Maine coast." They continue to fascinate me.

Islands of Time is the story of Ben Bunker, who comes from a long line of fishermen and ferry captains, and Becky Granger, the daughter of affluent summer people from New York City. After writing *Islands of Time* from Becky's perspective, I wanted to know Ben better. I wondered how he experienced their meeting and about the ways in which it affected him. I wondered who he had become. *Ben's Story* is my attempt to answer those questions and to better understand the life of a man from an island off the coast of Maine.

Telling Ben's side of the story also gives me the chance to look at the challenges fishermen and fishing communities face as the condition of the fisheries changes. What are the causes and effects of change, and what can we do to sustain the fisheries, fishermen, and communities that depend on them? I don't know, but I have learned we must face the realities of our damage to the ocean as we came to understand the ways we abused our rivers.

I've enjoyed the chance to write again about a place and people I love, and to learn a bit about fish, fishermen, and fishing. I'm sure that Maine fishermen and members of their families will agree that I have still a lot to learn, but I'm also confident that they will continue to help me as they have before. To them I give my deepest thanks.

Looking Out
by
William Bracken
of Mount Desert Island, Maine

William A. Bracken lives and works on Mount Desert Island in Maine, where he maintains a studio and gallery. His traditional, realistic paintings depict the landscape, architecture and people that surround him. He is a member of both the American Watercolor Society and the New England Watercolor Society. His contemporary American paintings have been included in regional and national juried exhibitions and are part of corporate, museum and private collections.

For more information, visit: williambracken.com.